THE VANISHING BOX

ELLY GRIFFITHS

ISIS
LARGE
PRINT

First published in Great Britain 2017
by
Quercus
An Hachette UK company

First Isis Edition
published 2020
by arrangement with
Hachette UK

A catalogue record for this book is available
from the British Library.

ISBN 978–1–78541–876–1

Published by
Ulverscroft Limited
Anstey, Leicestershire

Set by Words & Graphics Ltd.
Anstey, Leicestershire
Printed and bound in Great Britain by
T. J. International Ltd., Padstow, Cornwall

This book is printed on acid-free paper

For Veronique Walker and Julie Williams

THE VANISHING BOX

Christmas, 1953: Max Mephisto and his daughter Ruby are headlining Brighton Hippodrome, an achievement only slightly marred by the less-than-savoury support act: a tableaux show of naked "living statues". This might appear to have nothing in common with DI Edgar Stephens' current case of the death of a quiet flower seller, but if there's one thing the old comrades have learned, it's that in Brighton, the line between art and life — and death — is all too easily blurred. The victim has been posed in a tableau of her own: the death of Lady Jane Grey. Edgar doesn't like the coincidence. His suspicions of a connection are vindicated when another violent death occurs within the tableaux troupe itself, and Max finds himself once more drawn into a murder investigation . . .

CHAPTER
ONE

14 December 1953

Monday

It was like being in a forest of frozen women. Max walked across the stage and the girls didn't move, not even a twitch of a hand or an intake of breath. It was an odd feeling, walking fully dressed between naked women, none of whom paid him the slightest bit of attention. Their eyes were fixed on the back of the stalls, teeth bared in smiles, arms — variously — uplifted or on hips, feet poised in that curious position that is meant to be flattering to the leg, one toe forward, calf swivelled. There was a cold wind blowing from the wings but, apart from acres of gooseflesh, the only effect was to ruffle the feathers on the skimpy flesh-coloured pants that were the girls' only clothing.

"Didn't I tell you?" said Vic Cutler. "Didn't I tell you that I had them well trained?"

Max had once shared the bill with a lion tamer called Bill Tilsley who used to boast about his total control over the frankly sad and moth-eaten creature. Max had been quietly pleased when the animal had turned on Bill at the Embassy Theatre Skegness, almost ripping

1

the trainer's arm off. He supposed it probably too much to hope that one of the frozen girls would maul Vic Cutler.

He looked back at the girls. They all kept their positions, staring straight ahead. This was not only good training; it was imperative under the law. The Lord Chamberlain allowed naked women on stage, as long as they didn't move. The idea was that the performers created "*tableaux vivants*", living re-creations of famous paintings or classical statuary. The reality was that it was a rather sleazy way to allow people to stare at half-naked women. If Max had known that the bill at the Brighton Hippodrome featured a tableaux act, he might not have accepted the gig, but his agent Joe Passolini had conveniently forgotten to mention this fact. And now Vic Cutler was actually suggesting that Max should use some of "his" girls in his act.

As Max was thinking of a way to word his refusal, he noticed a slight movement in the serried ranks. The girl on the far right of the front row lowered her false eyelashes in a wink. This was unnoticed by Vic who was still boasting about his troupe: "At the Windmill I had them all in togas with nothing underneath, tasteful, you know . . ." Max smiled at the girl who smiled quickly back. She had one of the best figures — he couldn't help noticing that — and was tall, with dark hair piled up on top of her head. She also had a proud way of standing that transcended her surroundings, the cold stage, the empty auditorium. You could almost believe that she was a classical statue come to life.

2

"I'm sorry," said Max, "it wouldn't work. The girls would distract from the trick."

"I thought you wanted distraction," said Vic, his little eyes shrewd. "Misdirection and all that."

"There's such a thing as too much misdirection," said Max.

"I heard you were doing the vanishing box," said Cutler. "You need a good girl for that. One of my girls could do it."

"I'm performing that trick with my daughter," said Max. "She's a magician too, you know."

"The lovely Ruby," said Cutler. "I've heard that the two of you are going to have your own television show."

"That's right," said Max, though his heart sank whenever he thought of *Magician and Daughter*. Joe kept telling him that the show would make Max a star, not seeming to realise that he had been a star now for more than two decades.

"I'll let you get on with your rehearsal," said Max, preparing to take his leave. He didn't want to stand around watching the girls form silent tableaux of the vestal virgins or Cleopatra's handmaidens.

"Stay," said Vic Cutler expansively. "You're welcome."

"No, I must be going. Good day, ladies." If he had been wearing his hat, he would have raised it. As he passed the girl in the front row she gave him a quick smile, but back in his dressing room, Max put his hand in his pocket and found a piece of paper. "Florence Jones" it said, with a telephone number. Max was impressed. With sleight of hand like that, perhaps it was

Florence who should be a magician. He smoothed out the paper and stayed looking at it for some time.

Detective Inspector Edgar Stephens was looking at a dead body. He had seen death before, of course, in the war as well as in his police work but there was something about this corpse that made it especially disturbing. It wasn't just the stench that sent his sergeant, Bob Willis, retching to the window. It wasn't just that the deceased was young, blonde and — even in the late stages of rigor mortis — beautiful. It was the way the body had been found. Lily Burtenshaw was kneeling on a towel beside her bed, a strip from a white sheet tied around her eyes and one hand stretched out towards a box in front of her. In order to keep the body in this unnatural position, the stretching hand had been tied onto a towel rail and the body roped to the back of a chair. Lily's blindfolded head dropped forward and her golden hair fell across one shoulder. She was wearing a white nightdress and her skin was also deadly white, except for the dark bruising around her neck.

"Oh my God!" cried a voice in the doorway, which Edgar identified as belonging to the landlady, Edna Wright.

"Don't come any closer," said Edgar. "Bob!" Bob turned, his face almost as white as the corpse's.

"Have you got the camera?" said Edgar. "Take some photos."

Taking pictures of a crime scene was a relatively new police practice. Edgar's boss, Frank Hodges, deplored it. "All an officer needs are his own eyes and ears." But

Edgar knew that sight and memory could be tricky things. He remembered a Corporal Evans who swore that he'd seen a ten-foot angel beckoning to him over a frozen lake in Norway. Evans had tried to follow the apparition and had to be wrestled to the ground by his fellow soldiers. The point was that, even after he had been transferred to a field hospital on the grounds of complete mental collapse, Evans was still sure that he'd seen the angel, "All in white with a flaming sword." "People see what they want to see," said his friend Max and he should know, given that, as a magician, illusion was his profession. Far better to have solid evidence in the form of a photograph which could be studied and analysed later.

"I notice Superintendent Hodges assumes that the investigating officer is male," said Edgar's other sergeant, Emma Holmes.

Bob took out the box brownie and started snapping away, as instructed by Edgar. Edna, supported by her husband Norris, stayed sobbing in the doorway.

"Why don't you go downstairs?" said Edgar. "We'll meet you there in a few minutes. You've had a terrible shock."

"Come on, Edna," said Norris. "I'll make you a nice hot cup of tea."

Edgar heard their footsteps descending the stairs and hoped that Norris would make a pot that stretched to all four of them. The room was freezing with an icy wind coming in through the half-open sash window.

"Did you open the window?" he asked Bob.

"No, it was already open."

That possibly explained why the body wasn't more decayed. Where was the police surgeon? He was usually almost unnaturally eager to reach the scene of death. But, even as he thought this, Edgar heard the sound of a throaty sports car pulling up outside. There were voices on the stairs and then Solomon Carter burst into the room.

"What have we here? Ooh, a nice one."

Now Edgar did feel like being sick.

Edna and Norris were sitting in a little room next to the kitchen. "The lodgers don't come in the snug," explained Norris, "so we won't be disturbed." The house, off Western Road in Hove, accommodated six lodgers over four floors. Lily Burtenshaw had been in residence for almost a year. She worked in a florist's near the station.

"Such a nice quiet girl," said Edna. "Paid her rent on Saturdays regular as clockwork."

"Did she pay this Saturday?" asked Edgar.

"Yes," said Edna. "Left the envelope on the table in the hall as usual."

Edgar thought. It was now Monday and he believed that Lily had been in the room for at least two days. The cold had prevented too much deterioration but the body had started to decay and it was the smell that had led Norris to use his master key to open the locked door. One look at what was inside had been enough to send Norris running to the downstairs telephone to call the police. Edgar and Bob had driven round immediately. Edgar wondered why he hadn't taken

Emma, who had also been on duty. He thought it was because he had wanted to spare her the sight which he suspected would await them. He hoped Emma never found this out.

But, if Lily had been killed before Saturday, there was the chance that someone had paid her rent to make it look as if she were still alive. He asked if Edna had kept the envelope.

"No," she said. "I put the money in my strong box and just threw the envelope away."

"Did it look like Lily's handwriting on the envelope?"

"I couldn't say, I'm sure."

"When did you see her last?"

"I think it was Friday afternoon. We exchanged a few words in the hall. Lodgers cater for themselves, you see. There are gas rings in all of the rooms. People come and go as they please."

"And did you see or hear anyone going into Lily's room on the Friday or the Saturday night?"

"No." Edna looked outraged. "This is a respectable house. We don't have strangers letting themselves into rooms."

Except someone did let themselves into Lily's room, thought Edgar. What's more, they had locked the door after them. But Edna was looking tearful again and he thought that he should back-pedal a bit. The landlady had seemed to be recovering her equilibrium, helped no doubt by the tea (Norris had thoughtfully made enough for four) and by the fact that she was three storeys away from the ghastly scene in the top bedroom. The last thing Edgar wanted was to have her in hysterics.

"Tell me more about Lily," he said. "Do you know anything about her background? Did she have any family? We'll have to inform her next-of-kin."

"There's her mother, Cecily. She lives in London. I've got an address somewhere. Oh, poor lady. What will she think when she hears?" Edna's face crumpled and she held her handkerchief to her eyes.

"Was Lily friendly with any of the other lodgers?" asked Edgar, after a respectful pause.

"There were a few of them that used to go out together sometimes. Lily and Brenda and Peggy. Brenda and Peggy work in a bank by the Clock Tower. Then there were the two new girls."

"The new girls?"

"Betty and Janette. They're in the show at the Hippodrome this week. It's hardly decent, to my mind. But they seem nice enough girls. They're only here for a fortnight."

"But Lily was friendly with them?"

"I heard them talking and laughing a few times. Betty and Janette share a room on the second floor. I had to ask them to be quiet once because they were playing their wireless so loudly. Old Mr Entwhistle has the room below them and he's a light sleeper."

Edgar was glad to see Bob writing down these names and sketching a rough floor plan. They'd have to interview all the residents as quickly as possible.

"Did Lily have any . . ." He tried to think of the best word. "Any gentlemen callers?" He supposed that he was a gentleman caller at Ruby's lodging house but no one there ever paid him any attention. He suspected that Edna would be a beadier presence.

Sure enough, Edna looked outraged. "I never allow anything like that here. Like I said, this is a respectable house. Peggy's got a fiancé but he's never been further than the front parlour."

"But do you know if Lily was seeing anyone?"

"No. Like I say, she was a nice girl."

There didn't seem to be much more to say. Edgar needed to contact the mother of this nice, quiet girl and tell her that her daughter had been brutally murdered. He saw Solomon Carter hovering in the hall and took that as his cue to leave. On the way out, though, he was surprised to see a flyer for the Hippodrome on the hall table together with a couple of tickets.

"Are you going to the show then?" he asked.

Edna looked embarrassed. "I got free tickets because two of the girls are staying here. I don't suppose I'll go, what with everything that's happened."

Edgar sympathised but wondered whether Edna would go all the same. He too had complimentary tickets for tonight's show but doubted that he'd get to the theatre. He hoped Ruby would understand.

CHAPTER
TWO

Max was still looking at the piece of paper when, after a peremptory knock, the dressing room door opened and his daughter Ruby came in. She was wearing green slacks and a white shirt knotted at the waist. Max still couldn't get used to her wearing trousers but knew better than to say anything. He wondered what Edgar, her fiancé, thought. Probably didn't give it a thought. Edgar was only ten years younger than Max but sometimes it seemed like a different generation.

"I thought we were rehearsing at eleven," said Ruby, sitting on his dressing table.

"The girls are still on stage."

"Honestly," said Ruby, "I don't know why they need to rehearse at all. How hard can it be to stand still?"

You find it pretty difficult, thought Max. Ruby was moodily swinging her legs to and fro whilst fiddling with his tubes of greasepaint. He wanted to tell her to stop but as he hadn't been a father for very long, he was not used to saying this kind of thing. Ruby was the child of Emerald, an ex-snake charmer turned respectable Hove citizen, with whom Max had once had an affair. Max had only found out about Ruby's existence three years ago, and in that time, Ruby had been his assistant, his daughter and now his co-star. It all took a bit of getting used to.

"We need to get the vanishing box right," said Ruby. "I thought it was a bit sticky last time."

Max bit back his irritation. He had been performing the vanishing box for years. It had been a regular in his act when he had Ethel, his best ever assistant. But, though Ethel had twirled like a good 'un to mask Max getting the cabinet in place, when it came to the trick itself she disappeared through the doors like a ghost. Ruby insisted on bantering with him, ad-libbing and twinkling up at the boxes, which put his timing out. The trouble was that Magician and Daughter was meant to be a double act but Max was best working on his own.

"Maybe if you don't talk when the cabinet door is open," he said. "Then the audience won't get a chance to see the false back."

Ruby pouted. "Joe says I should talk more. He says audiences like the interaction between the two of us."

Max sighed. Joe Passolini was his agent as well as Ruby's and there was no doubt that Max owed his new television career entirely to Joe. On the other hand, he wished Ruby wouldn't quote Joe as if he was an expert on variety. Joe was in his twenties, he hadn't been born in the golden age of music hall, when Max Miller and Vesta Tilley were household names and when Jasper Maskelyne performed magic so incredible that it seemed almost satanic. Joe knew about television and about getting fat fees for his artistes (Max had to admit that he was a lot richer since he had met Joe) but he

11

knew nothing about the stage, about the thrill of persuading some two thousand people in an auditorium that you were actually making a girl vanish in front of their eyes.

"Well, just don't talk when you're getting into the cabinet," said Max. "We can interact all you like the rest of the time."

"Can we go through my trick again?" said Ruby. "The bit where I make your hat disappear. I keep getting it wrong."

Max recognised this as an olive branch.

"Is Edgar coming to the show tonight?" he asked.

"He said he would," said Ruby. She looked at him under her lashes. "What about Mrs M?"

Max had been — what was the right phrase? Stepping out? Keeping company? Having an affair? — with Joyce Markham for nearly two years but Ruby still referred to her as Mrs M, which is how she was known as a theatrical landlady. Max wondered if this was Ruby's way of distancing herself from the relationship although she always seemed to get on well with Joyce whenever they met.

"She's got tickets," he said. "All the landladies have free tickets for Monday." That was what made the Monday night audience so tough.

He might have said more but Toby, the ASM, banged on the door to say that the stage was free, so he and Ruby headed down the stairs to perform some magic.

Edgar drove back to the police station in Bartholomew Square, stopping only to let Bob collect two portions of chips from a stall by the West Pier. They both felt slightly ashamed of feeling hungry after attending a murder scene, but that was often how it was. Life must go on. It was sunny but cold outside, the wind making the awning on the pier billow like a ship's sail. People were hurrying along the promenade in fur coats and heavy jackets. Christmas lights were strung between the lamp-posts and there were posters for pantomimes ("*Snow White and the Seven Dwarfs*, featuring the Flying Fantinis") and the show at the Hippodrome. He remembered Max appearing in *Aladdin* two years ago. Edgar had been hunting a killer then, too, the streets swirling with snow, the icy chill that struck to the heart. He hoped Ruby wouldn't mind too much about him missing the show tonight.

Edgar parked on the pavement while they ate their chips. He felt self-conscious sitting in a Wolseley which had a police badge prominently displayed on the grille. Several passers-by gave them "Is this what I pay my taxes for?" looks.

"What do you think then?" said Edgar, searching for the last crumbs in the folds of newspaper. "Was it an inside job?"

"Could have been someone in the house," said Bob. "No signs of a break-in, the door was locked from the outside, landlady didn't hear anyone coming in. Unless it was her, of course. Or her husband."

In theory Edgar approved of Bob's propensity to think ill of everyone but sometimes his cheerful misanthropy was a little wearing. But he was right. Edna and Norris were definitely suspects.

"We need to interview everyone in the house, either today or tomorrow," he said. "You and Emma can start this afternoon. What do you think about the way the body was found, with the blindfold and everything?"

"Weird," said Bob, scrunching up his newspaper. "Killer must be some kind of pervert."

"It reminded me of something," said Edgar.

When they got back to the police station, Emma Holmes had a lot to say on the subject. "If the victim was blindfolded it could imply that the murderer knew her. That he couldn't stand to look in her eyes or for her to see him."

"Or maybe he was just a pervert," said Bob doggedly.

"Maybe it wasn't a he," said Edgar. "A strong woman could strangle a slight young girl like Lily." He had succeeded in tracking down Lily's mother. A local policeman would be on his way to her house now. He wished he could stop thinking about that.

"If Lily was tied to a chair then her pose must have been significant," said Emma. "I wish I could see the photographs. I couldn't really work it out from your drawing."

There was a darkroom at the station (actually, as the CID offices were underground, almost all the rooms were dark) but the only officer who knew how to develop photographs was out on another case. Edgar's sketch had looked like a horse with six legs. He looked apologetically at Bob.

"Do you think you could just show Emma . . .?"

Bob sighed but got up, turned his chair round and knelt in front of it. He extended one arm. "This arm was tied onto a towel rail thing."

"The pose was significant," said Edgar. "A lot of work obviously went into getting the position right and the window was opened so the body wouldn't decay too much."

Emma walked around the kneeling Bob.

"What was she pointing at again?"

"An empty crate," said Edgar, "with 'King Edward Potatoes' written on the side. Must have been from a greengrocer's, there was still some straw in it."

"Can I get up now?" said Bob, sounding long-suffering.

"Yes, thanks Bob."

Emma was still pacing.

"Have you got a photograph of Lily? When she was alive, I mean."

"No. I've asked the London police to ask her mother." Edgar wondered if the duty officer would have the nerve to make this request. It felt like an intrusion but it was vital that they had a good likeness to show visitors. Also, having a photograph staring down from the incident room wall did tend to focus the minds of the investigating team.

"She looked pretty," said Bob. "Long blonde hair."

It had been hard to tell, thought Edgar, given that Lily's face was half covered by the sheet, but he was willing to bet that she was very pretty indeed and that this had something to do with her death.

15

"Lily worked at the Rose Garden on Queen's Road," he said. "You two go up there now and break the news. See if Lily had any admirers or if anyone was hanging round the shop recently. Lily would have been pretty conspicuous working there. Then we can go back to the digs and start interviewing the lodgers as they come home from work. I'd better wait here for Lily's mother. The Clapham police are going to drive her down."

"Do you want me to wait with you?" said Emma.

"No, it's all right," said Edgar. "You two go and start interviewing people. That way we might stop someone else being killed."

Emma went red and Edgar wondered if he'd spoken too harshly. But it wasn't like Emma to be oversensitive. She and Bob gathered up their things and left, leaving Edgar to break the news to Superintendent Hodges that there was another murderer on the loose in Brighton.

The cabinet had been made by a specialist carpenter in Hove. The vanishing box, also known as the rattle box, was usually a table trick. The magician would put a ring or another valuable object in a small box, rattle it so the audience can hear it inside, then open it to show an empty box. In their act, Max and Ruby were using a human-sized version. They competed to make larger and larger objects disappear until, at last, Ruby stepped inside the cabinet. Then, as Max stepped inside to show that the box was empty, Ruby appeared around the side, shut the doors and opened them again to show that the great magician had vanished. Cue applause,

Ruby dimpling prettily and the doors opening again to show Max inside.

It was a simple illusion really. The cabinet had a false back that swivelled round, the person inside had to cling to the back until the doors were closed and then swivel themselves back inside. The trouble was that it was a manoeuvre best suited to a slight, athletic girl like Ruby and not to a man of over six foot. Max found it hard to stay attached to the back, clinging by his fingernails to the frame, until Ruby closed the doors again. The trouble was that she always strung out this bit of the show, enjoying her moment alone on stage, and a couple of times Max had fallen off, causing gales of laughter from Ruby and the backstage staff. He tried to laugh too but actually he hated being the butt of the joke, the stooge, leaving Ruby to win the last round. He was the magician. It was his job to fling open the cabinet doors with a perfectly timed double-take, grinning up at the royal box as he demonstrated his total control over time and space. "That great magician stuff is old hat now," Joe told him. "You've got to turn the trick on its head, bring the audience into the joke, the way Tommy Cooper does. This act shows that you can perform great magic but that you don't take yourself too seriously. That's what the public wants to see." The trouble was that Max suspected that he did take himself, or at least his magic, rather seriously. The reference to Tommy Cooper, an ex-NAAFI magician who was becoming famous by getting the tricks wrong, irritated him too.

But the rehearsal went well. The objects disappeared easily (the box had a false bottom too) and Max and Ruby walked in and out of the cabinet with perfect timing, laughing and exchanging backchat all the while. About halfway through Max noticed laughter coming from the stalls and wondered if the theatre manager, Dick Billings, had come front of house to watch the rehearsal. But, when the lights went up, he heard clapping and saw the familiar sallow features of Joe Passolini, the shoulders of one of his ridiculous suits up around his ears as he sat in the front row.

"Great stuff." The agent got up, still clapping.

"Joe!" Ruby ran to the edge of the stage. "Was it all right?"

"Perfect, beautiful. You'll kill them tonight."

Max was irritated that Ruby had asked Joe for his opinion. He spent his time double-checking the cabinet before climbing down from the stage and joining the others.

"I didn't know you were coming to Brighton, Joe."

"Always try to catch the first nights," said Joe briskly. He was carrying a Homburg hat and looked, as usual, like an American gangster on holiday. "That's when the press will be here."

"The *Evening Argus* perhaps," said Max.

"Don't knock the local press," said Joe. "They want to do a feature on you and Ruby. 'How I found my vanishing daughter.' "

Max groaned silently.

Joe offered to take them to lunch and Max agreed because Ruby obviously wanted to go. In the foyer, Joe stopped to ask about box office receipts and Max tried to avoid a huge poster of Vic Cutler's "girls", all legs, teeth and feather boas. If they were sold out, it was probably because people had come to gaze at half-naked women, not to watch finely judged magic tricks.

"A note was delivered for you, Miss French," said the front-of-house manager, blushing slightly.

Ruby opened it and her face darkened. "Edgar can't come tonight. He says something has come up at work."

"Shame," said Joe, slipping his arm through hers. "A copper's work is never done."

Max, following them, wondered what had happened to stop Edgar keeping his promise. Murder, at the very least, he thought. He'd been involved in a few murder investigations himself. He'd met Edgar in the war when they'd both been seconded to a secret service group called the Magic Men. The aim of the mission was to use magic tricks — sleight of hand, camouflage, misdirection — against the enemy. Max had already been using these tactics successfully in North Africa. Edgar was regular army, a captain with a good war record, brought in to provide respectability and military discipline. Despite this, Max and Edgar had formed a close friendship which had faltered after the war and strengthened again when Edgar, now a detective, had asked for Max's help in catching a murderer who became known as the Conjuror Killer. Max was surprised to find himself wishing that he knew more about the case that was stopping Edgar meeting Ruby tonight. It would be something big, he knew that much.

"Are you still with us, Maxie boy?" Despite many attempts, Max had not been able to break his agent's habit of calling him by this name.

"Sorry," said Max. "Where do you want to go?"

"What about Il Teatro?" said Joe, indicating the Italian restaurant next to the theatre. "They do good meatballs."

"Oh no," said Ruby. "They always make so much fuss of me in there."

"We could go somewhere where the waiters would ignore you," offered Max.

"No, it's all right," said Ruby, her hand on the door. "We're here now."

CHAPTER
THREE

The Rose Garden was full of holly wreaths and pine branches sprayed gold and silver. The owner, a plump woman in her fifties, was alone in the shop. She greeted them cheerfully but her smile sagged when she saw their warrant cards.

"Is there somewhere we can talk?" said Emma.

The owner, Mrs Catherine Edwards ("Call me Cath, everyone does"), led them into a back room. It was crowded with buckets full of Christmas roses, half-finished wreaths, ribbons, coloured paper and shiny baubles. It felt too cheerful a place for the news that they were about to impart.

Cath couldn't believe it at first.

"Lily was such a lovely girl. Her parents had a flower stall in Covent Garden. That's why she was called Lily. Oh, her mother will be heartbroken." She reached for a handkerchief.

"Would you like a glass of water?" said Emma. There was a sink in the room but it was full of roses. They smelt opulent and slightly sickly.

"Yes please."

Bob filled a mug and silently handed it over. Emma waited until Cath had taken a sip.

"Would you mind if we asked you some questions? I know you've had a shock but we need to find the person who did this terrible thing. That means we have to move as quickly as possible."

"What do you want to know?" asked Cath. The colour was slowly coming back to her face.

"How long had Lily worked for you?"

"Almost a year, I think. Yes, she started in January."

Lily was nineteen, Emma knew. She wondered what had prompted the girl to leave London and move to Brighton, living on her own in a rented room.

"Do you know where she worked before?"

"On her parents' stall. Then her father died and I suppose they had to close it down. She knew a lot about flowers though. You could tell she'd been brought up in the business."

"Why did she come to Brighton?" said Emma. "Did she have friends or family here?"

"I don't think so," said Cath. "I think she just liked the place. The sea," she added vaguely.

"When did you last see Lily?" asked Bob..

"On Friday. She came to work as usual. She was very reliable. That's why I was a bit worried when she didn't come in today. It was almost as if I knew." She took a meditative sip of water, marvelling at her psychic powers.

Emma made a note. That meant that the earliest Lily could have been killed was on Friday night.

"How did she seem on Friday?" This was Bob, doing his best to sound sensitive.

22

"The same as always," said Cath. "She was a quiet girl but we used to have some lovely talks. I'll miss her." She dabbed her eyes.

"What did you talk about on Friday?" asked Emma. "Can you remember?"

"The usual sorts of things," said Cath. "Christmas coming up. She was going to London to see her mother. We talked about making her a Christmas wreath. I'm famous for my wreaths."

"Did Lily have any brothers or sisters?" said Emma.

"I think there was a married brother," said Cath, "but it was really just her and her mum. Oh, poor lady."

It occurred to Emma that Lily's mother would have her wreath now. Her eyes pricked but it was probably just the overpowering smell of pine leaves and roses.

"Did Lily have a boyfriend?" she said, trying to make her voice sound cosy and all girls together.

"Not that I knew of," said Cath. "She was a very pretty girl but reserved, you know. In her looks too. You wouldn't necessarily look at her twice. She dressed modestly. She wasn't covered in make-up like some of the girls."

Emma wondered who these girls were. She never wore make-up at work, no matter how many times her mother tried to foist lipstick on her, and she hoped that her scrubbed face was winning her brownie points with Cath.

"What about girlfriends?" she asked. "Did anyone call for her at the shop?"

"She had a couple of friends who worked at the bank," said Cath. "Nice girls. They used to have lunch together sometimes."

"What about the other girls in her digs?" asked Bob. "The ones in the show at the Hippodrome?"

"Oh, them." Cath's mouth pursed. "They came in one day last week, covered in face paint. One of them was smoking openly in the street. And that show. Well, it's not decent, to my mind. The girls are practically naked. There ought to be a law against it."

"Was Lily friendly with them?" asked Bob. Emma noticed his ears redden at the mention of the nearly naked girls.

"She was too nice," said Cath. "She thought the best of everyone. I told her, 'You'll get taken advantage of.' "

Well someone had taken advantage of Lily, thought Emma, as they made their way out through the golden branches. She didn't think that this was the fate that her employer had had in mind though.

By the time Emma and Bob reached the digs on Lansdowne Road, Edna had obviously broken the news to some of the lodgers. An elderly man sat on the sofa in the front parlour with his head in his hands. Two girls, whom Emma identified immediately as the over-painted hussies from the Hippodrome, sat either side comforting him.

"I only saw her the other day," the man was saying. "She said, 'Good morning, Mr E' as nice as anything."

"We saw her on Thursday night, didn't we, Bet?" said one of the girls. "She was going to come to the show this week."

Emma and Bob took the sofa opposite.

"We're trying to build up a picture of what happened," Emma told the lodgers. "I know it's difficult and that you've had an awful shock but Sergeant Willis and I really need to talk to you all individually."

"Where's that other policeman?" said the landlady, Edna, who was standing in the doorway looking rather belligerent. "The detective inspector?"

"Detective Inspector Stephens will be along soon," said Bob, exchanging a glance with Emma. "He's asked us to conduct these interviews."

This word seemed to inflame Edna still further. "Interviews?" she said. "No one's interviewing me, thank you very much."

"It's not an interview," said Emma, trying for a soothing tone. "It's just a chat. After all, we need to find out who did this."

"Yes," said the girl addressed as Bet. "To think that someone came into this house and murdered her in her bed. I'll never sleep again."

Emma noted that Bet didn't seem to know any details of how Lily was found. "In her bed" sounded almost gentle when compared to the reality. She also didn't mention the rather more terrifying scenario. That the killer had come from within the house.

"You're quite safe here, Betty," said Edna, bristling. "Norris will sleep downstairs."

Quite how Norris, who was half Edna's size, would deter a ruthless killer was not explained. Emma said, "We can send police protection too. A constable can keep watch outside the house. Try not to worry too much, Miss . . ."

"Smith. Betty Smith."

The other lodgers identified themselves as Janette Duvall (which Emma suspected was a stage name) and Peter Entwhistle. After a brief discussion, Betty volunteered to take Emma to her bedroom for their chat, while Peter and Bob repaired to the room on the floor below. Edna and Janette remained in the parlour, sitting at opposite ends of the sofa.

The room Betty shared with Janette was large and depressing. It contained twin beds covered with grey blankets, several items of utility furniture and a fine crop of mould blossoming in the corner of the high ceiling. The girls' attempts to cheer the place up — a bunch of artificial flowers on the dressing table, a framed photograph of Errol Flynn — only served to make it seem sadder.

"Here you go," said Betty, pointing Emma to the only chair. "Home sweet home."

Emma sometimes fantasised about leaving her parents' house and getting a bed-sitter. Now, breathing in the scent of damp and cheap perfume, she thought of her bed with its patchwork quilt, her bookcase, her white-painted furniture. Her mother might drive her mad trying to make her wear skirts and go to tennis parties, but what would it be like to come back to a room like this every night?

"I suppose you have to move around a lot in your profession," she said to Betty, who was sitting on one of the beds filing her nails.

"This is fortnightly rep," said Betty. "It's not so bad. One week rehearsing, one week performing. A place can get to seem like home in two weeks. We've got a wireless and that makes a difference, though the old cat downstairs makes a fuss about the noise."

"What do you do in the show?" asked Emma.

"It's a tableaux show," said Betty, offering Emma a cigarette and then lighting one herself. "We go into these poses — you know, Cleopatra, Boadicea, Elizabeth and Raleigh, Hiawatha and Minnehaha — and we have to stand completely still. That's because of the censor, you see. It's harder than you think, staying completely still."

"I'm sure it is," said Emma. "How did you get into doing that?"

"I started as a dancer," said Betty, "chorus line and that. I joined Vic Cutler's Victories when I was sixteen. That was during the war, patriotic stuff, 'There'll always be an England' and all that. But there aren't the bookings any more. People don't want dancers. Apparently what they do want is to stare at naked girls standing still."

"Naked?" said Emma, remembering Cath's thin-lipped disapproval.

"As good as," said Betty cheerfully. "Just a few feathers and that. It's not bad work really. The other girls are mostly good fun and it's money in the bank."

27

"How long have you been doing it?"

"A couple of years. I don't want to do it for ever. I'm twenty-five now and I don't want to be taking my clothes off when I'm thirty."

That made Betty Emma's age. She looked older, or maybe it was just the sophisticated way she was smoking the cigarette.

"How well did you know Lily?" asked Emma.

"Not that well," said Betty. "Like I say, we've only been here for a week. But we got talking on the landing, you know how it is in digs. Janette and me, we tried to cheer her up a bit, get her to see a bit of the world. We'd got her tickets for the show. I suppose we wanted her to make a bit more of herself. She was a beauty, Lily, really, but she didn't have the first idea what to do with her face. I offered to lend her some powder and rouge but she said her employer wouldn't like it. That old biddy at the flower shop. We called in to see Lil once and the look that woman gave me!" Betty blew an eloquent smoke ring.

"Did Lily ever mention a boyfriend or even someone hanging around bothering her?"

She fully expected a variation on the theme that Lily was a quiet girl who kept herself to herself. Instead, Betty gave a short laugh.

"Well, there was the person who left flowers outside her door."

"What?"

"Yes, little bunches of flowers. Carnations and roses. We used to tease her about them."

"Did she have any idea who sent them?"

28

"No, but it must have been someone who knew how to get into the house."

It must indeed, thought Emma. "What about the other lodgers?" she said, looking at her notes. "Brenda and Peggy. Were they friendly with Lily?"

"Yes," said Betty. "They were quiet types too but Lily sometimes went to the Lyons' or to the flicks with them. Oh God," she looked at Emma, her eyes suddenly round with horror, "they don't know yet, do they?"

Emma looked at her watch. It was three o'clock. Brenda and Peggy wouldn't be home from the bank yet. She imagined that she and Bob would be at the house for a good few hours yet. They would probably have to break the news to the two bank clerks. When would the DI arrive? He was probably still with Lily's mother. Emma knew that he would consider it his duty to take Mrs Burtenshaw to see her daughter's body.

"When did you last see Lily?" she asked.

"Thursday night," said Betty. "Me and Janette had been to the flicks and, when we came back, we saw that Lily's light was on. We asked her down for some cocoa and a chat."

"What did you talk about?"

"The show. Vic Cutler's latest temper tantrum. Variety. Max Mephisto."

"Max Mephisto?" said Emma, more sharply than she'd intended.

"Yes, you know, the magician. He's top of the bill at the Hippodrome." Betty looked at her curiously. "You have heard of Max Mephisto, haven't you?"

"Yes," said Emma. "I've met him a couple of times."

"Really?" Emma thought that Betty looked at her with new respect. "Well, he's a gent, Max. Not like some. Janette thinks he's stuck up but he offered me a cigarette the other day, as nice as anything."

"Was Lily interested in the show?"

"Yes. She came in to watch a rehearsal last week. She used to go to variety shows with her mother in London. I think she said that her mother had been on the boards herself once."

"And when did you say goodnight to Lily?"

"Not that late. About ten. She said she had to be up early to sort out the flowers from the market. I didn't think there were any flowers in winter but she said that they were making Christmas decorations."

Emma thought of the shop with its glowing branches and decorated wreaths. She imagined Lily working away in the back room, twisting flower stalks onto a frame. Who would want to kill her, this shy hard-working girl?

"Thank you," she said to Betty. "Do you think you could send Janette up now?"

Peter Entwhistle gave his age as seventy which surprised Bob, who had thought it was nearer ninety. To him, the man seemed the epitome of old age: shaking, liver-spotted hands, quavering voice, ill-fitting false teeth. I hope I never get that old, thought Bob, without pondering too much on the alternative. He was twenty-five, he was never going to die.

Mr Entwhistle told Bob that he was a retired bookkeeper. He had no family and, unlike the other lodgers, he was a "half-boarder" at Lansdowne Road. "That means I get my breakfast and evening meal," he explained. "Edna's what my mother would call a good plain cook so I don't starve. I usually go to the Lyons' for my lunch."

"How well did you know Miss Burtenshaw? Lily."

"Not very well but we always chatted when we met in the hall and suchlike. She was a lovely girl." Peter's voice shook more than ever.

"Do you want a glass of water?" said Bob. He didn't want the old boy keeling over on him.

"No. I'll be all right. Worse things happen at sea, eh?"

There was no answer to that so Bob prompted gently, "When did you last see Lily?"

"I think it was Thursday or Friday morning. We met in the hall. I was looking to see if I had any post — there's a niece who sends me postcards sometimes — and she was reading a letter. I said, 'Good morning, my dear' and she said, 'Good morning, Mr E.' "

"Can you remember if this was Thursday or Friday?"

"I think it was Friday because I remember the smell of kippers. Edna always does kippers on a Friday."

"Can you tell me anything about Lily?" said Bob. "Did she have any friends? A boyfriend?"

"No." Peter looked quite shocked. "She was a nice quiet girl. An old-fashioned type. Reminded me of girls when I was growing up."

Did they have girls when Peter was growing up? wondered Bob.

"Was she friends with the other girls in the house?" he asked.

"Yes, I think she was friendly with the two girls who work in the bank, Peggy and Brenda. She knew the others too. They're a bit *fast*." He breathed the last word.

"In what way?"

"Oh, playing the wireless, running round the house in their petticoats, that sort of thing," said Peter. "And they're in that show at the Hippodrome. Have you seen the posters?"

"Yes," said Bob.

"Disgusting," said Peter. Then, on a ruminative note, "I'd love to see it."

Janette was not as pretty as Betty but there was a certain elegance to her that reminded Emma of girls in French films. She sat on the edge of her bed and smoked a cigarette, her legs wrapped round each other, one arm across her lap. Defensive, thought Emma, making a note of the pose. Janette had only been in the tableaux show for six months but had immediately "teamed up" with Betty. "Most of the girls share in twos. It's cheaper and more fun. Safer too if you get a landlord with wandering hands."

"Does that happen often?" said Emma.

Janette shrugged. "It happens a bit. The landlord here's all right though. He's too terrified of his wife to try anything."

"What did you do before the tableaux?"

Janette laughed and exhaled smoke. "I was married. Got married straight out of school. This was in the war when every girl was marrying the first man they saw. I met Larry at a dance and thought he was the bee's knees in his RAF uniform. After the war, crammed together in a one-room flat, he didn't seem so marvellous. I got out, worked as a waitress for a while, met Vic Cutler and the rest is history."

"Do you enjoy it?"

"It's all right," said Janette, echoing Betty. "I don't want to do it for ever, though. What I really enjoy is the business side. I'd like to run my own troupe. Vic takes too big a cut. Someone's got to pay for his cars and his mistresses. If I was running things, I'd put money back into the act."

She seemed quite animated now and uncrossed her legs, gesturing with one arm to show her limitless ambition. Ash fell from her cigarette onto the rug. Emma brought her back to earth by asking how well she knew Lily. Janette's face clouded immediately.

"Not very well. Poor kid. I just can't believe that she's dead. She was a nice girl. Pretty too. Betty and me, we wanted to bring her out of herself a bit. Otherwise I thought she'd be like me and marry the first man who asked her."

"Do you know if anyone did ask her?"

"No. I don't think she had a chance to meet anyone, stuck in that flower shop all day. That's why we took her out with us. We even took her to the theatre to watch a rehearsal one evening. She was really interested in the act."

Had Lily thought of going on the stage? wondered Emma. But, although the showgirls both seemed friendly, she didn't imagine that their life looked that enticing from Lily's angle.

"What about the person who left the flowers?" she asked. "Did Lily talk to you about that?"

"Yes," said Janette. "We used to laugh about it. Just shows you, doesn't it. Everyone's got a secret admirer somewhere."

Emma didn't like the sound of this at all. Bob often implied that she had her admirers amongst the younger police officers but, as far as Emma was concerned, they could stay secret.

"When did you last see Lily?" she asked.

"On Thursday night. Betty and I had been to the flicks. We were making cocoa here, on the gas ring, and we heard Lily moving about upstairs so we invited her to join us. We had a nice chat and then Lily said goodnight and went to bed. Oh God . . ." Janette put down her cigarette and stared at Emma with real horror in her eyes. "I never thought that I wouldn't see her again."

And Janette threw aside her showgirl sophistication and started to cry.

Bob was interviewing Norris in the snug. Edna had been initially reluctant to leave them alone and again expressed the view that no one was going to interview *her*, thank you very much.

"Sergeant Holmes will probably just have a chat in a minute," said Bob, trying for a soothing tone. Edna

34

reminded him of his own landlady, a terrifying woman known locally as Portslade Patsy.

Norris had been fairly equable though. He'd even made Bob a cup of tea and offered him a scone.

"I do quite a lot of the cooking," he said. "Edna doesn't really have much time, what with her work on the townswomen's guild and everything."

"How long have you lived here?" asked Bob.

"Ever since Edna and I got married, twenty-odd years ago. Edna inherited the house from her parents. They rented rooms out too so we're carrying on in the family tradition, as it were."

Not your family tradition, thought Bob. He asked where Norris was from.

"Surrey originally," said Norris. "My father was a vicar in Banstead. I worked in an insurance office after school but then the first war came and I joined up. Served in the navy and got pneumonia for my pains." He coughed a bit for good measure. "Weak chest. That's why I didn't serve in the second."

"What can you tell me about Lily?" said Bob. It always made him feel nervous to hear people talking about their war service. He couldn't help having been only ten in 1939.

"She was a lovely girl," said Norris, now sounding genuinely choked. "Edna knew her mother from way back. She looked on us as her family."

Perhaps she did, thought Bob. But people are often killed by their families. He asked Norris when he had last seen Lily.

"I think it was on Friday morning," said Norris. "I was putting out some crumbs for the birds and I saw her leaving for work."

"Did you speak to her?"

"Just 'cheerio', I think."

"What were you doing on Friday night?" asked Bob.

Norris blinked but answered quite calmly. "Edna and I had supper with Mr Entwhistle then we listened to the wireless."

"What time did you go to bed?"

"Quite early. About nine-thirty."

"And did you see or hear anything unusual? Anyone sneaking around outside, for example."

"No. I heard Brenda come in at about ten. Edna says she heard Peggy come in a bit later. But I was probably in the bathroom then. Performing my ablutions."

"Did you hear anything later in the night?"

"One of next door's cats knocked over some flower pots," said Norris. "That was in the early hours. I didn't get up though. It's always happening. They're pests, those animals. People should be made to have a licence, like they do with dogs."

"Can I go and have a look around outside?" said Bob. It might have been cats, he thought, but then again it could have been someone leaving Lily's bedroom. He was rather fond of cats himself.

Meanwhile, Emma was chatting with Edna in the front parlour. It was a pleasant room with two sofas, a large wireless and a cottage piano, its sides painted like a hurdy-gurdy. Emma commented on it.

"My father bought it in an auction," said Edna. "No one really plays it now except Mr Entwhistle sometimes."

"How long have you run a boarding house?" asked Emma.

"It's in my blood," said Edna. "My parents ran this house before me. My mother was a well-known theatrical landlady. We've had them all here. I've seen them come and I've seen them go. The Great Diablo. Lou Lenny and her unrideable mule. Charlie Haystack. The Diller Twins. I've had my share of pros too though I prefer long-term paying guests, like Mr Entwhistle. It's more stable."

"Must be an interesting life," said Emma.

"Oh it is." Edna showed her orange gums in a smile. "I'm like a mother to some of my lodgers. They tell me all their secrets."

"Do you have children of your own?" asked Emma.

"No." Edna's smile sagged a bit. "Norris and I were never blessed."

"How did Lily come to live here?" asked Emma. "I'm just wondering because she was from London."

"I knew her mother from way back," said Edna. "She was in the business. Cecily Harmond her name was then. She had a lovely little act. She used to have a swing with all flowers round it. She would swing out over the audience, singing all the while."

"And did Cecily stay here?" asked Emma.

"Yes, she stayed for a few summer seasons before the war. We kept in touch and, when Lily wanted to come to Brighton, Cecily wrote to ask if I had any rooms vacant. Such a lovely letter she wrote. Oh, poor Cecily." Edna's eyes filled with tears. "Does she know?"

"Yes," said Emma. "She came down to Brighton today to see . . . well, to see Lily."

This set the landlady off again and it was a few minutes before Emma could ask about the last time Edna saw Lily.

"I've been thinking about that," said Edna. "It was Friday afternoon. Must have been about half past five. Lily had just come back from work and I'd just had my hair set. Lily complimented me on it. She was such a nice girl."

Emma looked at the bluish waves balancing on Edna's head. Lily must have been very nice indeed, she thought.

"How did Lily seem?" asked Emma.

"Same as usual," said Edna. "A bit tired maybe. She was carrying some flowers, red and white roses. She often brought flowers back from work. I suppose they don't keep, do they? We just chatted about this and that. I asked after Cecily. Lily said she was looking forward to going home for Christmas." Edna threatened to be overcome yet again but, as she started to sniff, the doorbell rang. Edna and Emma both looked in its direction, like gundogs.

They heard Norris talking in the hall and then a voice that Emma recognised immediately.

"Is that the detective inspector?" said Edna, patting her hair.

"Yes," said Emma.

"I must go and say hallo." Edna got to her feet, every inch the welcoming landlady, but Emma stayed where she was. After a few minutes the DI came into the room, accompanied by Edna, Norris and Bob. He looked pale, thought Emma, but otherwise in control.

"Have you talked to everyone in the house?" He addressed the question to Emma but Bob answered.

"Yes. Peggy Barnet and Brenda Stebbings aren't back yet."

"Have you been up the top floor yet?"

"No," said Emma. The detective in her was longing to examine the murder scene, the other half was dreading seeing Lily's room.

"We'll go up now, do a proper search."

But, in the hall, they met with a traffic jam. Two young women in coats and scarves, laughing as they got back from work, meeting Betty and Janette, red-eyed and grim-faced, setting off for the theatre.

CHAPTER
FOUR

"Have you heard?" said Ruby. "Someone was murdered in one of the girls' digs."

Max stopped, halfway through applying greasepaint. "What?"

"You know Betty, the one with sausage curls? Well a girl was killed in her lodgings. Murdered in her bed, Betty said. She's very upset. Janette too. They share a room."

"Where are these lodgings?"

"Hove. Off Western Road. Do you think that's why Edgar couldn't come tonight?"

Marvelling afresh at the way that Ruby managed to turn everything, even murder, back to herself, he said, "I expect so. Poor old Ed. Another crazed killer on the loose."

"Do you think that's who it was?" Ruby gave a shiver. "A crazed killer."

"No," said Max. "It's usually the boyfriend or the father, someone like that. Murder's pretty boring on the whole."

"Edgar caught the Conjuror Killer," said Ruby. She was almost the only person who still used this name.

Max and Edgar talked about the case as little as possible.

"With a bit of help from Diablo," said Max. "Did you know he was coming tonight?"

"Uncle Stan?" Ruby brightened. "I can't wait to see him."

"He's with his landlady friend, Queenie."

"What about *your* landlady friend?" said Ruby, looking at herself in the mirror.

"She's coming," said Max, watching Ruby's refection. She was so pretty, with her dark hair and brown long-lashed eyes. Did she look like him? He couldn't see it although Joe said that they were "two peas in a pod". He couldn't see Ruby's mother, Emerald, in her either. Mind you, he could hardly remember what Emerald had looked like when she was young. She had been pretty, though, he was sure of that. When he thought of that far-off summer in Worthing, when he and Emerald had fallen in love, he could only picture impossibly good weather, making love on the beach, walking hand in hand along the promenade while the band played. He couldn't recall actual details like the colour of Emerald's eyes, though, curiously enough, he could remember the name of the python who had been her partner in the act. It was called George. Secretly he thought that Ruby probably resembled his mother, an Italian opera singer, who had died when he was six.

Ruby turned and grinned at him. She had an irresistible smile, with dimples appearing in each cheek.

"We'd better put on a good show then. Especially as the girls might be a bit below par."

Peggy and Brenda didn't seem to be able to take in the news at first. "But we only saw her on Thursday," said Brenda, a solid-looking girl with a fringe and pale, rather protuberant, eyes. "We went to the flicks together."

"I'm really sorry," said Emma, "but we need to get an idea of Lily's last movements. Would you mind answering a few more questions?"

"No," said Brenda. She started to rearrange a group of glass animals on her bedside table. Peggy and Brenda's room was the same size as the one shared by Betty and Janette but it was much more homely. There were chintz curtains at the window and matching pink candlewick bedspreads on the twin beds. The bedside table also had a ruffled chintz skirt. Emma wondered whether one of the girls had made it themselves — it didn't seem Edna's style somehow. The ornaments were obviously Brenda's: a horse with a green tail, an elephant with an orange trunk, three rather unpleasant-looking monkeys that were welded together. See no evil, speak no evil, hear no evil. Emma had never really gone in for toys herself, even as a child. Her favourite companion had been an imaginary horse on whom she used to gallop for hours, cantering down the corridors at school and changing into an embarrassed skip if she saw a teacher coming. She couldn't imagine transporting a menagerie like this from house to house. But

Brenda and Peggy had lived at Lansdowne Road for over a year so maybe it seemed like home to them now.

Brenda came from Shoreham, she told Emma. She'd worked at the local bank since leaving school but was offered the chance to transfer to the Brighton branch. "Senior cashier," she said, lining up the glass animals so that they could catch the light. "It was a real opportunity." She'd commuted from home at first but then Peggy, who worked at the same branch, had found the room with Mrs Wright and suggested that they share.

"It's a nice room," said Brenda, "and convenient for work. It's nice to have someone to share with as well." "Nice" seemed to be her favourite adjective.

"How well did you know Lily?" asked Emma.

"Quite well. She moved in about the same time as us. She's ever such a nice girl. Oh dear . . ." Brenda reached for a tissue from an embroidered box (chintz naturally). "I just can't believe she's dead. Who would do such a terrible thing?"

"That's what we've got to find out," said Emma. "Did Lily ever talk to you about work, about her life? Boyfriends, for example?"

"She didn't have a boyfriend," said Brenda. "Like I said, she was a quiet girl."

Being quiet doesn't stop you having boyfriends, thought Emma. She had been quiet herself but neither that, nor going to an all girls' school, had stopped her having several teenage romances. True, the boys involved hadn't always been aware of them, but the emotion had been real enough at the time.

"Betty said that someone used to leave flowers outside Lily's room," she said. "Did you know anything about that?"

"Oh, Lily mentioned something about it," said Brenda. "I don't think it was anything serious though. She used to giggle about it."

"But you had no idea who it was?"

"No. Every girl has something like that though. Someone used to leave love notes on my typewriter when I worked in Shoreham."

But you haven't been brutally murdered, thought Emma, so it's not relevant.

"Can we go back to when you last saw Lily?" she said. "I think you said it was Thursday night?"

"Yes. We'd been to the pictures. They were showing *The Robe*. Such a nice film, very religious. We came back at about nine. Lily went upstairs to her room but later I heard her talking to Betty and Janette in the hall."

"You didn't go out and join them?"

"No. I didn't really know Betty and Janette all that well. They're only staying for two weeks and . . . well . . . they're on the stage. They're not really our sort."

Betty and Janette had been to the cinema on Thursday too, remembered Emma. She was willing to bet that they hadn't seen *The Robe*. It was interesting that Lily, supposedly so quiet and shy, had apparently got on well with the two theatricals. She'd been interested in the show too, going in to watch a rehearsal and planning to watch a performance.

44

"What did you do on Friday night?" she asked Brenda.

"Went to see my mother in Shoreham," said Brenda. "I left straight from work and got back at about ten."

"And you didn't see Lily?"

"No, the house was quiet. Mr Entwhistle goes to bed early and Peggy was out with Steve."

But the house hadn't been completely quiet, thought Emma. They wouldn't know until they had the post-mortem results but it was probable that, at some time during Friday night, the quiet girl in the attic bedroom had been strangled.

Bob found Peggy rather more congenial. She was a pretty redhead who, in happier circumstances, was probably the sort of girl who laughed easily. Today though, she was shocked and tearful, putting her hand over her mouth if she thought she had spoken too loudly or too cheerfully. It was probably a good idea to speak quietly, Bob thought. They were in the snug and, although they could hear Edna crashing about in the kitchen, he wouldn't put it above her to listen at the door.

Peggy said that she'd liked Lily. Peggy, Brenda and Lily quite often went out together, to the flicks or to the Lyons'. She'd last seen Lily on Thursday night when the three of them had been to the pictures. They'd said goodnight but Lily had come down later to have cocoa with Betty and Janette. Peggy had been out with her fiancé on Friday night. His name was Steve and he was a printer at the *Argus*. They'd said goodnight on the doorstep — Mrs Wright wouldn't let Steve come in the house after lights out — and Peggy had gone to bed. She thought it was about eleven. Brenda was already asleep. No, she hadn't heard anything from upstairs. Shudder.

"Was that when it happened? When Lily was . . ."

"I can't say," said Bob, shutting his notebook. "Thank you very much for your help."

And then it was time to go upstairs. The DI was already there, standing thoughtfully in the middle of the room. Emma forced herself to look at the scene dispassionately: single bed with white eiderdown, bedside table with jam jar of flowers (red and white roses), chair, wardrobe, towel rail, chest of drawers, two windows with venetian blinds half-drawn. It was a big room, high-ceilinged and bitterly cold, the central light fitting swaying in a thorough draught. By the bed there was a large bloodstain on the bare boards.

"Was this where she was?" asked Emma.

"Yes." The DI seemed to wake from his reverie. "She was kneeling by the bed, tied to the back of this chair." He indicated the cane-backed chair. "Her arm was tied to the back of the towel rail to make it look as if she was pointing." The towel rail was just a wooden bar between two uprights. It was standing at right angles to the chair.

"Facing the bed?"

"Yes."

Emma turned to face the bed but all she could see was the wall opposite, painted cream above the wooden dado rail, green below. Why had Lily been posed in this way? What had she been pointing at?

"Where was the box? The vegetable crate?"

"Here. Beside the bed. I've sent it to the lab to see if they can dust it for fingerprints. There's still some straw from it over there." He pointed to the corner of the room where wisps of straw gave a strangely rural impression, as if they were in a barn.

"There aren't many personal items," said the DI. "Just a novel and a letter on the bedside table."

Emma went over to look. As well as the flowers in the jam jar, now dropping their petals, there was a letter in a lilac envelope and a paperback romance showing a yellow-haired nurse being embraced by a square-jawed doctor.

"Can I look at the letter?" she said.

"Yes," said the DI. "Wear gloves though." This was one of the DI's obsessions, not touching anything in the crime scene without wearing gloves. Emma pulled on her leather gloves. The letter was dated a week ago. It began, "Dearest Lily" and ended "Keep smiling, Mum." Emma felt her eyes beginning to prickle. She opened the book and found a dried carnation between the pages.

"Someone used to leave flowers outside Lily's room," she said. "Betty told me."

"Really?" The DI looked up. "That could be very significant. Did Betty have any idea who it was?"

"No," said Emma, "she seemed to treat it as a bit of a joke. Brenda did too. She said Lily used to giggle about it."

"Maybe," said the DI. "But that doesn't mean that the sender didn't have some sinister purpose in mind."

"Everyone says she was a quiet girl," said Bob, who'd just come in and seemed unwilling to touch anything in the room. "Quiet and shy with no boyfriends."

"That may be true," said Edgar. "Someone may have been attracted by her precisely because she seemed so shy and enigmatic. And she was a very good-looking girl. Look, her mother gave me this." He pulled a photograph from his inside pocket. It was a studio portrait showing Lily, three-quarter face, with her blonde hair flowing around her.

"She was beautiful," said Emma. "She looks more like an actress than the two that live downstairs."

"That's what her mother said." The DI held the picture up to the light. "She said, 'Lily could have been on the stage with looks like that but she wasn't interested in performing. All she wanted to do was work in a little flower shop.' "

"Were these the flowers that were left outside her room?" said Bob, pointing to the jam jar.

"Maybe," said Emma. "But Edna said she saw Lily holding flowers when she came home on Friday. Apparently she often brought flowers back from work."

"We don't have a time of death yet," said Edgar, "but Carter said he thought it could have been on Friday night."

"Brenda was visiting her mother on Friday night," said Emma. "She said the house was quiet when she got back."

48

"Peggy was out with her fiancé," said Bob. "She says the same."

Emma opened the wardrobe door. Inside were two black dresses, maybe the ones that Lily wore for work, three tweed skirts and a formal green suit. There was also a black overcoat with a green paisley scarf around the neck. On the floor were black boots, padded with newspaper to keep their shape, some brogues and a pair of court shoes. In the chest of drawers she found jumpers and blouses, all neatly folded. Underwear was in the drawer below together with a lavender bag. No love letters hidden under the lining paper, nothing untoward or out of place; it was all so ordinary and unassuming that it made Emma feel nervous.

"What was she wearing when you found her?" she asked.

"A white nightdress," said Edgar. "Linen, I think."

"There are pyjamas in the drawer here," said Emma. "Fleecy-lined ones. That's what she would have worn on a cold night. I think someone dressed her in the nightdress specially."

Bob was quiet and Emma thought that he might disapprove of her rummaging through Lily's clothing but it seemed she had misjudged him. After staring at the bedside table for a few minutes, he said, "Where's the letter?"

"What letter?" said Emma.

"Mr Entwhistle said that Lily got a letter on Friday morning," said Bob. "It's not here."

"I'll get someone to search the dustbins," said Edgar. "Come on. Let's go back to the station. There's nothing more to see here."

CHAPTER
FIVE

Max felt slightly awkward watching the act from the wings. He was uncomfortably aware that several other pros, and the ASM Toby, were also standing in the shadows as the girls took up their positions in the spotlight. Toby, to Max's right, seemed to be breathing particularly heavily.

The act was more complicated than it first seemed. The girls struck various artistic poses at first, feathers strategically placed. Then the stage darkened and the performers arranged themselves, with minimal props, into various scenes from history. There was a projection screen in place of a backcloth and Toby's job was to slot in slides showing various settings: the pyramids, Stonehenge, a seascape. Another stagehand was in charge of putting coloured filters on the pageant lamp.

Even with the slides it was sometimes quite hard to tell what was going on. Max found that the best clue was the music. A minuet and Elizabeth I, wearing a ruff and very little else, stood contemplating a curvaceous Walter Raleigh and his cloak. Some watery Debussy and the Lady of Shalott lay on a chaise longue, obviously meant to be a boat, while the other girls held branches of silk flowers over her. A martial tune and

Boadicea mounted her chariot, whip in hand. At band call that morning it had occurred to Max that the orchestra at the Hippodrome were better than the usual standard for variety, where disparate musicians at the lowest end of their union pay-scale gathered together to scrape out tunes that started quite hopefully but didn't always end in the same key. The conductor was a young man called Tommy Watson and he was playing the piano now. The Debussy had really sounded quite good.

Now Tommy launched into the "Grand March" from *Aida* and the death of Cleopatra was being enacted, with the aid of a large stuffed snake. This was, from Max's point of view, the most interesting tableau because it featured Florence in the role of the Egyptian queen. Florence lay on the chaise longue, wearing a gold headdress, with the snake arranged artistically across her breasts. Two of the other girls were her handmaidens and they reposed at her feet, intertwined in a vaguely Sapphic way. From the wings, Max could see Florence's dark hair almost touching the dusty stage and the sheen of perspiration on her outstretched leg, toes painted dark red. Her skin was golden-brown but he couldn't tell if this was natural or greasepaint. He thought about the girls whose housemate had been killed. Were they in this scene and, if so, how did they feel, re-enacting death when its shadow had come so close? It felt wrong to be looking at the women in this way and the snake reminded him of Emerald. Max turned and left the wings.

The girls were the last act before the interval. Max could hear the applause as he descended the stairs to his dressing room. Dick, the producer, had told him rather gleefully that he had had several letters of protest about Vic Cutler's Living Tableaux, including one from the League of Public Decency, but there was no doubt that they were getting a good reception tonight. In the corridor he found Ruby chatting with Stew Stewart, the young comedian who had second billing.

"Hallo, Max," said Stew, with a grin. "Been getting an eyeful of the natural wonders?"

As this was precisely what Max had been doing, he couldn't exactly protest his innocence, but he found Stewart's tone offensive. Stew Stewart was one of the new wave of comics, trousers slightly too short and jacket slightly too big, full of naturalistic banter that bordered on the surreal. Ruby clearly found him highly amusing.

"Can I have a word about the act?" he said to Ruby. "Excuse us, Stew."

"Don't mind me," said Stewart, chortling as if this was a brilliant piece of repartee.

Apart from the desk sergeant on reception, the police station at Bartholomew Square was deserted. The CID rooms were dark and cold, even when Emma plugged in the two-bar electric fire. Edgar would have to call in reinforcements tomorrow, get some officers to guard Lansdowne Road, call in specials to go door-to-door asking if anyone had seen anything suspicious on Friday night or Saturday morning. He thought back to the house, the warmth of the downstairs rooms, the chill in the attic, the rose petals falling, the blood on the floorboards. He thought of Cecily Burtenshaw's face when she had seen her daughter's body in the mortuary. "She was so beautiful," she said, again and again, touching the cold face. Yes, Lily had been beautiful. Was that why she had been killed?

Emma and Bob still had their coats on but Edgar knew that they would be prepared to work through the night if he asked them to. But there would be time enough for that when they had the post-mortem report and the photographs of the crime scene.

"Did you get anything interesting from the flower shop owner?" he asked.

"Not really," said Bob. "Lily was a nice girl, worked hard. No followers or anything like that. She went out to lunch with the girls from the bank sometimes."

"Betty and Janette called for her once," said Emma. "The owner didn't seem too keen on them."

"Well, they're showgirls, aren't they?" said Bob. "She wouldn't like them. Mind you, I thought they seemed very nice, very ladylike."

Sometimes, when Bob spoke, Edgar could hear Bob's mother's voice, although he had never met her.

"I thought it was interesting that Lily, who was supposed to be so shy, got on so well with Betty and Janette," said Emma. "After all, she'd only known them a week and she was meeting them for lunch and having late-night cocoa with them. She even went to watch a rehearsal. Maybe she was more interested in the theatre than she seemed."

54

"Her mother had been on the stage," said Edgar, "so surely Lily could have gone into show business if she'd wanted. In fact, Cecily seemed a bit disappointed that she hadn't."

"She went into her father's business instead," said Emma. "I wonder if there's anything significant in the flowers."

"Do you mean the flowers left by the mysterious admirer?" said Bob.

Emma was frowning as she often did when she was thinking. "I just wonder if there was a clue in the actual flowers. She was called Lily, after all. The flowers by her bed were red and white roses."

"What do they signify?" asked Edgar. "Apart from the Wars of the Roses?"

"I think they're bad luck," said Emma. "My cousin Pandora had them in her wedding bouquet and Mummy said that it was a mistake."

Edgar saw Bob's lips twitch at "Pandora" and "Mummy" but wisely he said nothing.

"We should have the photographs developed tomorrow," said Edgar. "And the lab will have dusted Lily's clothes for fingerprints. There's nothing more we can do tonight. Let's go home and get some sleep."

There was always a slight frisson before the first night, especially a Monday when you knew that the audience was going to be full of stern-faced landladies with their handbags on their laps. Max and Ruby waited in the wings and, on stage, Jim Jones drank a pint of beer while Reggie, his dummy, sang the national anthem.

"God save our gracious Queen." There was a slight gargle but it was still rather impressive. It still felt odd to hear "Queen" instead of "King", not that Max was much of a royalist. He looked behind him to check that the vanishing box was in place and was surprised to see, next to Toby, a willowy figure in a gold dressing gown. Florence Jones. Her dark hair was loose and her face looked very pale in the shadows. When she saw Max looking, she waved, just a small movement of her fingers. Max normally didn't allow the other pros to watch him backstage. The last thing he wanted was for the whole world to know how he did his tricks. Magic was still about mystique, whatever Joe said. But, as he had watched Florence earlier, he didn't feel that he could object. Even so, he felt slightly jolted.

"Say goodnight to the nice ladies and gentlemen," Jim was telling Reggie.

"Goodnight, nice ladies and gentlemen."

Applause, not over-generous but not niggardly either. Jim bowed and Reggie inclined his wooden head. Jim came off and Max murmured, "Well done."

"Not bad for a Monday," said Jim. "Do you think I could milk another bow?"

"Give it a try."

Jim went back for another bow and the applause just covered his exit. In the orchestra pit, Max saw Tommy Watson lifting his baton. There was a definite whisper of anticipation in the audience and suddenly Max longed to be out there, alone on stage in the circle of light. This was why you performed; why you put up with the travelling, the depressing digs, the eccentric

56

pros, the loneliness, the lack of security. This moment, waiting in the wings for your entrance, the stage empty but charged with a magic more potent than anything Max could create. The orchestra was beginning his signature slow version of the "Danse Macabre". "Break a leg," whispered Ruby behind him. Max felt his sleeves and pockets for props, then he touched the silver Madonna that he kept next to his heart. Finally, he walked round in an anticlockwise circle. Widdershins. For luck. Then, as the music faded, the curtain rose and he walked out onto the stage.

Emma walked home. Her father was always telling her to get a taxi when it was dark but she preferred to take the bus or walk. You were alone with your thoughts that way and didn't have to make conversation with a cheerful cabbie ("Been working late, love?").

"After what happened last year," said her mother, "you'd think you'd be more careful."

"I am careful," said Emma. And she was. The memory of last year's attack still had the power to wake her up at night, sitting bolt upright and groping for the light switch, but she would never admit this to anyone, least of all her parents. But she kept to the well-lit roads as much as possible, fingers clasped around the keys in her pocket. As she cut up behind Marine Parade she thought of Tol and Astarte. Should she pop in to see them? Astarte would know whether red and white roses were bad luck or not. She'd met the Bartons, father and daughter, on a previous case. Tol (short for Ptolemy) was a chef who had recently bought a coffee shop in Brighton, a place that was becoming increasingly popular with the town's young people. Astarte was a clairvoyant, one of a long line of gypsy women with "the sight". Emma was never sure that she believed in Astarte's visions but she had grown fond of the Bartons. The thought of coming in out of the cold, perhaps being asked to stay for supper, was a beguiling one but Emma kept walking. They were sure to want to know about the case and, although Astarte was meant to have second sight, it was Tol's perception that she was worried about. He always knew when she was hiding something and would ask awkward questions. Better keep going. It was a cold night and the roads were deserted but, walking along St James's Street, she could hear people in the pubs, a beery convivial hum that made her almost want to join them, although she always turned down Bob's invitations to join the other young officers in the Bath Arms.

Despite everything, it felt quite exciting to be working on a serious case again. She liked the intimacy of discussing the evidence with Bob and the DI, the three of them alone in the basement room with the two-bar fire. The DI was going to marry Ruby in the summer. She knew she had no chance of ever winning his love but at least she had this, a professional closeness that excluded even Ruby. She was sure that, when Edgar and Ruby were together, the conversation ran on lighter topics, the main topic probably being Ruby herself, Edgar would never tell his fiancée the gory details of a murder. Gory details were probably not an ideal basis for a relationship but they were better than nothing and Emma had a stronger stomach than Bob, or the DI himself, come to that. She was ashamed at the shot of pleasure that had run through her when she realised that Edgar was not going to be able to attend Ruby's show that night.

But the case was unsettling too. Of course it was. A young woman had been murdered. A mother had lost her child. The DI said that the interview with Mrs Burtenshaw had been "tough" and Emma could only imagine how tough. The DI always insisted on seeing the relatives himself although Emma knew that he hated that part of the job. Well, if all they could do for Lily's mother was find her daughter's murderer, that was what they would do. This was why Emma had joined the police, in the face of strong parental opposition, rather than going to university or finishing school. Most of her classmates at Roedean had gone on to be presented at court as debutantes and many were now married with children. Only Emma was walking the mean streets of Brighton, searching for a killer. The thought made her feel strong and self-reliant.

She passed Upper Rock Gardens, where Joyce Markham had her boarding house. She liked the landlady who, in her own words, had taken quite a fancy to Emma. Would Mrs M be at the show tonight? She thought of Betty and Janette, standing totally still on the stage while thousands of eyes stared at them. To Emma, this was a more frightening thought than being attacked again. Even so, she quickened her pace as she passed the golf course. Too much space and darkness, too many places to hide. Where had Lily's assailant hidden? According to Bob there were several places where an intruder could have got in. The side door was usually kept unlocked and there was another entrance through the scullery. The house was large and rambling with lots of rooms on different levels. Next to Lily's bedroom was a bathroom and an airing cupboard. The killer could easily have hidden there, crouched below the clean sheets, waiting for Lily's return.

Now she could see the lights of her house. Her mother never stinted on electricity. Ada, the housekeeper, would meet her at the door and fuss about her supper. Her duffel coat would be taken and aired in front of the Aga. Her father would try to make her drink a glass of sherry, "keeps out the cold". She thought of Betty's descriptions of life in Lansdowne Road: the wireless playing, laughter on the landing, late-night chats over cocoa. Despite the squalor of the rooms — despite even the murder in the top bedroom — Emma briefly wished that this was what awaited her at the end of her walk.

The act went well. Max could always feel when the crowd were with him, and even with all the landladies sitting on their hands, the audience at the Hippodrome were with Magician and Daughter all the way, carrying them on great waves of approval. They laughed at every quip and gasped at every trick. Finally, when Ruby opened the doors to show that the vanishing box was empty and that Max had disappeared, there was almost a howl of bewilderment and appreciation. Then, when Max re-emerged and took Ruby's hand, the audience cheered them to the rafters. Max had meant to kiss Ruby on the cheek but, in the excitement of the moment, he gave her a hug that lifted her off her feet. More cheers.

In Max's dressing room, Joe poured champagne and prophesied a glittering future.

"To Magician and Daughter."

"Magician and Daughter," echoed Diablo, draining his glass in one easy movement. "You were magnificent, dear boy. And Ruby . . ." He kissed his fingers at her. "You were superb."

"Thank you, Uncle Stan." Ruby twinkled prettily at him from across the room. The old magician, wearing a rather threadbare velvet smoking jacket and matching bow tie, was sitting next to Queenie on the sofa and Max knew that he did not intend to move for hours (or until all the alcohol had been consumed).

"They'll love this act on TV, Maxie boy," Joe was saying. "Think of the business the two of you can do. All the father and daughter stuff but with magic thrown in. It's a winner. Did you hear how they cheered when you gave Ruby a hug? People are seeing the real Max Mephisto for the first time."

"How do you know which is the real Max Mephisto?" said Mrs M from the dressing-table chair, slotting a cigarette into her amber holder. She sounded amused.

"It doesn't matter," said Joe, dismissing this with one of his exuberant Latinate gestures. "What matters is that they *think* they're seeing the real Max."

"Maybe I should have a spot on my own first," said Ruby, "then people could get to see the real me."

"Are you sure that's a good idea, dear?" said Mrs M.

"Maybe later," said Joe. "This is the act for now. A week in Brighton, a week in the West End after Christmas, then the TV spot in the early spring. Perfect. I'd better see Don from the *Evening Argus* now. I want you two on the front page tomorrow."

"Did you hear about the murder?" said Ruby. "Won't that be on the front page?"

Joe's face darkened when Ruby told him about the death in Betty's digs.

"The Wrights' place," said Mrs M. "I know Edna. Her mother used to run the house before her. Quite a few pros have stayed there over the years."

"Is there any link to the show?" asked Joe, tapping his programme against his leg.

"Not really," said Ruby. "It's just that Betty and Janette knew the girl."

"Good," said Joe. "I don't want you or Max mixed up in anything like this. Wholesome's the name of the game from now on."

"Wholesome!" Diablo gave a laugh that turned into a coughing fit. "You'd better hope the public haven't got long memories then," he said, wiping his eyes.

"Don't you worry," said Joe. "The public will remember what I tell them to remember."

62

"You're very confident," said Ruby, looking at him under her lashes.

"Of course, I'm confident," said Joe. "I've got two artistes here — two *stars* — who are going places. Today Brighton, tomorrow the world."

Max could never work out whether Joe meant this sort of thing to be funny or not. At any rate, Diablo seemed to find it highly amusing. He said, wiping his eyes, "You remind me of a playbill I once had. It said, 'The Great Diablo, a star in Sheffield *and* Darlington.' "

"You were a big star once, Stan," said Queenie, patting his arm.

"I've had my moments," said Diablo. "Last one approximately 1928."

He leered affectionately at Queenie, which made Max feel rather uncomfortable. What was the relationship between those two? He had stayed at Queenie's boarding house once and she had made it abundantly clear that, should Max so desire it, he could move from his guest bedroom into her four-poster with en-suite bathroom and sea views. Diablo was seventy at the most charitable estimate but the lure of the landlady was not to be underestimated. Look at him and Mrs M.

"Shall we go out to eat somewhere?" he said. "Unless you want to be getting back to Hastings."

"Oh, the night is young," said Diablo, draining his glass. "Besides, Queenie's driving."

Somehow Joe managed to invite himself along to the meal. Max didn't mind too much, at least he provided Ruby with some younger company. They walked along

63

the seafront, Max and Mrs M in front, followed by Queenie and Diablo, with Joe and Ruby bringing up the rear. There was a new moon over the sea, a sliver of silver, and they all had to stop while Diablo wished on it.

"Make a wish," Joe urged Ruby.

Max saw her shut her eyes like a child as her lips moved silently. Though he couldn't have said why, he suddenly felt anxious for her. He made a wish of his own, "Please look after Ruby." It was the first time in his life that a wish of this kind hadn't involved fame and fortune.

They went to an Italian restaurant in the Lanes where Max knew the owner, one of the few places still open at ten o'clock on a Monday night. Joe spoke in Italian to the waiter and a bottle of champagne appeared, as if by magic.

"Oh, you're another Italian, are you?" said Diablo. "That's probably why you get on so well with Max."

"I'm Sicilian," said Joe. "A Sicilian is an Italian with a knife in each hand."

"I think that probably sounds better in the original Sicilian," said Max.

Dinner was convivial enough. Diablo kept up a continual flow of show-business reminiscences and Mrs M and Queenie chimed in with tales of their respective lodgers. "I found him in bed with two of the dwarves from Snow White . . . I wouldn't mind but it was only a single bed." Max let the conversation wash over him and watched Ruby, her face vivid and changeable in the candlelight, listening as Joe sketched out her brilliant career: "Television but that's just the start, with your looks and talent you could go all the way . . ." It was true, thought Max, Ruby did have a glittering future ahead of her. She had the perfect show-business temperament: charming, tough and resilient. She wasn't afraid of hard work either. Well, both of her parents had been in the business after all.

He realised that Diablo was speaking to him.

"This murder," he said, leaning forward across the table, "is Edgar handling the case?"

"I think so, yes."

"Poor boy. He always takes these things so hard. Remember those two children a few years ago?"

"Yes," said Max, hoping that Diablo wasn't about to go into more detail.

"I like Edgar," said Mrs M. "He's always so polite and considerate. Good-looking too."

"Who's this?" Queenie pricked her ears up.

"Ruby's fiancé," said Mrs M.

Ruby heard her name and turned round. "Are you talking about me?" she said.

"About your handsome policeman," said Mrs M. "When's the big day?"

"June, I think," said Ruby, gouging wax out of the candle in front of her.

"You think? Aren't you sure?"

"June the twelfth."

"A June bride," said Queenie. "How romantic. I was married in February. It rained solidly all day. We were happy though." She sighed and absent-mindedly ate a piece of bread.

"Will it be in Brighton?" said Joe. "We should get the *Argus* to cover it."

"In Hove," said Ruby. "At the church my parents go to. Edgar wants a small wedding though."

"We can't have that," said Joe. "You should book the Grand. I know the manager there."

"Big weddings can be a bit of an ordeal," said Max.

"How do you know?" Ruby turned on him. "You've never been married."

"That's true," said Diablo. "And when you think of the number of girls who've tried to drag him to the altar."

Joyce winked at Max across the table but he thought it was probably time to bring the conversation to a close. He signalled to the waiter for the bill.

"No, Maxie boy." Joe reached for his wallet. "Let me. I insist."

Joe could be hard going, thought Max, as the agent brought out a fat roll of notes, but there were compensations.

CHAPTER
SIX

Tuesday

The post-mortem reports were on Edgar's desk in the morning. The coroner estimated that Lily had been dead for at least forty-eight hours which could still put time of death on Friday afternoon. Death was by manual strangulation, killer possibly left-handed.

"There's something odd about left-handers," said Bob.

"An interesting survival of an old superstition," said Emma briskly. "Left is *sinistra* in Italian, hence left-handers being seen as sinister and Catholics being called left-footers."

"The bend sinister," said Edgar. "That's what they call it in heraldry." He remembered this from his Oxford days. Max was left-handed, he said it was an advantage in tricks requiring sleight of hand. He was a Catholic too.

"Solomon Carter also thought that she could have been drugged," he said. "Maybe with chloroform. There were traces about her mouth, apparently."

"So someone drugged her, then strangled her, then arranged her body in the kneeling position," said Bob.

You could always rely on Bob to state the obvious, but somehow, this flat sequence of events, relayed in Bob's most wooden voice, was curiously chilling.

"It's hard to believe that no one in the house heard anything," said Edgar.

"Betty and Janette got back from their rehearsal at eight," said Emma, looking through her notes. "Then they listened to the wireless for a while. Maybe that was pretty loud. Edna used to complain about it apparently. At any rate, when Brenda got in at ten, she said that the house was quiet."

"Peggy said goodnight to her fiancé at eleven," said Bob, "and she said the same."

"We should interview the boyfriend," said Edgar. "It's a long shot but he's another person who knew the house well. He could have had a secret crush on Lily."

"Norris said that he heard cats knocking over some flower pots in the early hours," said Bob, "but when I looked outside there was no sign that anything had fallen over. There was no sign of any intruders either but it was getting dark by then. There is a shed with a flat roof. Someone could have stood on it to get in through one of the first-floor windows but it's hard to see how anyone could have done that without being noticed. I mean, the house was full of people."

Yes, the house was full of people, thought Edgar. It was like a picture he'd once seen in a children's book, a tall house with lots of shutters which could be folded back to reveal different rooms, each one concealing a different person. The old man, the showgirls, the bank clerks, Edna and Norris. Who knew what else could be concealed?

"We'll search the garden again today," he said. "It's possible someone got in that way. But if not that leaves just two possibilities: the murderer had a key or it was someone in the house."

Emma was collating the witness statements. "On Friday night, Edna and Norris were listening to the wireless in the front parlour, Mr Entwhistle was in his room, Betty and Janette were rehearsing at the theatre until eight, then they were in their room. Peggy was out with her fiancé and Brenda was visiting her mother in Shoreham. No one remembers seeing a stranger about the place."

"Let me look at the plan again," said Edgar. Bob produced a neat drawing of the house in Lansdowne Road. On the ground floor was the kitchen, with the snug leading off it, dining room and front parlour. There was a toilet in an outside passage which Edgar remembered had a china plaque on the door saying "Little Boys' Room". Mr Entwhistle slept on the first floor, as did Edna and Norris. There was a bathroom and lavatory on this floor too. Betty and Janette and Brenda and Peggy had two rooms on the floor above. Lily's room was in the attic where there was a second bathroom and airing cupboard.

"I keep thinking about Lily's room," said Emma. "Lily was earning six pounds a week and her rent was four pounds. That's quite a lot for a single girl. Why did she want such a big room all to herself? Surely it would have made more sense to share like the other girls."

"Maybe that was the only room available," said Edgar. "Didn't you say that Lily's mother wrote to Edna?"

"Yes, she did," said Emma. "Cecily Burtenshaw had stayed with Edna before the war, when she was on the stage. But I still wonder why Lily came to Brighton in the first place. It isn't as if there aren't flower shops in London."

"Maybe she just liked Brighton," said Bob. "People do."

"But it takes some nerve for a quiet, shy girl like Lily to leave her family home and rent a room somewhere," said Emma. "I just wonder if she did have a boyfriend, someone she didn't want anyone to know about."

"It's possible," said Edgar. "Lily was a very pretty girl. She could have had a secret admirer. And that's a third possibility. Lily could have admitted her murderer herself."

He looked up at the photograph which was now pinned to the incident board. Was it his imagination or did Lily's half-smile seem to hide something? You think you know me, said the dead girl, but you don't.

"We'll need to speak to her family," said Edgar. "I didn't want to bother her mother with too many questions yesterday."

"If she did have a secret," said Emma, in the voice of one who knows, "the last person she'd tell would be her mother."

Edgar was about to answer when PC Hobbs put his head round the door and said that the photographs had been developed. The prints were slightly wet and smelt of chemicals. Edgar spread them out on his desk. The black and white images shone with a ghostly luminosity. The girl kneeling by the bed in her nightdress, her eyes bound by the white cloth, hand outstretched. Emma pushed her chair back.

"I'm going out," she said, "won't be long."

"Where are you going?" said Edgar. He supposed that, technically, she should have asked his permission.

"Library," came back Emma's reply. She was already halfway up the stairs.

Edgar and Bob looked at each other. "Did she say the library?" said Bob.

Max always liked to pop into his dressing room the morning after the first night. There he would check his post, go back over the act to see if any modifications needed to be made, maybe even catch the first of the reviews. Theatres usually had a friendly atmosphere in the mornings, not the frantic preparations of the evening, more a pleasant buzz of activity: flats being painted, costumes being repaired, pros wandering around wondering whether it was time for the first drink of the day.

Max walked briskly along the seafront. The clouds were low over the sea and a bitter wind was blowing. Max didn't mind though. He felt that his head needed clearing, in more ways than one. When they left the restaurant last night, Joe had walked Ruby home and the long-suffering Queenie had driven Diablo back to Hastings. Max and Joyce had gone back to Upper Rock Gardens where they had drunk brandy and repaired to bed. Joyce had been in the mood for sex and he had been able to perform, but only just. It was the drink, he told himself, and the fact that he was forty-four, not twenty-one. But, all the same, there had been a desperation about their lovemaking that he didn't quite like. Joyce had never made any demands on him; it was one of the things he liked about her. They had never spoken of love; she had never asked him to forsake all others. But, last night, in the dimly lit bedroom (Joyce was too old a hand to have the central lights on), Max had been seized by a sudden fear which, if he could have put it into words, would have sounded something like: is this it? Maybe it wasn't such a bad fate, settling down with a good-looking woman who had a comfortably flexible moral code, but it wasn't quite what Max had envisioned when, as a younger man, he had pictured his future wife. "How would you know?" he heard Ruby's voice. "You've never been married." The trouble was that, whilst there had been many love affairs, there had never been anyone with whom Max had contemplated sharing his life. Perhaps that was because a pro's life wasn't worth sharing. You did get married couples sometimes, double acts who made each dressing room a home from home, with tablecloths and drapes and patchwork cushions. But, by and large, variety performers were a solitary bunch, moving from town to town with their belongings on their backs. Like snails, except that they didn't leave a trail. Max didn't want to be a snail all his life, that was partly why he had agreed to make the television programmes. Sometimes he thought that he'd like a flat in London — or Paris or Rome or New York — where he'd never have to be more than a few hundred yards from a taxi or a restaurant. But, even in his fantasies, he was living in his city eyrie alone. Mrs M had never featured in his dreams. Did he feature in hers?

The Hippodrome theatre was in a back street at the end of the Lanes. From the outside it was solid and uncompromising, two squat towers framing a flat façade. A wrought-iron canopy provided some decoration but there was none of the Regency glamour of the Theatre Royal near the Pavilion. But inside — inside was magical. The Hippodrome had originally been designed for circuses and there was still something of the amphitheatre about the space; this wasn't a cosy theatre, it was made for spectacle. A fantastically decorated domed ceiling ensured great acoustics and the seats raked dramatically upwards. On stage last night, Max had been aware of the need for grand gestures, for noise, colour and trumpet blasts. This was why the tableaux act worked so well here. This wasn't a place for subtlety.

Passing the auditorium now, he heard a piano playing. A Chopin waltz, he thought. He stood for a moment, listening to the notes rising and falling, evoking images of ballrooms, chandeliers, doomed officers riding out into the snow. He entered through the stalls and saw Tommy Watson in the orchestra pit, lit only by the blue light over the music, his fingers a blur.

Max sat three rows back, listening. When Tommy had finished he called "Bravo". The conductor turned, his face flushing.

"I didn't know anyone was there."

"You're very good," said Max. He walked towards the front of the stalls. Tommy twisted round on his piano stool. He looked older than Max first thought, in his thirties rather than twenties. It was the untidy dark hair and boyish face that made him look younger.

"I was at music college before the war," said Tommy, "but then I was called up and afterwards it seemed too trivial a thing to return to. I couldn't do anything else though so ended up conducting dance bands."

This was very much what Edgar had said about going back to Oxford after the war. It occurred to Max that Tommy reminded him slightly of Edgar.

"Your orchestra is a class above the usual," said Max. "Sometimes I'm left on stage waiting for a drum roll that doesn't come."

Tommy laughed. "I was almost too busy watching the tricks last night to cue in the drums. Your act is incredible."

"Thank you," said Max. "It's the first time I've performed in a double act. Takes some getting used to."

"But Ruby's your daughter," said Tommy, "that must be different, surely?" He blushed when he said Ruby's name. Not another one, thought Max.

"Yes," said Max. "It's a lot more difficult. What do you think of Vic Cutler's girls?"

Tommy shrugged. "Gives me a chance to play Debussy and Verdi but it's not my taste. I know Vic from way back. He can be an ugly customer."

An interesting phrase, thought Max. Cutler wasn't exactly ugly but there was a darkness about him,

74

something almost Mephisophelean. He wondered when the brash showman and the shy pianist had met.

In his dressing room, Max lit a cigarette and looked through his post. There wasn't much — an invitation to open a Christmas fair in Alfriston, a postcard from an ex-girlfriend called Sandra now living in Wootton Bassett — but he always hoped that one day there would be an invitation to tour America or a letter from a Hollywood agent. He propped the postcard up against his mirror and vowed to answer the Alfriston letter, whilst knowing that he never would.

He'd asked Toby to make him some coffee but, when the door opened, it was Dick Billings, the theatre manager, carrying a mug and a copy of the *Evening Argus*.

"Got an early copy," he said. "Thought you'd like to see it."

Joe Passolini was in luck. The murder hadn't made the papers yet and, on the front page, was a picture of Max in top hat and tails accompanied by Ruby in a red dress. The headline was: MAGICIAN AND DAUGHTER WOW THE CROWD.

"Show got a good write-up too," said Dick. "Even though he did say that the tableaux act was vulgar. Bloody provincial hack. What does he know?"

Max was looking for the review. "What could be better than a headline act from the great Max Mephisto?" he read. "Max Mephisto plus his beautiful, talented daughter, Ruby French. The existence of this lady has been kept a secret until now and her appearance on stage at the Hippodrome last night was a *coup de théâtre* worthy of Mephisto at his best."

"He fancies himself as a writer," said Max.

"He'll be one of those university types," said Dick. "Imagines he's working for *The Times*. What's he called?"

"Sam Collins," said Max, looking at the byline. He continued to read, "Mephisto and French produced a fresh and unusual take on the tired old theme of a lady vanishing. With their lively repartee and skilful conjuring, I foresee a glittering future for Magician and Daughter."

"You must be pleased with that," said Dick, watching him.

Max hesitated. He was pleased with the publicity, of course he was, though he thought that he looked rather old in the photograph beside Ruby's fresh-faced beauty. But there were things in the review that he didn't quite like: the assumption that he was better with Ruby than on his own, the "tired old theme", the prophecy of a glittering future when, in truth, he'd had a pretty good past.

"Yes, it's pretty decent," he said. "As long as they get your name right, eh?"

Sam Collins had praise for Stew Stewart, "one of the exciting new breed of comedians", and moderate praise for the jugglers who opened the second half. But his greatest scorn was reserved for Vic Cutler's Living Tableaux. "Have we really progressed no further," he asked rhetorically, "than grubby men in raincoats paying a shilling to leer at naked girls, their fading charms inadequately masked by historically inaccurate costumes?"

"A shilling," said Dick. "He doesn't know the prices in Soho these days."

Max had no doubt that Dick did know the going rate. He was a good theatre manager, but he wasn't exactly wholesome, to use Joe's word. In the evenings, dressed in the traditional dinner jacket, Dick Billings was an impressive figure. This morning, in flannels, a threadbare jumper barely covering his paunch, the manager looked decidedly seedy.

"The girls got a good reception last night," said Max. "Though they might not be Mr Collins's cup of tea, they're probably the reason why the show's doing so well."

He waited for Dick to say that he, Max Mephisto, was the reason for the "Sold Out" boards appearing in front of the theatre but the manager did not appear to have heard his cue.

"Fading charms," he said. "Bloody cheek. Vic Cutler will have his guts for garters."

"Don't show him the review then," said Max.

"You're joking," said Dick. "Vic Cutler knows every newspaper editor in the country."

"Vic's got influence, has he?"

Dick laughed without humour. "He's got influence everywhere, that man. I just told him about that murder, the one in Hove, and he was talking about going to see the detective inspector."

"Was he?" said Max. An encounter between Edgar and Vic Cutler would be interesting.

"Sam Collins will be out of a job tomorrow. You mark my words."

Later, drinking his lukewarm coffee, Max thought that Dick hadn't cared when the League of Decency had complained about the tableaux act but the reporter seemed to have struck a nerve. Could Vic really get him sacked? He hoped not. Collins had, at least, described his conjuring as skilful.

Emma was back twenty minutes later. She was out of breath and carrying a hardback book which she slammed down on the incident room table.

Bob, who was laboriously typing up his notes, read the title aloud, *"England's Forgotten Queen.* What the . . ."

Edgar looked up from the post-mortem report.

"What have you got there, Emma?"

"It's a book about Lady Jane Grey," she said.

"Who?" This was Bob, of course.

"She was Queen of England for nine days after the death of Edward VI," said Emma. "He wanted a Protestant to succeed him instead of his Catholic half-sister, Mary. But the people rallied to Mary and Jane Grey was arrested and executed."

"Thank you for the history lesson," said Bob, in the tone he used whenever he thought that Emma was trying to make him look stupid. "But what's that got to do with this case?"

"This," said Emma. And she opened the book at a double-page colour illustration.

Bob leant over to look at it. "Good God," he said.

Intrigued, Edgar came over. The picture showed Lady Jane Grey kneeling, wearing a white dress. Her long blonde hair fell over her shoulder, her eyes were covered by a white cloth and one hand was reaching out towards the block where she would soon place her head.

"It's Lily," said Emma. "Lily was posed to look like this painting."

"But why?" said Bob. "Why would anyone do that?"

Edgar looked at the illustration, which was a glossy reproduction of a painting. A man was leaning over the blindfolded girl, guiding her hand, his manner a horrible mixture of solicitude and coercion. On the right stood a young man in red tights and, on the left, a lady-in-waiting who looked to be almost fainting with grief. But it was the central image that held the eye. Even though her face was half-covered, there was courage and pathos in every line of the girl's figure. Her white dress glimmered in the darkness, her extended hand seemed to reach out towards the observer. Help me.

"Who painted this?" he asked.

"It's Victorian, not Tudor," said Emma. She peered at the caption below the picture. "Paul Delaroche, 1833. But it's quite well known."

"I knew the crime scene reminded me of something," said Edgar. He fetched the photographs from the case file and put them beside the picture. Although Lily was on her own, and the background was of a dingy attic bedroom, the similarities were striking. Lily was even kneeling on a green towel to match the cushion in the painting. There was straw around the block as there had been around the potato box. Lily's hair was arranged to fall forward exactly as Jane's had. Edgar remembered one of the girls saying that Lily usually wore her hair up.

"Why?" said Bob again. "Why would anyone kill a girl then make it look like some old painting?"

But Edgar was remembering the flyer on Edna's hall table.

Vic Cutler's Living Tableaux: scenes from the past brought to life.

CHAPTER
SEVEN

In the props room Max checked the vanishing box, swivelling the back to and fro and making sure that the false floor was still working. Idly he put in his cigarette case, shut the door and opened it again. It was . . . *gone*. Cue double take, applause, etc.

"Very impressive."

Max wheeled round. Florence Jones was standing watching him. She was wearing a black coat and a fur hat that made her look vaguely Russian.

"I do my best," said Max. He opened the door again and took out his case. He offered a cigarette to Florence but she shook her head.

"Can you make me disappear?" she said.

Max didn't know what possessed him. He was used to people wanting to know how his tricks worked and he usually repelled them with polite blankness or a bland assurance that it was, in fact, magic. But he found himself saying, "Be my guest" and opening the cabinet door. Florence stepped inside. She was taller than Ruby but carried herself well, with a grace and fluidity that made Max wonder if she'd been a dancer once.

"Press the back," said Max. Florence did so and gave an exclamation as the solid wood started to move.

"Is that it?" she said. "A false back?"

"What did you expect?" said Max. "The trick is to swivel round with the door in one easy movement."

Florence tried. She made quite a good attempt but couldn't keep her balance and stepped off, laughing.

"That's the end of my career as a magician's assistant."

"Is it?" said Max.

There was a short silence and then Florence said, "You must be wondering why I gave you my number."

"I enjoy a mystery."

"I think I might be able to explain myself better over lunch," said Florence. "Would you join me? I know a nice café near here."

Max prided himself on knowing the best cafés and restaurants in every theatre town but he'd never been invited to lunch by a single woman in a way that was neither flirtatious nor awkward. In a funny way Florence reminded him of Joe when he'd first approached Max about becoming his agent. There was something businesslike about her, notwithstanding the fur hat and the long, dancer's legs.

"I'd like that," he said.

Florence's café turned out to be near Bartholomew Square, where Edgar and his team lurked in the town hall basement solving dastardly crimes. Max must have walked past the café a hundred times but he'd ignored it because, with its bay window and hanging baskets,

Susie's hadn't looked like a place where you could get a decent Chianti or a plate of tagliatelle. This was probably true but you could get a surprisingly good bowl of soup served with home-made bread. The interior might have had more gingham and chintz than Max was strictly comfortable with but it was clean and the waitress efficient. He thought he might bring Ruby here one day. At least here the waiters wouldn't flirt with her.

"How do you know this place?" he asked Florence. "Are you from Brighton?"

"No," said Florence. "I was born in Wales but I've spent quite a bit of time here."

There was a faint Welsh lilt to her voice, now that Max noticed it. There was something altogether mysterious about Florence Jones, he thought. Her black hair could be Italian or Spanish but her eyes were a striking, witchy green that seemed more Celtic. Her face was classically beautiful, with full lips and high cheekbones, but there was something closed about it as well. She looked like a woman who knew how to keep a secret.

"So how did you come to be one of Vic Cutler's Living Tableaux?" said Max as they waited for their soup.

Florence took a sip of water. She had taken off her coat and underneath was wearing a green jumper and tweed skirt. Unremarkable clothes except that the tweed was beautifully cut and the jumper brought out the colour of her eyes. "I was trained as a ballet dancer," she said, "but I got too tall. I was part of a

Spanish dancing act for a while but my partner got married. I was just about to give up, go home and get a boring job when I saw Vic's advertisement. I thought I'd just do it for a while, to tide me over, but I've been in the troupe for over a year now."

This raised a lot of questions for Max, not least how did a woman who looked like this get to her twenties (he guessed about twenty-five) without being married? He noted that her options had included a boring job but not matrimony.

"It's a hard life, touring," he said. He meant, for a girl like you.

"I enjoy it," she said. "I like seeing new places. Of course, Brighton is wonderful. You can't exactly say that about some of the other theatre towns."

"No, you can't," said Max feelingly. Their soups arrived, smelling extremely good. Florence crumbled her bread but didn't put it in her mouth. Max wished she would start eating so he could.

"The other girls are nice," Florence was saying, "but Vic . . ."

She lapsed into silence and spooned up some soup.

"I can't imagine he's a very savoury character," said Max, following suit.

"No," said Florence. There was another pause before she said, "I've written some scripts."

Whatever he had expected, it wasn't this. "What sort of scripts?"

"Comedy scripts," said Florence. "For the radio. I thought, well I know your agent's Joe Passolini. I wondered if you could show them to him."

So it was business after all. Max felt strangely disappointed as well as intrigued.

"Have you got the scripts with you?" he said.

Florence opened her handbag and took out a sheaf of typewritten paper. "I've got lots of ideas," she said. "The new comedians like Stew Stewart, they're moving away from a string of gags, telling more of a story. I've written some sketches with different characters and settings. I think they'd work really well for someone like Spike Milligan. But it's impossible to get the BBC to look at them, especially if you're a woman."

Max had seen Spike Milligan perform once and thought that he was probably mad or a genius. He still couldn't get used to the idea that the glamorous woman opposite was a budding scriptwriter, a job that seemed the very antithesis of glamour.

"I'll be happy to look at the scripts," he said.

"And show them to Mr Passolini?"

"Yes, all right," said Max. He thought he could imagine Joe's reaction if he ever caught sight of Florence. "She's wasted on writing, Maxie boy, get her on stage in a basque and tights pronto."

"Thank you." Florence gave him a dazzling smile. "I'm sorry if I've been a little forward."

"Not at all."

"Of course, I wanted to meet you too. I've been a fan ever since I was little."

Max winced inwardly. He beckoned for the bill.

"Let me," said Florence. "Lunch was my idea."

"I wouldn't dream of it," said Max. He put some coins on the table, including a generous tip. He never wanted anyone to say, "I had that Max Mephisto in my cab/café/restaurant and he was a stingy bastard."

"I could write a script for you and Ruby if you like," said Florence, as they made their way back to the theatre. The sky was greyer than ever and it looked as if rain, if not snow, was on its way.

"I think Joe has some scriptwriters in mind," said Max. "But I'm not sure if the double act will be a regular thing."

"I'm sure Ruby wants it to be," said Florence.

Max looked at her. Florence had sounded rather tart and he wondered if she had crossed swords with Ruby during rehearsals. Ruby was always very charming but, having once been at the bottom of the bill, she was rather enjoying her celebrity status.

Outside the theatre, Max raised his hat and said goodbye. "If I can give you a piece of advice in return," he said, "don't stay with Vic too long. Not that you don't make a very good Cleopatra."

Florence laughed. "I saw you backstage last night. What was the sudden interest in tableaux?"

"I don't know," said Max, "maybe I was interested in you."

He said it lightly but Florence looked up, eyelashes fluttering. "I'm interested in you too."

"I know," said Max, "you've been a fan ever since you were little."

"I'm not interested in you as a fan," said Florence.

Max looked at her, wondering what to say next. He was relieved, as well as irritated, to hear a familiar voice hailing him from across the street.

"Max!"

"Ed. What are you doing here?"

Edgar shouted something back but Max didn't catch it and, by the time Edgar had crossed the road, Florence had gone.

"Max." Edgar came loping towards him. "I need to talk to you."

"What's it about?" said Max. But he knew that it had to be about the murder and he felt a slight stirring of excitement at the thought of being involved with an investigation again.

"Can we go somewhere private?" said Edgar.

"We'd better go to my dressing room," said Max. "We won't be disturbed there."

"Things have changed then," said Edgar. "Your dressing room's usually about as busy as Piccadilly Circus."

"Dear old Dilly," said Max. "How I love London."

He led the way through the stage door and past the mysterious boxes and hampers that always seemed to appear in the backstage corridors of theatres. They passed Stew Stewart flirting energetically with one of Vic Cutler's girls and Dick Billings shouting at the stagehands because someone had put their foot through a backcloth. Edgar was more used to backstage now, because of Ruby, but he still looked out of place with his policeman's overcoat and fresh-faced smile. There was always something innocent about Edgar, Max thought, no matter how many horrific murders he solved, and innocence was in short supply on the variety circuit.

In his dressing room, Max poured himself a whisky and offered one to Edgar.

"Keep the cold out."

"I can't," said Edgar. "I'm on duty."

"So, what's all this about?" Max sat at the dressing table and lit a cigarette. Edgar sat on the sofa opposite.

"Have you heard about the murder in Lansdowne Road?" he said.

"Yes, Ruby told me about it. She'd heard from one of the girls."

A familiar worried look came over Edgar's face. "I haven't been able to get hold of Ruby. Was she all right about me missing the first night?"

"She was fine," said Max. "She understood. Diablo came. Not that he was a substitute for you, of course."

Edgar laughed. "Good old Diablo. Surprised you've got any whisky left."

"This is a new bottle. We went out for a meal afterwards. Diablo was talking about you."

"He was? Why?"

"He'd heard about the murder. He was concerned about you."

"No need to worry about me," said Edgar. "Worry about the poor girl who was killed."

"A bit late for that, I suppose."

"Yes." Edgar sighed and looked, despite his protests, very worried indeed. Diablo was right, thought Max, Edgar always took things hard. Even so, he was tougher than he looked.

"I wanted to talk to you about the Living Tableaux," said Edgar.

Now Max really was surprised. To his annoyance, he found himself feeling slightly guilty.

"The Living Tableaux? Why?"

"The girl who died," said Edgar. "She was called Lily Burtenshaw. She was strangled and her body was arranged in an odd way. I shouldn't really be showing you but this is a picture of the crime scene."

Max looked at the black and white photograph. "Jesus," he said, "that's horrible. Why is she tied to the chair like that?"

"Now look at this." To Max's surprise Edgar produced a book from his briefcase. It opened at an illustration that was vaguely familiar, a highly romanticised Victorian painting of a kneeling girl and an executioner's block. He looked at Edgar.

"You think the girl was posed to look like this picture?"

"Don't you?"

"Well, now I see them together . . ."

"Then I thought of the Living Tableaux," said Edgar. "Two of the girls are staying at the house where it happened. I wondered, do they re-create the death of Lady Jane Grey?"

Max thought. "I don't think so. I watched nearly the whole show last night. Jane Grey is a bit obscure for Vic Cutler. They do Elizabeth I and Cleopatra and the Lady of Shalott."

Edgar looked disappointed. "It was just an idea. There was something so odd, so theatrical about it. Why arrange the body like that? What does it mean?"

"He's a showman," said Max, "whoever did this. He wants an audience."

Edgar looked at the photographs, seeming somehow even more poignant in this alien environment. Who was the intended audience? Was this somehow for *his* benefit?

"But why?" he said. "And why this particular scene?"

"I don't know," said Max. "But there's something odd about the tableaux too. Living women trying to look like dead ones. There's a lot of death in the act, it's all part of the prurience, of course. It's a bit like people in the last century queuing up at the Paris morgue to see suicides fished out of the Seine."

"What about the man who puts on the show? What do you know about him?"

"Vic Cutler? He's pretty successful, not very likable. You know the sort — handmade shoes, Rolls Royce, gold signet ring and cigarette case. I've never heard any actual scandal about him, though, apart from the obvious stuff about him seducing the prettiest girls."

"Was that girl you were speaking to earlier one of the Tableaux girls?"

"Yes."

"And one of the prettiest?"

"Naturally."

Edgar put the book and the photograph back in his bag, looking disappointed. "Apparently Lily came to see the girls rehearse last week," he said. "You don't remember seeing her?"

"No. I only arrived in Brighton on Sunday."

"Are you staying with Mrs M?"

"Yes. You must come round one night. She'd like to see you."

"I'd like to see her," said Edgar. "I'll try to get to the show but it will be difficult with this investigation going on."

"You'll solve it," said Max. "After all, you've got Emma to help you."

"And Bob," said Edgar.

"Yes," said Max. "Somehow I always forget Bob."

CHAPTER
EIGHT

Emma was very surprised when the DI suggested it.

"You want us to go to the theatre. Together?"

"Not together," Bob protested. "Just at the same time."

Emma shot him a look. "You want me and Bob to go to the theatre tonight. Together. At the same time."

"Yes," said Edgar. He was sitting at his desk and the lamp was on but it only lit his hands drumming gently on his papers. Emma couldn't see his face. Why wasn't he going to the theatre? she wondered. Had he had a fight with Ruby?

Luckily Bob was on hand to ask the obvious question. "Why can't you go, sir?"

"I'm going to London," said Edgar. "I want to talk to Lily's mother and her brother."

"Now?" said Bob. He looked at the window which, as the room was below ground level, only showed a sliver of the outside world. It was dark now, booted feet walking past, dirty snowflakes gathering on the basement steps.

"First thing in the morning," said Edgar. "I'm still curious about Vic Cutler and his Living Tableaux. There's a link with Lily. The girls, Betty and Janette, staying in the same house. The constables who searched the garden this morning found a place where someone seemed to have broken through the hedge. It's possible that there's been an intruder. I've set a guard on the house for tonight."

"But what's that got to do with the show?" said Bob.

"I'm not sure," said Edgar. "But there's something theatrical about the whole thing. The way the body was posed, everything. Even though the Living Tableaux don't re-create the Jane Grey painting, they do show the deaths of famous women. I think it's worth you going and taking some notes. Keep your eyes open. Talk to the girls afterwards. Max has spoken to the theatre manager so you can go backstage."

So the DI had been to see Max. Emma wondered again why he wasn't going to see the show himself. Was it just that it wouldn't look good, the detective inspector in charge of a murder case out watching half-naked girls in a theatre? That was probably it. She felt the tiny spark of hope, that she had stupidly allowed to flare into life, flicker and go out.

Bob's eyes were round. He had a puritanical side, Emma knew, but he was probably looking forward to the evening's entertainment all the same.

"Do you really think someone in the show killed Lily?"

"Not necessarily," said Edgar. He adjusted the picture of Ruby on his desk. Emma wished that she could read his expression. "But someone could have watched the show in rehearsal and got the idea from it. Ask around. Talk to the performers."

Bob's face was an almost perfect blend of excitement and unease. Emma hoped that he wasn't going to embarrass her at the theatre.

Edgar watched them leave at six. On the way out he heard Bob asking Emma if she was going home to change. He regretted that he couldn't hear Emma's reply. Bob would definitely think Emma's jersey and slacks unsuitable for the theatre, he'd be hoping that she would be planning to change into a little black dress, preferably accessorised with pearls. Edgar had once seen Emma dressed up for the evening, when they went to a pantomime two years ago, and he had been surprised at how different she had looked, poised and rather beautiful. Ruby always said that it was a shame Emma didn't make more of herself, "she could be quite a pretty girl if she tried", but Edgar rather admired Emma's refusal to compromise, about her appearance or anything else. And, though he didn't want to admit it even to himself, he didn't like the thought of a glamorous Emma accompanying Bob to the theatre. Far better for all of them to keep their minds on work.

He wasn't sure why he had decided not to attend the show himself. Partly it was because he didn't want people to recognise him and write angry "why do I pay my taxes?" letters to the *Evening Argus*. Partly it was because he knew that, as soon as he saw Ruby, he would lose the focus he needed for the investigation. And partly it was just because he felt that he didn't deserve it. Max always said that Edgar had an overdeveloped sense of guilt. "There's me with my

Catholic upbringing," he would say, "and not a shred of guilt. You, riddled with it." And it was true that Edgar would feel deeply uncomfortable sitting on one of the plush chairs at the Hippodrome while Lily's killer remained at large.

And it was good for Emma and Bob to go off on their own. He knew he could rely on Emma's powers of observation; she would be watching those tableaux like a hawk. Bob, too, could be very shrewd. He would also be determined not to be seduced by any show-business charm. Edgar wondered what Ruby would think when she saw Emma and Bob in the audience. He had left a message at her lodgings explaining and he tried to imagine her reading it with an understanding smile. This last vision stubbornly refused to come to life. All he could see was Ruby's face, eyes huge, lips trembling. "You can't possibly love me if you don't come and see the show." Truly, he was a terrible person.

Outside, the snow was still falling. The area steps were almost completely white. He'd better leave soon. The last thing he wanted was to be snowed in at Bartholomew Square. He'd freeze to death in the basement rooms, even with the two-bar fire. He made a telephone call to the Hove police station to check that there was a constable in place outside the house on Lansdowne Road. "They'll love you," said the desk sergeant cheerfully, "doing sentry duty in this weather."

"No one needs to do more than a two-hour stint," said Edgar, "but we do need to keep the house under observation." He didn't think that the killer would strike in the same place twice but, with four young women in the house, it wouldn't do to be complacent. And there were those signs that someone had been in the garden. He checked that he had the car keys for tomorrow, plus addresses for Lily's mother and her brother, Carl. He hoped the roads wouldn't be blocked in the morning.

But, when he finally emerged from the building, the snow had stopped. It was a cold, clear night, the stars bright and high, the roads icy and white. Edgar hated snow. It reminded him of 1940 and being sent to Norway as part of the Allied expeditionary force. The Arctic landscape, for which the British troops had been woefully unprepared, still featured in his nightmares: ice floes, glaciers, the blue light in the mornings, the bodies of his comrades falling to freeze where they lay. He'd been lucky to escape with frostbite that caused him to lose a toe. More recently, snow had covered the bodies of two murdered children in Brighton and made the hunt for their killer almost impossible. Edgar had been taught at Sunday School that hell was a fiery furnace but he had a sneaking suspicion that, should he ever arrive at those dolorous gates, he would feel an icy chill that promised snow in its wake.

Cold also reminded him of his childhood. Their first house in Willesden where there were icicles on the inside of the bathroom window and getting up in the morning required a superhuman effort of will. Funnily enough, though, he had warm memories of that time: sharing a room with his brother Jonathan, playing cricket in the garden with Jonathan and their sister, Lucy, making paper chains at Christmas, roasting chestnuts on the open fire in the kitchen. But then they had moved from Willesden to a modern bungalow in Esher. For Edgar's mother, Rose, the new house meant a significant rise in social status, but Edgar had never liked Esher. It was too neat, too antiseptic, a place of hushed voices, antimacassars and net curtains. His father had died not long after the move to Surrey and now Jonathan was dead too, killed at Dunkirk. Lucy was married to a doctor and was the mother of two young sons. And Edgar, who had shocked his mother by winning a scholarship to Oxford before the war, was a policeman. He knew that his mother thought his job sordid and somehow disreputable and she was probably right. Even so, after the war, after the Norway debacle and his subsequent adventures with the Magic Men, Edgar had known that he didn't want to go back to university or settle into a respectable job. "I want to make a difference," he'd once said to Max who had, quite rightly, laughed.

Edgar walked back along the seafront. The pavements here had been gritted and people were out and about, muffled up against the cold. The West Pier, twinkling with lights, looked like an ocean liner setting out on its maiden voyage. The *Titanic*, "Nearer, My God, to Thee", another time when ice had killed. Edgar almost wanted to warn the families heading towards the end-of-the-pier pantomime: "Don't get on board." But, of course, they were just looking forward to a night at the theatre, a bit of traditional Christmas cheer, slapstick and double entendres and sweets thrown by the Dame. Edgar was the only person walking through the night thinking about death.

He had recently moved to a flat in Brunswick Square, Hove. It was a far smarter area than his old haunt in Hanover and, in his darker moments, he wondered if he was becoming like his mother, talking about "going up in the world". He missed his old flat more than he thought he would, although he didn't miss the slog up one of the steepest hills in Brighton to get there. But at least when you got to the top there had been the wonderful view as a reward, the rows of terraces stepping down towards the beach, the seagulls hanging in the air, the sea wider and bluer than you could possibly imagine. The Brunswick Square flat had a sea view if you leant far enough out of the sitting room window but the rooms at the back faced more apartment blocks and were dark winter and summer. He had rented the flat because it seemed a more suitable place to bring Ruby after they were married. In his wilder moments, he imagined Ruby pushing a pram in the square or greeting him at the door with a dry martini. The reality was that Ruby would probably be working every night and he would still come home to paperwork and the dregs at the bottom of the whisky bottle. Recently, Ruby had talked about moving to London because it was easier for her television work. "What would I do?" asked Edgar. "Transfer," said Ruby. "There's lots of crime in London," she added, as if promising him a rare treat.

It was quite pleasant though to open the front door and not be assailed by the strange smell that always haunted his Hanover flat. Edgar went into the kitchen and made himself a sandwich. He couldn't get used to the luxury of having a fridge and a modern electric oven. There was even a washing machine in the basement. He poured himself a whisky and went into the sitting room, not turning on the lights so that he could see the stars. He thought of Lily's mother, Cecily. What would she be doing this evening? Sitting looking at pictures of her golden-haired daughter and mourning the future that had been stolen from her. "She never wanted to go on the stage," said Cecily, still blonde and pretty in her forties. "She just wanted a nice job and to meet a nice man." Had Lily met a man, one who was demonstrably not very nice? Edgar agreed with Emma that it was important to find out why Lily had come to Brighton. It did seem a rather bold move for a girl described variously as "home-loving", "shy" and "quiet". Maybe her brother would be able to shed some light on the matter. Was there any link with Vic Cutler and his Living Tableaux? Edgar sat at the window, drinking his whisky in the dark, allowing his thoughts to drift back to the Hippodrome and the entertainment awaiting his sergeants.

Emma did get changed in the end. This was partly because she wanted a lift from her father and she knew that Archie would complain if she wore trousers. She didn't want to wear anything too eveningy though, nothing that showed her arms or cleavage (not that she had much to show). In the end she settled on a dark green dress, quite smart but high-necked and

99

respectable. It certainly met with her father's approval. "Now you look like my little princess again," he said, as she came down the stairs. "You'd better borrow my mink," said her mother, Sybil. "You can't wear that old duffel coat to the theatre." Emma wanted to say no thanks; she hated wearing fur, she felt self-conscious and sorry for the animals — "Mink aren't very *nice* animals, darling," her mother had said when she voiced this thought — but it would have been churlish to refuse so she sat in the front seat of her father's Rolls, swathed in blonde fur, praying that Bob would not witness her entrance. "You can drop me on the coast road," she told her father, "it's hard to turn round in Middle Street."

She was hoping that she could get to the theatre and take off the fur before Bob saw her but, when she reached the foyer, he was already there, looking uncharacteristically smart in a dark suit with his hair slicked back.

"Blimey," he said, "I hardly recognised you."

"Thank you," said Emma, struggling to shrug off the coat. Bob didn't help her, of course, just stood there with his mouth slightly open and arms hanging at his sides.

"I've got programmes," he said. "Do you want a drink first?"

Emma didn't know whether she should refuse because they were, strictly speaking, on duty but Bob seemed anxious that they should do the thing properly and, besides, she thought a gin and tonic might help her get through the evening.

100

Bob fought his way to the bar and came back with their drinks, plus a small bag of nuts.

"I say," he said, grinning at her, "this is something like."

And Emma couldn't help herself smiling back. After all, it was odd, but slightly exciting, to be at a theatre surrounded by well-dressed people. It felt even odder to be there with Bob, now opening the packet with his teeth. Odd, but not actually unpleasant.

"It's a good bill," said Bob, opening his programme. "A juggler, a comedian, somebody called Madame Mitzi and her performing poodles. And Max Mephisto, of course."

Behind Bob's shoulder Max and Ruby loomed out from a life-size poster. Magician and Daughter. Ruby peeping out from behind a top-hatted Max, her eyes dancing.

A bell rang. "Come on," said Emma, "let's go in."

The complimentary seats were good ones, Row H of the stalls. The first seven rows were reserved for exclusive seats called "special fauteuils". Emma was surprised how opulent the place looked inside: the domed ceiling, the ornate balconies, the swagged velvet stage curtains. You hardly noticed the fact that the seats were a little threadbare and that some of the gilt cherubs had lost their noses.

"My parents used to come here before the war," she told Bob. "They saw Max Miller and the Crazy Gang."

"Variety isn't what it used to be," said Bob solemnly. But, sitting in the theatre, listening to the orchestra playing "Happy Days Are Here Again", it didn't seem that variety was dead and buried just yet. The audience were surprisingly elegant too, lots of jewellery and bow ties, swirls of velvet and satin. You could almost imagine that you were back in those pre-war days when people dressed for dinner and tailcoats were not exclusively worn by musicians or waiters.

"It's starting," said Bob. He looked so excited that she could not stop herself smiling back.

The show was entertaining enough too. Emma found Stew Stewart quite funny though Bob stayed stony-faced throughout. He did laugh at Madame Mitzi and her poodles, slapping his thighs as they pushed each other through paper hoops. The animals were rather too anthropomorphically knowing for Emma's taste although she did think it was clever of them to be able to count. Then there was a dance act, vaguely balletic with lots of arm-waving. Emma didn't think much of the dancers but the orchestra seemed rather good. Then there was a definite buzz of excitement in the audience.

"It's the Living Tableaux next," whispered Bob.

"I know," Emma told him but Bob, leaning forward, his face intense, seemed not to have heard her.

The red light went on and the curtain went up to show a blue-lit stage and girls holding strategically placed feathers. Emma was sure that she could hear heavy breathing all round her. Was this what Emily Wilding Davidson died for? she thought. The right to stand stock-still while men strained their eyes to see if they could see your nipples? The stage darkened and the figures rearranged themselves. The pianist played

102

something Elizabethan and a girl stood spotlit, wearing a ruff and holding a fan across her breasts. The music changed and a different girl lay on a chaise longue surrounded by flowers. These last, though clearly artificial, reminded Emma of Lily. She also thought she recognised the recumbent girl. She mouthed "Betty?" at Bob and he nodded. Betty was wearing a long blonde wig that also reminded Emma of Lily. She couldn't see which of the shadowy figures was Janette. Another scene change and a dark-haired Cleopatra lay on the chaise longue, a stuffed snake preserving her modesty in a rather Freudian way. The final tableau was Minnehaha (the music, confusingly, was Liszt's "Hungarian Rhapsody Number Two") and showed a woman in an Indian headdress with other women at her feet, apparently frozen in the act of rowing a canoe. This was the most salacious scene yet as Minnehaha's pigtails did not quite cover her breasts. The performers held their positions for what seemed like an eternity, then the lights dimmed and they were in their showgirl poses again, feathers aquiver. The applause rang out from all sides.

Bob insisted on buying ice creams in the interval. He seemed determined that they should have the full theatre experience, not that Emma was complaining too much. They discussed the tableaux in lowered voices.

"It's not really that shocking," said Bob. "I mean, you can't see much." He scooped up some ice cream, his ears going red.

"I think it's horrible," said Emma, "staring at women as if they're objects."

"Do you think that's what our killer did? Kill Lily so that he could stare at her like that?"

Emma looked round nervously but the seats behind them were vacant, their occupants either queuing up at the bar or the lavatories.

"I don't know," she said, "but he had definitely created a tableau of some kind. It was a shock to see Betty looking so like Lily, wasn't it?"

"It's just the hair," said Bob. "She doesn't look like Lily really. Hair changes a woman."

"Are you an expert on women now?"

Bob blushed. "Take you, for example. You look completely different with your hair down."

Emma didn't quite know what to say to that. Did he mean better, different? She was rather relieved when the bell rang and they were forced to keep bobbing up and down to let people past them into their seats. She looked at her programme. Magician and Daughter was the last act.

The glamour of show business was wearing a bit thin by the time Max and Ruby took to the stage. After the juggler, a second dose of the dancers and a truly terrifying ventriloquist, Emma was beginning to wonder if variety was really worth saving. Then, the orchestra began a slow sinister version of the "Danse Macabre" and a whisper ran through the theatre. *Max Mephisto is next.*

Emma had never seen Max on stage. She had almost seen him perform in a television programme called *Those Were the Days* but the rather pressing appearance of an unexploded bomb had distracted her. She knew that he was considered a great magician, her parents' generation spoke about him with awe, but she honestly hadn't expected him to be this good. He conjured birds from the air, he prowled amongst the audience making pearl necklaces and cigarette cases disappear. At one point, he came very near them and flashed Emma a smile. She felt both disappointed and relieved that he hadn't made any of her possessions disappear.

Then Ruby pranced onto the stage. Emma had seen *her* perform before and so was expecting the smiles, the twirls, the rapport with the audience. She and Max exchanged some very funny backchat and then they were engaged in a competitive game with the vanishing box. Hats, fans, capes all disappeared and finally Ruby danced into the box. A flash of light and she was gone. Then it was Max's turn. It seemed almost impossible that so commanding a presence could vanish from sight but vanish he did, leaving Ruby temporarily in control of the stage. But then he was back and the audience was stamping and cheering.

"Wasn't that amazing?" said Bob.

"Yes," said Emma. "Let's hurry up and go backstage."

It was difficult fighting their way through the laughing, idling crowds but eventually they found themselves at a discreet door by the entrance to the

Royal Box, "the pass door" Edgar had called it. Emma knocked and, after mentioning Max's name, they were ushered in.

If she had been dazzled by the old-style glamour of the auditorium, Emma was shocked by the dinginess of backstage. They walked along a narrow corridor, exposed pipes gurgling overhead, uneven floorboards underneath. When they climbed the stairs to the dressing rooms, though, the drab surroundings were transformed by the glittering creatures fluttering to and fro. "You were wonderful, darling." Dancers in gauzy ballet dresses, black-jacketed musicians, Madame Mitzi with a yapping dog under each arm, Jim Jones, the ventriloquist, carrying his monstrous dummy.

There were names taped to the doors and Emma walked quickly, Bob in her wake, looking for Vic Cutler's troupe.

"Emma!" It was Ruby in her red dress, eyes huge with mascara, accompanied by a dark-haired man in tails.

"Hallo, Ruby," said Emma. She knew Edgar's fiancée quite well by now. "You were great."

"Thank you." Ruby lowered her eyelashes as Bob added his congratulations.

"Is Ed here?" asked Ruby. Her sudden look of excitement made Emma feel bad, despite herself.

"No," said Emma. "He had to work. We're here on official business really."

She'd meant to make Ruby feel better about Edgar but was taken aback by the expression of fear and curiosity that now appeared on her face. "Is it about the murder? Do you suspect someone here?"

"Don't worry," said the man. "It's probably just routine."

"Yes, it is," said Emma gratefully. The man held out his hand, "Tommy Watson."

"He's the musical director," said Ruby. "And he plays the piano."

"I thought the music was really good," said Emma truthfully. "We're looking for the Living Tableaux. Do you know where their dressing room is?"

"It's upstairs. The last on the left," said Ruby, still looking as if she wanted to know more.

Emma thought it was time to say goodbye. "She's *so* pretty," said Bob as they walked away. Emma ignored him.

The dressing room door was open and Emma spotted Betty, wearing a rather grubby red satin robe, taking off her make-up. She was still wearing the blonde wig but it looked whiter and more unreal away from the lights.

"Hallo," said Emma. "Do you remember me?"

In the mirror, Betty's face grew pale. "Has anything else happened?"

"No," said Emma, "we just thought we'd come and say hallo. It was a great show."

Betty put her hand over her heart. "Oh, you did give me a turn. Did you really like it? Not too raunchy for you?" This last was addressed, rather saucily, to Bob.

"No," said Bob hoarsely. "Enjoyed it a lot."

"Who are your friends, my dear?" A large man had somehow insinuated himself between Betty and Emma. Betty gestured rather helplessly. "This is . . . er . . ."

"Detective Sergeant Emma Holmes," said Emma briskly, "and Detective Sergeant Bob Willis."

The man didn't bat an eyelid. "Police sergeants are certainly getting prettier. Vic Cutler at your service."

So this was the famous showman. Vic Cutler was younger than Emma had imagined, probably in his late forties, and handsome in a fleshy sort of way. He also held her hand for slightly too long.

"To what do we owe this visit?"

"We're investigating the death of Lily Burtenshaw." Edgar had told them to be discreet but Emma found herself wanting to shake Cutler out of his suavity. Cutler's expression certainly changed but she couldn't read what she saw there: tension, anger, maybe even fear.

"What's that got to do with Betty?" he said, the bantering note gone from his voice.

"She was in my digs," said Betty. She pulled off her wig and her bubbly curls sprang out again. "I'm scared to go home, I really am."

"We've got a police constable watching your house," said Emma. "You're quite safe."

"It's the walk back. It's so dark along Western Road."

"I'll walk you home," said Bob. "I live in Hove."

Emma looked at him in surprise but Cutler smiled, smooth as silk again. "There you are, Betty, you'll be quite safe with this strong young policeman."

Cutler looked like he was about to say more but then, suddenly, his expression seemed to change again. The suave mask slipped and was replaced by something cold and watchful. He reminded Emma of a cat at a mousehole.

Emma followed his gaze and saw the dark girl who had played Cleopatra slipping out of the door. On an impulse, she left Bob talking to Betty and followed her.

The corridor was now empty and Emma watched as Cleopatra knocked on one of the dressing room doors and was admitted. Walking quietly past, she was not surprised to see the name on the door. Max Mephisto.

Emma had meant to get a taxi but, when she left the theatre, her father was waiting for her in the Rolls. She got in, glad that the street was now deserted.

"You must have been waiting ages," she said. "Are you frozen?"

"I'm fine," said Archie. He was wearing a heavy sheepskin coat and smelt of brandy. Emma knew he had a flask in the glove compartment.

"It was very kind of you to fetch me," she said.

"Anything for my princess."

As the Rolls purred along the seafront Emma thought of Bob walking Betty home. Presumably Janette would be with them, playing gooseberry. Was Bob slightly sweet on Betty? If so, he would surely be doomed to heartbreak when she left for the next fortnightly gig. Bob would be far more suited to someone steady and reliable, a girl he could take home to his mother in Maidstone. Still, he had been a good companion tonight. Emma wished him success in his courtship, however brief it turned out to be.

She certainly didn't expect to hear from Bob again that night but, when Emma was in bed, having drunk the cocoa forced on her by Ada, the family maid, she heard the telephone ringing. Her father went downstairs, massive in his camel-hair dressing gown. "Holmes," he barked into the receiver.

Emma and her mother went onto the landing to listen.

"Emma," shouted Archie, "it's for you. Fella called Bob."

Emma ran downstairs. "What is it?"

"It's Betty," said Bob. "Someone's left flowers outside her room."

CHAPTER
NINE

Wednesday

Edgar heard the news when he telephoned from a police box on Clapham Common. He'd made good time on the drive and it was still only eight-thirty in the morning. Too early, he thought, to call on Cecily Burtenshaw. He might as well telephone the station and find out if there was any news from last night. He wasn't surprised to hear that Sergeant Holmes was already in. It would take more than a night out at the theatre to make Emma late for work.

He *was* surprised, though, to hear about the flowers.

"And the officer at the door didn't see anyone enter the house?"

"No. I talked to him and he said he'd kept watch all the time."

"Who was it?"

"PC Barnes, from Portslade."

"He's pretty reliable, I think. Did Betty call you when she saw the flowers?"

"No, Bob was with her. He walked her home."

"Did he?" Alone, in the freezing police box, Edgar allowed himself a grin. "That was very gallant."

"You know Bob," said Emma, "ever the gentleman. Betty was worried about walking home alone. I think all the girls are pretty shaken up. Bob said Betty was terrified when she saw the flowers."

"What sort were they?"

"Red and white roses."

"Like the ones Lily was carrying on Friday evening."

"Yes. And, last night, on stage, Betty was wearing a blonde wig that made her look a bit like Lily. I was wondering if there could be a link there."

"Do we know who the flowers were for: Betty or Janette? They share a room, don't they?"

"No. There was no note."

"We need to speak to everyone at Lansdowne Road. The flowers could have come from outside but the most likely explanation is that they were put there by someone in the house."

"Bob's going there this morning."

"Is he now?"

Edgar heard an answering laugh in Emma's voice but she answered primly, "I'm writing up my notes from last night."

"Find out anything interesting?"

"We talked to the girls. They remembered Lily coming in to watch a rehearsal. And I met Vic Cutler. He seemed a bit slimy."

"Max says he's quite an unpleasant character. Did you see Max?"

"Just on stage. I didn't speak to him backstage. I saw Ruby, though. She seemed well."

Edgar wanted to ask if Ruby had asked after him but it didn't seem an appropriate question somehow.

"Hold the fort there," he said. "I'll be back by early afternoon."

"Good luck," said Emma.

"Thanks," said Edgar. He could see the shopkeepers opposite opening their shutters. He realised he'd been putting off the moment of knocking on Cecily Burtenshaw's door but it was too cold to keep standing in a telephone box. He'd just have to get on with it.

Cecily lived in a street just off the common. They were pleasant little houses, with neat gardens and net-curtained windows. Edgar wondered again why Lily, who seemed like a girl who would appreciate a nice home, would up sticks, move to Brighton and live in a dingy attic room.

Cecily answered the door wearing an apron over a black dress. She ushered him into a small sitting room where the furniture had all but disappeared under huge mounds of flowers: roses, chrysanthemums and — above all — lilies, their scent rich, sweet and cloying. Cecily shrugged slightly. "I know a lot of florists," she said.

She offered him a cup of tea and he accepted, not just for politeness but because he was absolutely freezing. He would rather have sat in the kitchen, or anywhere but this flower-bedecked shrine, but Cecily seemed to feel that only the front room was suitable for guests.

Edgar gave his condolences again. "I'm so sorry to be here asking you questions again but, if we're going to catch the person who did this, we need to act quickly and the smallest piece of information might turn out to be vital."

"It's all right," said Cecily. She was very pale but extremely dignified, sitting on the edge of the sofa in her good black dress. Edgar was struck once more by how attractive she was, and how like her daughter.

"Can you tell me a bit more about Lily? I know you said she was rather a quiet girl."

"Yes," said Cecily, putting down her cup and patting her lips with a lace handkerchief, even though Edgar hadn't seen her drink. "She was always such a good girl. She helped out at home and on the stall. Never any trouble. All the teachers liked her at school but she wasn't bookish, if you know what I mean. All she wanted to do was work with flowers. She was ever so upset when I sold the stall after Burt died."

"What about friends? Did Lily have any close friends?"

"Everyone liked Lily. People have been bringing flowers round ever since . . . ever since it happened. But close friends? I don't know. She was more one for the family. Maybe there were a couple of girls that she'd been at school with."

"It would be great if I could have their names later," said Edgar. "What about boyfriends? Sorry, but I have to ask."

To his surprise, Cecily smiled. "That's all right. I wish Lily had had a boyfriend, to be honest. It's only natural, isn't it, and she was such a pretty girl. And a boyfriend might have protected her from . . . from whoever did this. But Lily used to say she wasn't interested. She was a real innocent. 'I'm not like you, Mum,' she used to say. Joking, you know."

"I'm sure you had lots of admirers when you were on the stage," said Edgar.

"Well, yes, I did," said Cecily, casting an involuntary glance at a large photograph on the wall. This showed Cecily on her famous swing, head back, blonde hair streaming out. "I did have a few. But that's what the business is like. Or what it used to be like, at all events. Stage-door johnnies, you know. They used to leave flowers and cards but they would never do anything bad to you."

The words hung in the pollen-heavy air while they both thought of Lily, to whom someone had done something very bad indeed.

"Mrs Burtenshaw," said Edgar, "why did Lily move to Brighton? It seems surprising for someone who was so family-orientated."

"I was surprised," said Cecily. "It was just after her eighteenth birthday and she announced that she wanted a place of her own. I suggested that she rent a room round here but, no, she wanted to move to Brighton."

"Did she say why?"

"Not really. Just said that she liked Brighton and she liked the sea. We used to go down for days out when she was little. Her dad had a car. But, suddenly, Lily

115

wanted to move there, if you please. She was determined. So I wrote to Edna."

"You'd stayed with Edna when you were on the stage?"

"Yes. This was before the war. I used to do summer seasons at the Hippodrome and I stayed with Edna's mother at first. Then her mother died and Edna took over the house. We were good friends, though Edna was older than me. We had some fun in those days. Then Edna got married so I couldn't stay with her any more. I moved to London, met Burt and got married too. Babies came along and I had to leave the business. I kept in touch with Edna, just cards at Christmas but, when Lily was looking for somewhere to stay, I thought of her. I wish to God I hadn't," she said, with sudden vehemence.

"You can't blame yourself," said Edgar. "Sometimes terrible things just happen."

"Yes," said Cecily, "they do. I'm just glad Burt's not alive, that's all."

This always seemed an odd sentiment to Edgar. Her mother often said she was glad his father hadn't lived to see Jonathan die. It seemed strange, in the face of bereavement, to be glad of another death.

"What about Lily's brother, Carl," he said. "Were they close?"

"Well, Carl is two years older," said Cecily. "They didn't play together much as children. Carl was very much one for boys' games. But he was protective of his little sister. He's just devastated by this." She gestured at the flowers and cards. *In sympathy. So Sorry. A new angel in heaven.*

"Carl lives nearby, doesn't he?"

"Yes. On the south side of the common. He's a greengrocer. He's got a lovely wife and a baby."

Edgar hoped that her grandchild would be a comfort to Cecily but, when he said goodbye and left her in the grief-scented house, he doubted it somehow.

Emma put the receiver down wondering if she'd struck the right tone with the DI. "Ruby seemed well." What sort of a phrase was that? Ruby had actually seemed excited and keyed up, disappointed that Edgar hadn't been there and both frightened and fascinated by the murder. But she didn't really feel that she could say any of this. At least the DI had thought it was funny about Bob. She had heard the laugh in his voice. Oh, for goodness sake, she told herself, stomping to the kettle to make herself a cup of tea, it's pathetic to hang on his words like this. He was her boss and he was engaged to someone else. And, besides, she had work to do.

She was looking at the list she had written last night with the names of Vic Cutler's girls.

Betty
Janette
Fenella
Patty
Florence
Joan

117

Barbara (Babs)
Rose

Emma looked at the names, trying to match them to the women in the dressing room last night, taking off their make-up, tying scarves round their hair, shouting news or gossip across the room. Patty was a redhead. Fenella had a nice line in sarcastic banter. Joan was apparently sweet on one of the musicians. Florence was the Cleopatra girl who had disappeared into Max's dressing room. None of them had much to add to the investigation. They remembered Lily coming in to watch a rehearsal. "Seemed like a nice girl," said Fenella, "and nice girls are a rarity around here." "Speak for yourself," said Babs. None of them had seen anyone sinister hanging around the stage door. "You always get these queer types," said Babs, "but most of them are harmless." *Most of them?* thought Emma.

At the bottom of the list Vic Cutler had written his name in a flashy blue scrawl. "Call me if you need any help," he'd said to Emma with a rather routine leer. "Always happy to help a pretty policewoman."

Bob was going straight to Lansdowne Road this morning. Were Betty and Janette in danger because of the flowers laid at their door? Which of the girls were they for anyway? Could someone be transferring their affections from Lily to one of the showgirls? Emma had wondered about Rose, who had a flower name like Lily. She'd checked and Rose was living in digs in Kemp Town. Maybe she ought to ask a PC to call round and make sure that she was all right tonight. All the girls were living in digs apart from Florence, who had given an address in Montpelier Crescent, a rather upmarket part of Hove. How could a showgirl afford a place like that? Emma resolved to do some research on Florence. She hadn't emerged from Max's dressing room by the time that Emma and Bob had left.

Emma had found the tableaux curiously unsettling. It wasn't just the lascivious expressions on the faces of the men around her, it was the girls themselves. They had been so still, so inert in their stylised positions, they reminded Emma of the time that she had visited Madame Tussaud's in London. The trip had been a thirteenth birthday present and, for her parents' sake, Emma had tried to hide the horror and revulsion she felt towards the wax figures frozen in the same pose for all eternity. The worst part had been the Chamber of Horrors, where murderers stood poised in the act of killing, their sightless eyes staring defiantly at the crowds on the other side of the glass case. *You find this fascinating, don't you? You know you shouldn't, but you do.* Burke and Hare, Charles Peace, Mary Ann Cotton. How is this suitable for children? she'd thought at the time, but she'd said nothing because the day was also to include a trip to the zoo and tea at the Ritz. She'd read recently that the exhibits now included John Christie, hanged that summer for the murders in Rillington Place. The Living Tableaux had had the same eerie neutrality as the Chamber of Horrors. This is what happened, your reaction is up to you. Emma thought of Lily Burtenshaw, whose dead body had been manipulated to resemble a young girl about to be executed. Was this what the killer was trying to say? That the onlooker was also guilty?

This isn't getting me anywhere, thought Emma. She sat down to write up her notes from last night. She hoped Bob would be back soon. She hated to admit it but she didn't like being in the underground offices on her own.

Carl Burtenshaw did not look much like his sister. At only twenty-one his dark hair was already thinning slightly and the stocky body encased in brown overalls seemed to be heading rapidly towards middle-aged spread. Carl left an individual identified only as "the boy" in charge of the shop and spoke to Edgar in the small yard at the back which was crammed with Christmas trees, their roots wrapped in hessian.

"Don't feel much like celebrating Christmas," said Carl, lighting a cigarette, "but there you go."

"I understand you've got a baby," said Edgar. He'd refused a cigarette but his breath was smoking all the same. "That must make Christmas special."

"Poor little Gracie," said Carl. "She'll never know her auntie."

"I'm sorry," said Edgar.

"Mum's all set on giving Lily a big funeral," said Carl. "Plumed horses, glass coffin, the lot. But, at the end of the day, she'll still be dead, won't she?"

"I'm sorry," said Edgar again. "I know it's not much comfort but I won't rest until we've found Lily's killer. And it would help if I could ask you a few questions about your sister."

120

"Ask away," said Carl, taking a deep drag on his cigarette.

"Your mum said that Lily was a quiet girl, with not many close friends. I wondered if there were any friends that you knew about that maybe her mother didn't. Boyfriends even."

"She had friends at school," said Carl. "She was always off giggling somewhere with a group of girls. But boyfriends? No. She wasn't the sort."

Everyone said that, thought Edgar, but you didn't have to be a particular sort of girl to have a boyfriend. His own sister, Lucy, had been strictly brought up but she'd had boyfriends, lovelorn lads passing her notes on the bus, youths knocking on the door asking her to go to the pictures with them.

"Do you know why Lily wanted to go to Brighton?" said Edgar. "It seems out of character somehow."

Carl finished his cigarette and ground the stub underfoot. Edgar wondered if he was buying himself a bit of time before answering. "It was unlike her," he said, at last. "She seemed quite happy living at home with Mum. We sold the flower stall after Dad died but she could have worked with me here or found a job in a dress shop or something. She was a pretty girl, nicely spoken too."

"Did she ever say anything to you about why she wanted to go to Brighton?"

"Not really. Just once she said something a bit strange."

"What was it?"

"We were talking about whether we were cockneys or not. You know, that old thing? You're a true cockney if you were born within the sound of Bow Bells. Well Dad was, he was born in Whitechapel, but I said that I didn't qualify because I was born at King's College Hospital in Camberwell. And Lily laughed and said that she certainly didn't qualify because she was born in Brighton."

"And was she?"

"No, she was born in King's College Hospital too. I told her so."

"Didn't she know where she was born?"

"Of course she did. There was never any secret about it. Mum gave me my birth certificate when I was married. She gave me everything, health certificates, the lot. She kept them in a special box."

"And you don't know where Lily got this idea from?"

"No. But that was the only time Lily mentioned Brighton to me."

Edgar asked a few more questions but the weather was becoming colder and Carl was obviously itching to get back and relieve the boy in the shop. It was only when Edgar was heading south along the Brighton Road that he thought of the yard behind the greengrocer's shop. The Christmas trees and the boxes of fruit and vegetables. Apples. Cauliflowers. King Edward Potatoes.

CHAPTER
TEN

Bob couldn't help being pleased at the stir his arrival caused at Lansdowne Road. "It's the police," Norris called up the stairs. Edna fussed around making him tea while Betty, Janette and a confused-looking Mr Entwhistle congregated in the front parlour. Peggy and Brenda were at work.

"Do you want the snug for your interviews, Sergeant Willis?" said Edna. "You'd be more private in there." Bob thought that the last thing the landlady wanted was for the interviews to be private but he accepted her offer all the same.

He spoke to Betty first. This was a formality because he'd been with her last night but she confirmed that they'd got back to the house at about eleven. She'd said goodnight to Bob on the doorstep and she and Janette had gone up to their room. The flowers had been outside the door. Betty had screamed and Janette had run down the stairs and out of the front door to call Bob back.

"And you've no idea who sent them?"

"No," said Betty. She looked less glamorous this morning, thought Bob, but more approachable. Her hair was tied back in a snood and she was wearing a black skirt and a white jumper. She'd smiled at him when he came in but now she looked serious, her eyebrows drawn together in a way that made her look much younger.

"Were they similar flowers to the ones that Lily received?"

"Lily had all sorts of flowers," said Betty. "But she was sent red roses a few times, I know that."

Janette's story was the same. She'd seen the flowers and called for Bob. She told her story impatiently, tapping a foot. Bob didn't find her nearly as attractive as Betty.

Bob spoke to Edna and Norris together. It wasn't ideal but he thought that he'd never get Edna to agree to separate interviews, given her aversion to the word. The landlord and landlady sat close together at the round table, presenting a united front. They were an odd couple, thought Bob. Edna was a large woman with a frankly terrifying bosom but there were signs that she might have been handsome once. The hair which was now built into a towering beehive was probably once dark and lustrous, her eyes, hidden now behind half-moon glasses, still retained a bit of fire. Norris was far less impressive, a small man with a quivering moustache and anxious eyes. But there was a slight twinkle which suggested that, away from Edna's chaperonage, Norris might possess the beginnings of a sense of humour.

The twinkle was markedly absent this morning. Norris said that he and Edna had been in bed last night when they'd heard Betty scream. "I came down to investigate," he said. "I've been keeping a poker by the bed and I brought that with me," Bob remembered seeing Norris, in his pyjamas, clutching this weapon. Edna had been there too, alarming in curlers.

"Did anyone call at the house earlier in the evening?" asked Bob.

"I don't think so," said Norris, looking at Edna for corroboration. "Peggy and Brenda stayed in all evening. I think they were shaken by . . . by what happened to Lily. Their light was off when we went to bed."

"What time was that?"

"About ten-thirty."

"What about Mr Entwhistle?"

"We ate together," said Edna, "and listened to the Light Programme. He went to bed at about nine."

"Have either of you got any idea who left the flowers outside Betty's room?" said Bob.

"No," said Edna. "I thought she was making it up at first. You know, to get attention. But she did seem properly upset."

"Yes," said Bob. "She did. Were you aware of the flowers that used to be left for Lily?"

"For Lily?" said Norris. "No."

"Neither of you ever left her flowers? Outside her room?"

"Why would we do that?" said Edna. "She worked in a flower shop. She had more flowers than she knew what to do with."

She crossed her arms as if declaring that the subject was at an end. Bob tried another tack. "Tell me about

Mr Entwhistle," he said. "Has he ever behaved in a strange way towards any of your lodgers?"

"Never," said Edna. "He's always been quite the gentleman. Of course, he has his little ways."

"Like what?"

"Well, he takes things sometimes."

"Takes things?"

"Yes, there's a word for it. Klepto-something. You'll be missing something — something ordinary like a hairbrush or a butter dish — and it'll turn up in his room. We've never said anything to him, Norris and me. We just let ourselves into his room every now and again and take our things back."

Bob interviewed Mr Entwhistle in his room because the old man seemed rather agitated. He had a surreptitious look around to see if he could see anything that looked stolen but the place was full of what Bob thought of as "old people's stuff": tobacco tins, pipe cleaners, books, china mugs, photographs of people who looked as if they had never been alive, ashtrays, pill bottles. It would be impossible to spot a pilfered item in amongst that lot.

Bob asked Peter Entwhistle what he had done last night. "I had supper with Edna and Norris. Shepherd's pie. Very nice. Afterwards, we listened to the wireless. Then I went to my room, read a bit of my book and went to bed."

"What time was that?"

"About nine-thirty. I go to bed early because I'm a light sleeper."

"Mr Entwhistle," said Bob, trying to think of the best way to frame his next question, "I know you said that you were fond of Lily."

"She was a lovely girl," he said, reaching for his handkerchief. "We were all fond of her."

"Did you ever buy her flowers?"

"What?" Peter Entwhistle looked at him and suddenly the rheumy eyes looked much sharper and much colder.

"Did you ever buy her flowers? You know, just as a gesture of affection."

"No." Once again the tone was gentle and quavering. "I never did anything like that."

"Do you know anyone else who could have bought her flowers? Maybe someone who left them outside her room because they didn't want to be identified."

"That's what that girl was shouting last night," said Peter. "She was saying that there were flowers outside her room."

"Yes," said Bob. "Do you know who could have left flowers for Lily or Betty?"

"It could have been the man from the show."

"What man from the show?"

"The man who was here the other day," said Peter. "He said that he was from the show."

There were innocent reasons for visiting a woman's flat in the middle of the morning, thought Max, but he couldn't think of any offhand. Pros were always at a bit of a loss during the day. Some played golf, others stayed in their dressing gowns until the evening, drinking endless cups of tea and cheating at patience. Max despised all athletic pursuits — if golf can be described as such — but he prided himself on being washed, dressed and shaved by nine a.m. He spent his days in cafés and restaurants, preferably establishments run by Italians. It was as near to content as he could get, sitting at a table with the sign on the door turned to closed, drinking grappa and playing scopa with a restaurateur from Naples or Sardinia. So Mrs M did not ask him where he was going when he set out from the house in Upper Rock Gardens. She obviously assumed that he had found some congenial hostelry where English was a second language. Her cheerful farewell ("See you later, darling") was a reproach that followed him all the way along the seafront and through the increasingly grand streets towards Montpelier Crescent.

"I'll be on my own," Florence had said. She had simply invited him round for a coffee ("I have the beans sent from Paris") but there had been an unspoken message that had hovered in the air from the moment she had entered his dressing room last night and shut the door behind her. Max had poured her a glass of champagne and they talked about the show. Florence was wearing a gold silk robe and still had the Cleopatra diadem in her hair. Max had been unable to look away from her long shimmering legs.

"I watched you from the wings," she said, "and I now think you must be magic."

Max remembered her watching him that first night and the slight jolt it had given him. He said, "I told you the trick of the vanishing box."

"There must be more to it than that."

"True magic is usually very simple."

"I'll drink to that," said Florence, raising her glass in a semi-ironical salute. She seemed quite unselfconscious, sitting opposite him in the small dressing room. She didn't fiddle with her hair or cross and uncross her legs. She simply looked at him with those amused green eyes. She'd taken off her stage make-up but her eyelashes were still dark and her lips smooth and red. Thinking of those lips now, Max found himself quickening his pace.

Montpelier Crescent was a half-moon of gracious white houses overlooking a grassy open space. Max walked past the wrought-iron railings, looking up at the tall windows, some shuttered, some with velvet curtains tasselled back to show chandeliers, Regency furniture, decorated Christmas trees. This was a step up from most theatrical digs and no mistake. There was obviously some mystery attached to Florence Jones. The thought made Max want to see her more than ever. He called it "intrigued" to himself. He was intrigued by her. The word had a comfortingly detached, intellectual ring to it.

"Number twenty, first-floor flat," Florence had said. By the time Max found the house she was watching him from the balcony.

"I'll throw the key down."

Thank God he caught it, one-handed. Nothing would have looked less dignified than to have fumbled and found himself scrabbling about on the pavement in the dirty snow left over from last night.

The flat was as opulent as it had looked from outside. The sitting room was a dream of symmetry with high ceilings and windows on either side of the balcony doors. The winter sun made a chessboard of the parquet floor and turned the brocade sofas into gold.

"This is quite some place," said Max when Florence came in with the coffee in exquisite lapis lazuli cups.

"Yes," was all Florence said. She sat opposite him, arranging her legs to their best advantage. She was wearing a dark blue dress, tight-fitting and pulled in at the waist with a white belt. Her hair was loose and she wore discreet gold earrings. Apart from her shoes, which were blue and white leather, very high, she looked like a perfect society beauty and nothing like a showgirl.

"Are you just staying here for the fortnight?"

Florence looked at him. "It's Victor's flat."

It was a few seconds before the name registered with Max and, when it did, it was with the dull realisation that he should have guessed.

"Ah," he said.

"Yes," said Florence. She put her cup down on the spindly table beside her. "I've been Vic's mistress for nearly a year now, ever since I joined the troupe really. Vic's got a few of these flats dotted around the place but Brighton's always been his base. It's not an exclusive position, you see, being Vic's mistress."

"Why are you telling me this?" said Max.

"Because I want you to know what you're getting into."

"I'm not getting into anything," said Max. But, even as he said it, he knew it wasn't true. He knew that, as soon as she got up, he would follow those wonderful legs out of the room and into whatever fantasy boudoir Vic Cutler considered suitable for his kept woman.

"What man?" said Bob, more sharply than he had intended.

"The man who was here," said Mr Entwhistle. It reminded Bob of a nonsense rhyme that he'd learnt as a child. "When I was going down the stair, I met a man who wasn't there."

"When did you see this man?" he asked.

"I don't know. Last week. Thursday or Friday or Saturday."

Bob counted to ten silently. "Can you remember which day? It might be important."

"I think it was Friday."

"The day you had kippers for breakfast?"

"What?"

Bob tried again. "What was the man doing?"

"He was standing in the hall. At the bottom of the stairs. I asked him if he needed any help because he looked a bit lost and he said he was from the show. I assumed that he was here for the girls. The ones from the Hippodrome. You know —" he mouthed the words at Bob — "the show where they *take their clothes off.*"

Bob found himself wanting to defend the Living Tableaux. He'd found the act rather tasteful although

Emma had had all sorts of objections to it, of course. But he didn't want to distract Mr Entwhistle.

"Can you describe this man?"

"He was youngish. Quite tall. Smartly dressed."

"Dark or fair?"

"Dark, I think."

"And can you remember what time of day it was when you saw him?"

"I think it was teatime because Edna always makes a pot in the snug."

"What time is teatime?"

"Four o'clock," said Mr Entwhistle, as if this was a stupid question.

"And what did the man do after you'd spoken to him?"

"I don't know," said Mr Entwhistle. "I left him standing there."

There didn't seem to be much further to be gained from the conversation, especially as Mr Entwhistle was looking rather worried. Bob thanked him and went back into the hall, where Edna was hovering.

"Mrs Wright," he said, "Mr Entwhistle says that there was a man in the house on Friday afternoon at about four. A strange man. He said that he was from the theatre. Do you remember seeing anyone like that?"

Edna seemed to swell, resembling Portslade Patsy more than ever.

"A strange man in this house! What sort of a landlady do you think I am? What are you implying?"

"I'm not implying anything. It's just that Mr Entwhistle said —"

Edna leant closer. "Mr Entwhistle," she said in a savage whisper, "isn't right in the head. I can't have you bothering him like this. Now, is there anything else?"

"No," said Bob.

As Bob left the house he noticed with disfavour that there was a group of reporters hanging about outside.

"I've got nothing to say," he told them. "Can't you leave these people alone?"

"Come on," said Don from the *Argus*, "just tell us how the investigation's going."

"No comment," said Bob, tying his muffler tighter.

"Sergeant Willis?" It was the police constable assigned to guard the house. "Can I have a word?" They walked a little way down the street. Behind the policeman's head, Bob could see the sea, sparkling blue like an advertisement for the joys of the seaside.

"Why haven't you chased the press away?" said Bob.

"It's a free country," said the policeman. He looked cold and fed up. "I've got a message for you from my sarge."

"What is it?"

"Your boss, DI Stephens." He assumed the la-di-da voice often adopted for impressions of the DI, although he wasn't posh, not really. "He told us to go through the dustbins. We get all the best jobs."

"Did you find anything?"

"That's just it. The sarge said that if you would honour us with your presence at the station, he's got something to show you."

Bob saw Don looking over towards them. "All right," he said. "Just tell me where to go."

It wasn't far away, an unprepossessing building near the cricket ground. Sarge, a burly man who, rumour had it, had once been a circus strongman, greeted Bob with exaggerated respect.

"What have we done to deserve this visit from CID?"

"The constable on duty outside Lansdowne Road said you had something to show me."

"Yes, come this way." He led Bob into a back room where newspapers had been spread on the floor. Piled on top was a noxious heap of vegetable peelings, tea leaves and other nameless items of household rubbish. Bob recoiled. Did they expect him to search through this lot?

Sarge pointed to the newspapers. "Best use for them, am I right?"

Bob relaxed slightly. "You're right. There was a gang of reporters outside the house."

"Vultures. Anyway, your boss told us to look out for a letter and we found something."

"You did?" Bob felt his heart beating faster.

"Not a letter. This." He handed Bob an envelope, originally white but now spattered with what looked like tea. Bob read the handwritten address, "Miss Lily Burtenshaw, 12 Lansdowne Road, Brighton."

In capital letters at the top were the words, "Private and Confidential".

CHAPTER
ELEVEN

Max hated himself for asking it. "When are you expecting Vic back?"

"Not until four o'clock," said Florence, stretching out on the bed. The sun slanting through the shutters drew straight lines on her body. She was entirely unselfconscious about being naked, not surprising really for someone who made their living out of appearing on stage wearing only a stuffed snake.

"What time is it?" Max reached for his watch which was on the bedside table beside his cigarette case. "Jesus, it's half past one."

"Time goes quickly when you're having fun," said Florence, raising herself up on one arm to look at him through her hair.

"Fun is an understatement —" Max leant over to kiss her — "but I should go."

Max started to dress, feeling the awkwardness that always accompanied the post-coital practicalities. Florence watched him, still naked, still devoid of embarrassment.

"I'll see you tonight," she said.

"I want to see you again," said Max, realising that he meant it. "And not just on stage dressed as Cleopatra."

135

"Oh, you'll see me again," said Florence, reaching for her robe with a lazy hand. "I'm not going to vanish."

"What about Vic?" said Max. "Is he going to vanish?"

"I can take care of Vic," said Florence. "What about Mrs Markham?"

Max didn't know that Florence knew about Joyce. Hearing her name on Florence's lips made his betrayal seem worse.

"Joyce and I are both adults," he said. "It's all very civilised."

"Sex is never civilised," said Florence, standing up. In her gold silk robe with her black hair loose, she looked far more like the Egyptian queen than she had on stage. She disappeared into the bathroom which, having visited it earlier, Max knew was straight out of Hollywood, all glass and marble with dark blue tiles and goldfish swimming in a bowl on a plinth.

Max searched for his tie before finding it encircling the head of a plaster bust of Cicero. Where had Vic Cutler found such an object? The whole flat looked like it had been ordered, lock, stock and barrel, from a theatrical designer. He stared at his reflection in one of the room's many mirrors. Not bad, slightly dishevelled by his standards, perhaps. Florence's words nagged at him. Would he have preferred it if she had said love instead of sex or would that have sent him into a panic? Florence was a beautiful woman and the time they had spent together had indeed been unforgettable. He knew that he wanted to sleep with her again but where did that leave his relationship with Joyce? And what about Vic Cutler, a man who wouldn't take kindly to being

136

cuckolded? A sensible man would walk away now, Max thought, adjusting the knot of his tie. Thank God he had never been sensible.

The DI was back by the time that Bob returned. He and Emma were sitting at the table in the incident room looking at the crime scene photographs. Typical of them to be working and not talking. He betted that neither of them had even put the kettle on.

"How did you get on at Lansdowne Road?" asked the DI.

Bob produced the tea-stained envelope with a flourish that he hoped was worthy of Max Mephisto himself.

"The Hove police found this in the rubbish. Sergeant Jenks says don't mention it, happy to help."

The DI laughed, smoothing out the paper. "Good old Jenks. One of nature's gentlemen."

"It doesn't get us very far though, does it," said Bob. "The envelope without the letter."

"Wait a minute," said Emma. She was leafing through her endless pages of notes. Really, thought Bob, she could paper the CID offices with them by now.

"Here." She was showing them a list.

"Those are the names of the girls," said Bob, "the girls in the tableaux act." Betty's name was at the top, he noticed.

"Not there, *there*." She pointed to the bottom of the page where there was some different handwriting. "Vic Cutler wrote his name there."

Edgar and Bob looked closer.

"It could be the same writing," said Edgar.

"It is the same," said Emma. "Look at the Os and the Is. The way the dot is over to the right. I'm sure of it. It's even the same blue pen."

"But why would Vic be writing to Lily?" said Edgar.

"He could have been the man Peter Entwhistle saw in the house," said Bob. "Mr Entwhistle said that he saw a strange man at Lansdowne Road last week. When Mr Entwhistle challenged him he said he was from the show."

"Did you get a description of the man?" asked the DI.

"A very vague one." Bob rifled through his notebook (See? I take notes too, Emma). "Here it is. 'Youngish. Quite tall. Smartly dressed. Dark.'"

"And Entwhistle spoke to him?" said Edgar.

"Yes, the man was standing in the hallway and Mr Entwhistle asked if he could help him. Probably being a bit nosy. The man said that he was from the show and Mr Entwhistle assumed that he was waiting for Betty and Janette."

"Could it have been Vic Cutler?" said Edgar.

"But he's not young," said Emma. "He's in his forties, I'm sure of it."

"Believe me," said Bob, "everyone's young compared to Entwhistle."

"Did he say when he saw this man?" said Edgar.

"Friday," said Bob. "At about four o'clock in the afternoon. I asked Edna but she flatly denied that anyone had been there. You know what she's like, 'this is a respectable house'." He attempted to copy the landlady's nasal tones.

"So we've only got Entwhistle's word that anyone was there?" said Edgar.

"Yes, but he seemed pretty certain. Edna tried to say that he wasn't right in the head but I think he's reliable enough. A bit confused at times, maybe, but he wouldn't just imagine meeting someone in the hall."

The DI still looked dubious so, of course, Emma did too.

"He might have been confused about the day though," she said.

"I suppose so," said Bob, "but I think it's worth following up. Friday night could have been when Lily was killed."

"But Lily wouldn't have been back from work at four," said Emma. "Edna saw her at half past five when she complimented her on her hairdo."

"Maybe the man didn't know that," said Bob.

"But he said he was from the show," said Emma. "Why would someone from the show want to see Lily?"

"I don't know," said Bob. "But I still think it might be important."

Emma looked like she wanted to argue some more but the DI lifted his hand. "It might well be important," he said. "Good work, Bob."

Bob tried not to look too smug.

"What about Vic Cutler?" said Emma. "We need to find out why he was writing to Lily."

"Yes," said the DI. "We certainly do need to talk to Mr Cutler. Did he write his address down for you, Emma?"

"No, just a telephone number. It's a London exchange."

Emma went to the telephone and dialled. They all listened to the numbers clicking into place, then they could hear the phone ringing. No answer.

"See if you can get an address from the theatre," said Edgar. "If not, we'll go to the Hippodrome later. I'm sure he never misses a performance."

Emma started to dial again. The DI looked at Bob. "Good work," he said again. "Did you find out anything else?"

"Norris and Edna Wright, Brenda, Peggy and Peter Entwhistle were all in the house last night. Any one of them could have left the flowers. I asked Mr Entwhistle, very tactfully, if he'd ever left flowers for Lily and he denied it."

"Did you believe him?"

"I think so. He seemed quite shocked at the idea. Mind you, Edna says that Entwhistle steals things."

"Steals things?"

"Yes. He's a kleptowhatsit. He takes odd things. Nothing of any particular value but the Wrights keep finding their belongings in his room."

"The Wrights just let themselves in?"

"Yes, remember they told us they have keys to all the rooms."

Emma was still on the telephone. Bob could hear her asking someone for Vic's address. Those cut-glass tones that always assumed — rightly — that they would instantly be obeyed. He looked at the photographs on the table.

"What were you looking at when I came in?"

"This." The DI pointed to one of the pictures showing the crime scene. "The box in front of Lily. Remember it had 'King Edward Potatoes' written on it? Well, her brother's a greengrocer and I just wondered if there was a possible link."

"You think her *brother* could have done it?"

The DI shrugged. "It was just a rather wild thought but nothing doing. The box in Lily's room was from Perkiss and Sons, a greengrocer's on the Western Road. It's not the same shop that usually delivers to the Wrights though."

Bob heard Emma saying, "Thank you so much." He turned.

"Got an address?"

"Yes, Montpelier Crescent."

Emma looked like she had more to say so Bob obliged her. "What's significant about that?"

"One of the girls gave that address too." Emma was looking at her list. "Florence Jones."

"Which one was she?"

"Cleopatra."

"Oh." Bob remembered her all right. She was one of the best-looking girls in the show but she hadn't been in the dressing room afterwards.

"You two go round there now," said the DI. "Ask Vic Cutler about his association with Lily. You ask the questions, Bob, as you got this lead."

Bob didn't dare look at Emma.

★ ★ ★

By the time that Florence emerged from the bathroom she was, mysteriously, fully dressed. Max was pleased. It would be too much like a French farce if she was half-naked while he was putting on his coat. As it was, he said, slightly awkwardly, "I'll see you at the theatre then."

"I'll walk downstairs with you," said Florence. "I've got a letter to post."

Max wondered about the wisdom of this but they met no one on the stairs. As they left the building the bells were ringing in a nearby church. Two o'clock.

At the corner of the street, Florence stopped. "I'll leave you here then."

"The mission bells told me that I mustn't stay," said Max, quoting an old song. To his surprise, Florence's face clouded.

"Why did you say that? Is this goodbye then? Goodbye and thanks for a lovely morning."

"Not at all," said Max. He reached for her gloved hand and kissed it. "I told you, I want to see you again."

Florence seemed to have recovered her poise. She smiled up at him. Not that there was a great difference in their heights. In her high heels, Florence could almost look him in the eye.

"Oh, you'll see me again," she said. "I promise."

"In that case —" Max raised his hat — "it's *au revoir*."

"See you later, Max." And Florence swept off down the street, her black coat billowing around her. Anna

Karenina in Hove. Max stayed watching her for quite some time.

It was nearly three o'clock by the time Bob and Emma reached Montpelier Crescent. The sky was already darkening and it looked like there might be more snow by nightfall. Emma had her duffel coat on and after a while she put the hood up, presumably to protect her ears but it had the effect of making her seem unreachable, wrapped up in her own thoughts. Bob was wearing the heavy jacket that his mother said made him look like a dustman. How different Emma had looked in that fur coat at the theatre, her blonde hair loose. She had behaved differently too, relaxing, even laughing with him. He felt proud to be seen with her, he really did. Of course, afterwards, when they were interviewing the girls in the dressing room, she was back to her old bossy self but he thought that he'd been given a glimpse of the real Emma and the thought made him feel oddly protective towards her.

"That policewoman's a bit of a madam, isn't she?" Janette had said on the way home. They had walked in an awkward threesome, Bob in the middle, a girl on each side.

"She's all right," said Bob. "She's very good at her job."

"Oh, are you sweet on her then?" Bob had ignored this comment and the laugh that went with it. Betty had squeezed his arm as if she understood.

Montpelier Crescent wasn't that far from Bob's lodgings on Third Avenue but it was a million miles away in terms of desirability. The smooth shuttered façades seemed to sneer at them as they slogged past. "You will never be able to live here," they said, "never have a lift or a dumb waiter or the key to your own private garden. You'll be sharing a bathroom until you die." Unless you were Emma, of course. You could probably fit two of these houses inside her family mansion in Roedean.

But Emma was thinking along the same lines. "Of course, this explains why Florence could afford to live here."

"Why?" said Bob, partly just to see if he could embarrass her.

"If she was Vic Cutler's mistress," said Emma, without missing a beat. "This must be the house."

"What number is the flat?" said Bob, finger poised over the buzzer.

"First floor, number one," said Emma. Bob rang and they listened to the sound reverberating. No answer. Bob looked up at the wrought-iron balcony. The curtains were open but there was no light inside.

"He must be out," said Bob.

"I'll ring for the porter," said Emma.

"How the other half lives," muttered Bob. He wouldn't have thought of the porter.

At first it seemed that this mythical personage wasn't going to appear but after about five minutes the door opened to show a small man in a rather rumpled green uniform. He looked like an angry leprechaun.

"Police," said Emma briskly, showing him her warrant card. "We need to see Mr Cutler in flat one."

144

"He's out," said the leprechaun, trying to shut the door.

"Did you see him go out?" asked Bob.

"No."

"Did you see him come in?"

A reluctant nod. "About half an hour ago."

"Then can you let us into the flat?"

"Mr Cutler will kill me."

"Do you want us to arrest you for obstructing the police?" said Emma. The man shot her an unfriendly look but stepped back to let them into the hall. In silence, they followed him up the wide staircase to the first floor.

The porter knocked on the door. "Mr Cutler!"

When there was no answer he took out an antique-looking fob and, after some fumbling, selected a key and turned it in the lock.

"Mr Cutler?" Emma stepped inside. The flat was completely silent but, for some reason, Bob felt a sudden reluctance to follow her. Go on, he told himself, you can't let her go first. Bob forced himself to shoulder past Emma and so was the first to enter the sitting room and see Vic Cutler sitting on the sofa with a knife in his chest.

CHAPTER
TWELVE

"Holy Mary Mother of God." This was the porter, becoming religious with shock.

"Don't come any closer," said Emma.

Bob was leaning over the body. "He's dead all right."

Vic Cutler was sitting upright in a ghastly semblance of his old overbearing manner. Emma half expected him to turn to her with his trademark leer. *Always happy to help a pretty policewoman.*

"Have you got a telephone?" she asked the porter.

"Yes," he said, standing ashen-faced in the doorway. "It's downstairs."

"You go," said Bob. "I'll stay here with . . . I'll stay here."

"Yes," said Emma. She was very grateful to Bob for offering to stay with the effigy that had been Vic but didn't quite know how to say so. She followed the porter, whose name she learnt was Norman, to his basement apartment. There she rang the DI and refused Norman's offer of a whisky "for the shock".

"How well did you know Mr Cutler?" she asked as the porter poured himself a large glassful.

"Not very well. He could be quite harshly spoken at times but he was generous with the tips."

"What about the lady who lives in the flat? Miss Jones."

"Ah, she's a lovely lady. She could be a film star." Emma was slightly surprised that Norman considered Florence a "lady" but she supposed that looks and money together had bought her respectability.

"When did you last speak to Miss Jones?" she asked.

"Today. This morning. She said that she was expecting a friend to call round."

"Did she say who this friend was?"

"No."

"But you saw them, didn't you?" said Emma, suddenly sure of this.

"Just a glimpse, going upstairs," said the porter. "She threw the keys down to him."

Somehow Emma had been sure that it was a him.

"Can you describe the man?" she said, getting out her notebook.

"I can do better than that," said Norman, draining his glass. "I recognised him. It was that magician from the show at the Hippodrome. Max Mephisto."

Edgar commandeered a squad car to drive him to Montpelier Crescent. He didn't want to waste any time and already the sky was an ominous dark pewter colour. He brought the box brownie with him, grimly determined to photograph this new crime scene.

He was met at the door by Emma. "I've interviewed the porter," she told him, as she led the way upstairs. "He saw Vic Cutler come in at about two-thirty. He didn't hear anything else or see anyone come in.

147

Florence Jones, the girl from the show, lives here whenever she's in Brighton. Today, the porter saw her go out at about two thirty-five."

"Just after Cutler got in?"

"Yes."

"Did anyone else visit the flat today?" said Edgar. He was surprised to see Emma blush fiercely. Surely the question wasn't that shocking?

They had arrived at the flat but Emma stood in front of the door as if she wanted to keep him from entering. "Yes," she said. "Florence had a visitor this morning. He arrived at about eleven. The porter saw him going upstairs."

"Did you get a description?"

"It was Max."

"*Max?*" Edgar stared at her, half hoping that this was a joke. "Max Mephisto?"

"Yes. The porter recognised him."

"Why would he . . ." Edgar stopped. He knew quite well why Max would have been visiting Florence at eleven o'clock in the morning.

"The thing is . . ." said Emma. She was blushing harder than ever. "Last night, at the theatre, I saw Florence going into Max's dressing room."

And Edgar remembered seeing Max outside the theatre talking to a woman in a fur hat. He was willing to bet that had been Florence Jones. *Was that girl you were speaking to earlier one of the Tableaux girls? Yes. And one of the prettiest? Naturally.*

"So Cutler got here at two-thirty and was dead by . . . what time did you arrive?"

148

"It was ten past three by the time that we got into the flat. The body was still warm."

"Let's go in then," said Edgar.

Bob was standing by the window. Edgar knew that he wouldn't have thought it appropriate to sit down in the presence of the corpse. He hadn't turned on the lights either and the shape on the sofa was sinister in its stillness. Edgar reached for the switch and the chandelier overhead sparkled into life. Edgar and Bob looked at each other, momentarily dazzled.

"We've called for Solomon Carter," said Bob.

"Well done," said Edgar. He approached the body but didn't touch it. The knife hilt was embedded in Victor's white shirt front but there was surprisingly little blood. Someone had known exactly where to strike.

Edgar handed the camera to Bob. "Can you take some pictures? Let's try to touch as little as possible." He looked around the room. There were two coffee cups on a small side table and a cigarette butt in the ashtray as if Vic had just stubbed it out. Cutler sat at his ease, looking almost ridiculously unprepared for the assault that had killed him.

"We need to talk to Florence Jones immediately," he said. "She's our main suspect. There's no sign of a struggle and she was seen leaving the house soon after Cutler came in. Emma, let's go down to the theatre and see if we can find her there. Bob, you wait for Carter."

Bob looked as if he wanted to protest but said nothing. Edgar knew that he would feel that he was missing out on the chase but he wanted Emma with him when he interviewed Florence. Was he also trying to save her from the gruesome wait with the dead body? Perhaps.

The squad car was still waiting outside and they were at the Hippodrome in ten minutes. The lights were on in the foyer but Edgar suggested they went round to the entrance that he had used with Max. As Edgar and Emma approached, two women wearing headscarves scuttled past them and in through the stage door. Were they performers, Vic Cutler's girls perhaps? It was impossible to tell. Maybe they were cleaners or box office staff. Edgar asked the commissionaire if Florence Jones was in.

"Who's asking?" said the man, with studied truculence.

"Police." Edgar produced his warrant card.

"I'll get Mr Billings. He's the theatre manager."

A scared-looking runner was dispatched and returned with a large man wearing a dress shirt and braces.

"I'm Dick Billings. What's all this about?"

"DI Edgar Stephens. I'd like to speak to Florence Jones."

"Why?"

Edgar stared him down. "I'm not at liberty to say."

Dick Billings opened his mouth and shut it again. He looked like a man used to blustering and bullying but he obviously decided that he couldn't shout at a detective inspector so he shrugged and said, "This way. She'll be in her dressing room. Third floor."

"Is there somewhere private that we can speak to Miss Jones?"

Billings's eyes bulged. "You can use my office." He was obviously desperate to know more but Edgar just thanked him and they carried on up the stone stairs.

The dressing rooms had names stuck onto the doors. Edgar spotted "Miss French" and "Max Mephisto" as well as "Jim Jones" and someone called "Madame Mitzi". Max's door also bore a rather tattered gold star. Billings stopped at a sign saying "Living Tableaux". He knocked once and entered without waiting for permission to do so.

A dark-haired woman was alone in the room, sitting at a dressing table. Edgar saw her face in the mirror before she turned: pale face, green eyes, red lips. What had she been doing? Just sitting there looking at her reflection?

"It's the police," said Billings, seeming to enjoy the drama of the statement. "They want to talk to you."

Florence stood up. She was tall and slim and, Edgar couldn't help noticing, extremely beautiful. There was also a poise and grace that he hadn't expected.

"Why do you want to talk to me?" Her voice was low-pitched and attractive with a hint of an accent, Welsh, Edgar thought. She seemed completely in control.

"Let's go into Mr Billings's office."

Dick Billings's office was little more than a glorified cubbyhole. Edgar squeezed behind the desk, Florence sat opposite and Emma stood by the door. Billings remained outside but Edgar didn't hear his footsteps retreating.

"Miss Jones," Edgar began, "can you confirm your address for me?"

Florence's eyes widened but she answered composedly. "Flat one, number twenty Montpelier Crescent, Hove."

"What time did you leave Montpelier Crescent today?"

"Just after two."

"Are you sure?" The porter had said that he had seen her leaving at two thirty-five. He'd been quite specific about it, according to Emma. Five minutes after Vic Cutler had arrived.

"Quite sure," said Florence. "Why are you asking me?"

"You share the house with a Mr Victor Cutler, is that right?"

Florence coloured slightly but answered in the same calm, low tone. "When he's in town, yes."

"I'm sorry to tell you, Miss Jones, but Mr Cutler has been found dead."

He said it deliberately baldly because he wanted to gauge Florence's reaction. For a moment she did not seem to take in the news although her face drained of colour.

"Victor?" she said. "That's not possible. I saw him this morning."

"I'm sorry," said Edgar again.

"How did he die?"

"He was murdered," said Edgar, watching her closely.

"Murdered?" Florence turned to look beseechingly at Emma. "Is this true?"

"Quite true," said Emma. Edgar was glad that she didn't give away any more information. He wanted to see what Florence would ask next.

"Where did this happen?" she said, pressing a lace handkerchief to eyes which, as far as Edgar could see, were completely tearless.

"At number twenty Montpelier Crescent," he said.

"At the flat?" A different tone, sharper, more panicky. "When?"

"This afternoon. Can you confirm again what time you left the flat?"

"It was just after two. I went to post a letter."

"Can anyone confirm this?"

A flicker. Florence's long dark eyelashes came down over her eyes. Then she looked up at him. "No," she said.

"What did you do next?"

"Walked around by myself for a while then came on to the theatre."

Edgar hesitated. Florence was the main suspect for Vic Cutler's death but he doubted that he had enough evidence to arrest her on the spot. Besides, it might be good to let her sweat for a little longer. There was also the nagging suspicion that Cutler's murder might not be just the age-old story of a mistress stabbing her lover but something altogether more complicated.

"That's all for now," he said. "I must ask you not to leave the area though. We'll be asking you some more questions over the next few days."

"I won't go anywhere," she said. "I don't know who the flat belongs tonow."

"Did Mr Cutler have any family that you know of?"

"He's got a mother in Manchester. She must be in her eighties."

Edgar would have to get an address for Cutler's elderly mother and ask the local police to break the news. He was relieved that he wouldn't be making the call himself.

"Miss Jones," said Emma from the doorway. "That black coat in the dressing room, was that the one you were wearing when you left the house today?"

Florence turned to face her. "Yes," she said. "Why?"

"Just a question," said Emma. Edgar raised his eyebrows to ask if Emma had more questions but she shook her head at him.

"That's all for now, Miss Jones," he said. "Just to let you know that my officers are still at Montpelier Crescent if you're thinking of going back there."

Florence sat up straighter in her chair and tossed her hair back. "I'm not going home yet," she said. "We've got to do the show first."

After Florence had left, Edgar allowed Dick Billings back into his own office and told him the news.

"Blimey," said Billings, mopping his brow with a red handkerchief. "Cutler murdered. Well, it couldn't have happened to a nicer bloke."

154

"You didn't like him?"

Billings sat heavily in the chair behind his desk. Edgar thought that the manager looked deeply shaken, whatever his protestations to the contrary.

"Cutler was a tough guy," he said, attempting a James Cagney accent. "He wasn't in the business to make friends. He always wanted the best deals for his girls, that's fair enough. He specified how big their name would be on the posters and all that stuff. But he was pleasant enough if he got his own way."

"What about his private life? Was he married?"

"Married? No. I think he had a mistress in every town. Treated them well by all accounts, fur coats, jewels, the lot. Then, when he was bored with them, it was on to the next girl."

"Does he have a mistress in this town?"

The manager eyed him shrewdly. "I'm imagining that's why you wanted to talk to Florence."

"Were there rumours about Cutler and Florence Jones?"

"Not really. I mean, I assumed he was sleeping with one of the girls and she was the obvious choice. Not my type though. Too tall."

"Have you any idea why anyone would have killed Cutler?"

Billings shrugged. "Like I say, if you're asking me if anyone had a grudge against him, I'd say there was a queue a mile long. But I don't know who could have hated him enough to kill him."

"Has Cutler argued with anyone at the theatre this week?"

"He's argued with everyone. Me, the stage manager, the musical director, most of the girls."

"What did he argue with you about?"

"He wanted to close the show but that had to be Mephisto. I mean, the girls are a big draw but Mephisto's a star. He's top of the bill, he closes the show. Have you seen the new act he does with his daughter? Now she's a beauty, if you like. Trim little figure too."

Edgar didn't like the way Billings's voice thickened when he said this. He thanked the theatre manager and stood up to take his leave. Outside in the corridor he told Emma to get back to the station and start coordinating the investigation.

"What about you?" Emma looked like she wanted to refuse.

"I've got someone else I need to see."

"Ed! What are you doing here?"

Max was sitting at his dressing table reading the paper. There was a black coffee next to him and a half-smoked cigarette in the ashtray. Edgar thought of all the times that he'd seen his friend relaxing like this: in the Caledonian Hotel at Inverness, where the Magic Men used to gather to plan their next deception, in various dressing rooms and hotels, at Mrs M's house. Max was a man without a home so he was at home anywhere.

"I want to talk to you," said Edgar.

"This sounds serious."

"Max —" Edgar sat on the sofa — "where were you this morning?"

Max put down the paper and stared at him. "What's this about?"

"Where were you today between eleven and two-thirty?"

Max looked at him as if he'd guessed the card that Edgar had hidden in his hand.

"I think you know where I was."

"Can you tell me, please?"

"All right. I was visiting a lady."

"Florence Jones?"

"Yes. Ideally you shouldn't have given me the name so early. It ruins the trick."

"This isn't a trick. What time did you arrive at Miss Jones's house?"

"About eleven."

"And when did you leave?"

"About two o'clock."

"Alone?"

"Florence left with me and we walked a little way together. She wanted to post a letter."

"And you're sure about the time?"

"Yes, a church bell was ringing when we left the flat. I made a joke about 'South of The Border'. You know the song. 'The mission bells told me that I mustn't stay.' Florence didn't think it was funny."

"What did you do next?"

"Went for a coffee at Aldo's and then walked to the theatre. I was here by three. Ed, what is this about? You look like my answer was tremendously significant."

157

"It was. A man was murdered today."

"My God. What's this got to do with Florence and me?"

"It was Vic Cutler. He was killed between two-thirty and three. You're Florence's alibi though she didn't mention you when I talked to her just now. I think she may have been trying to save your reputation."

"Vic Cutler. Good God." Max's face was hard to read at the best of times and Edgar couldn't guess at his emotions now. Max took a cigarette from his case, stared at it and then seemed to change his mind. He reached for the whisky bottle.

"I think we need a drink."

"I can't. I'm on duty."

"I need a drink then."

He poured himself a generous measure and drank most of it in one swallow. "How did he die?"

Edgar thought he probably shouldn't say but the habit of sharing his cases with Max was too strong. "He was stabbed."

"Someone meant business then."

"It wasn't an accident, if that's what you mean."

"Have you seen Florence? Is she all right?"

"I've just spoken to Miss Jones. She seems remarkably composed."

Max shot Edgar a hard look. "Oh yes, of course, she's your main suspect, isn't she?"

"We needed to talk to her," said Edgar levelly. "She shared a house with Cutler, after all."

There was a short silence, during which Max finished the rest of his whisky.

"You said that I was Florence's alibi," he said at last, "so does that mean she's in the clear?"

"Not entirely," said Edgar. "She could have walked to the post box with you and then gone back and killed Cutler but it makes it less likely. There was no sign of her when my officers got there at ten past three."

"Cutler was a man with a lot of enemies," said Max. "He had a tough reputation in the business."

"So I've been hearing."

"And Florence . . ." Max hesitated. "Florence didn't speak of him with dislike. She didn't have any reason to kill him."

"Except that she'd just met someone else," said Edgar.

"For God's sake." Max stood up. "We'd only just met. Florence wouldn't have killed Cutler over me."

Stranger things have happened, thought Edgar. Florence could have returned to the flat, Vic could have seen something that made him suspicious — crumpled sheets, an extra glass — and confronted her. Except that there was only a window of about twenty minutes for this to have happened and the room had shown no sign of a violent argument.

"We don't know what happened yet," he said. "We'll need to talk to Miss Jones again."

"How did she seem just now?"

"Like I said, composed. She was thinking about the show."

Max gave a short laugh. "Pros are a hard-hearted bunch. You must know that by now."

Edgar stood up. "I need to get back to the station."

159

"This is turning into quite a week for you."

"I've had better." At the door he turned. "Keep your eyes open, Max, will you?"

"I always do."

"And be careful. Whoever killed Cutler was ruthless and determined. They could kill again."

CHAPTER
THIRTEEN

"It's a woman's crime, that's what Carter said."

Edgar sighed. He could just imagine Solomon Carter saying something like that. They were back at the police station in Bartholomew Square. It was already dark but officers would be standing outside the flat on Montpelier Crescent and the house in Lansdowne Road. And, somewhere in Manchester, a police constable was on the way to Mrs Cutler's house to break the news of her son's death. Bob had left Solomon Carter supervising the removal of the body to the mortuary.

Emma had made tea and Edgar warmed his hands on the mug. "How does Carter make that out?" he said.

Bob took a sip of his tea. "Stabbing's personal. You have to get up close to do it. It's a crime of passion."

"Florence Jones is certainly our main suspect," said Edgar. "She says she left the house at two and Max confirms that. But the porter saw her leaving at two thirty-five, about five minutes after Cutler got in."

"Except . . ." said Emma. She was looking flushed and important. Edgar knew that she had been saving this up for his return.

"Except that the person the porter saw leaving was wearing a fur coat. He was quite specific about it. Florence was wearing a black cloth coat. Dior's New Look, I think."

Edgar suppressed a smile. "So that's why you asked about the coat."

"Yes, all someone needed to do was put on the coat and a black wig. Florence is a tall woman. It could have been a man."

"Why would somebody do that?" Bob had his stubborn look on.

"Dick Billings, the theatre manager, said that Cutler had a lot of enemies," said Edgar. "I suppose it's possible that someone came to the house and stabbed him. The porter didn't see all the comings and goings. There's also the link to Lily Burtenshaw. Cutler wrote to her and now he's dead. That's a coincidence and I don't like coincidence."

"This is a very different sort of murder though," said Bob.

"That's true," said Edgar. "Lily's was so carefully staged. That must have been for a reason even if that reason only existed in the killer's mind. But this crime could have been one of expediency. Maybe someone needed to silence Cutler quickly."

"Because of what he wrote to Lily?" said Emma.

"Perhaps."

"Could still have been the girlfriend," said Bob, reluctant to let go of his *crime passionnel*.

"Why would she kill him though?" said Emma. "It looked like she had a very comfortable life with him."

"Well, if she'd met someone else . . ." said Bob, his ears reddening. He shot a look at Edgar. Both sergeants had so far avoided mentioning Max.

"She had only just met Max," said Edgar. "It seems a bit extreme to murder because of him. Besides, there was nothing to stop her being with Max. Neither of them are married, after all." He thought of Mrs M, whom he'd always liked. He hadn't expected her relationship with Max to last for ever but it still shocked him slightly to think of Max leaving the landlady's house and walking across town to have an illicit liaison with a woman he barely knew. He heard Diablo's voice in his head, "You're too easily shocked, dear boy." Diablo, he was sure, had slept with plenty of showgirls in his time.

"We need to find out if Cutler really was at Lansdowne Road last week," said Edgar. "Let's go back and talk to the Wrights and Mr Entwhistle tomorrow. We'll see if Mrs Cutler has anything to tell the police about Vic's past. Not that she'll be in much of a state to talk to them, poor woman."

"What about the link to the Living Tableaux?" said Emma. "There were the flowers left for Betty and now Cutler's dead. We ought to keep an eye on the girls."

"I'm going to the show tonight." Edgar avoided looking at Emma. "I'll keep my eyes open."

The dressing room door was open and Florence appeared to be in the middle of a pep talk.

"Vic's not here but we know the routine backwards. We'll just have to look out for each other to make sure we don't miss any cues. I've asked Tommy to take the Hiawatha music more slowly to give us time to get into position."

Did the girls know that Vic Cutler was not just absent but dead? wondered Max, standing in the doorway. Well, if they didn't, they soon would. Edgar had told Dick Billings and Max had already heard Jim Jones and Stew Stewart discussing it in the corridor. Soon the whole theatre would know that Vic Cutler, the brash showman with his handmade suits and bruiser's face, had been murdered.

He beckoned to Florence. "Can I have a quick word?"

"It'll have to be quick," said Florence. She was wearing her gold wrap over — he assumed — not very much. "Madame Mitzi's on now. We're next after the dancers."

They went into Max's dressing room. "Are you all right?" said Max, as he closed the door.

Florence shrugged, a one-shouldered movement that made her look curiously young. "I haven't really taken it in yet. The police were here earlier. Apparently I'm the prime suspect."

"Speaking of the police, why didn't you tell them that you left with me at two o'clock?"

Florence looked away. "I didn't want to involve you."

"Florence." Max put a hand on her shoulder, turning her to face him. "This is serious. It doesn't matter a damn about me. I'm your alibi. I've already told Edgar that I was with you."

"Edgar?"

"DI Edgar Stephens. We're old friends. You can trust him."

"He clearly thinks I did it. After all, what was to stop me going back after I left you and killing Victor?"

"Did you?" said Max.

"No," said Florence. The flat monosyllable convinced him more than a vehement denial. "If people are lying, they repeat themselves," that's what Tony "The Mind" Mulholland used to say. And he knew about lies.

"Do you know who did?"

"No." Florence's heavily mascaraed eyes filled with tears. Max handed her his handkerchief and she blotted them carefully.

"Victor had a lot of enemies," she said, at last, "but he was always good to me, in his own way. He was generous with money too. I was able to send some back to my parents every month."

"I'm sorry," said Max. "Look, you shouldn't go back to the house tonight."

"I won't. I'm going to stay with Rose. Elizabeth the First."

"Do the other girls know what happened to Vic?"

"No, I'll tell them after our spot. I don't want them upset before we go on."

"Let's talk tomorrow. Eleven o'clock at the café you took me to before?"

"All right," said Florence. "I'd better go now."

Max watched as Florence walked back down the corridor. The high heels made her hips swing with exaggerated provocation. "Of course," Florence had said to him that day over lunch, "Cleopatra *would* have been wearing six-inch court shoes. To say nothing of Minnehaha." He liked Florence. He liked her intelligence and style. He liked the way that she had talked about her scriptwriting. He didn't think any the worse of her for having been Vic Cutler's mistress. It had been a good business move on her part and it clearly allowed her to support her ageing parents in Wales. But did he trust her? He wasn't sure.

"Mr Mephisto?"

Max turned. A woman stood facing him. She was youngish, probably in her mid-twenties, with thick brown hair tied back in a ponytail, wearing slacks and a shapeless winter coat. For a moment, Max just stared at her. Women were rarities backstage, unless they were pros, of course. And, if there was one thing he was sure of, it was that this woman wasn't a pro.

"Sam Collins." She held out her hand. "From the *Evening Argus*."

"Sam . . . ?" Max knew that he was still staring. Was this the reporter who had praised his magic tricks and found the Living Tableaux "vulgar"? This small, badly dressed woman with bright eyes and a firm handshake?

"Yes," she said, with a quick smile. "The androgynous name is quite useful in my line of work. I wanted to talk to you about Vic Cutler."

"What about him?" said Max.

"Well, is it true that he's been murdered, for one thing?"

"I'm sorry," said Max. "I don't think I'm the person you should be talking to."

166

Sam Collins mimed writing on an invisible notepad. "Max Mephisto . . . did not deny the rumour . . ."

"With a courteous bow," said Max, bowing, "the magician made his exit."

He could still hear Sam Collins laughing as he shut his dressing room door. It occurred to him that it was rare to hear unforced laughter backstage. The sound was almost shocking.

Edgar was surprised to find himself enjoying the show. Despite everything that he knew about the dark side of show business, there was still something magical about sitting in a darkened theatre when the curtains open and the empty space in front of you becomes . . . well, anything really. He laughed at Stew Stewart, a comedian with a surreal line in patter that seemed lost on some of the audience, and even enjoyed the manic poodles jumping through paper hoops. He had been expecting the tableaux to be rather tacky but, actually, the music and the still shapes on the stage created something rather beautiful. He recognised Betty in her blonde wig and Florence, queenly and mesmerising as Cleopatra. He thought of Lily tied to her chair. Was this scene what the killer had been trying to create, with humdrum domestic objects like towels and greengrocers' crates? Next to Edgar, two young men were leaning forward, open-mouthed, obviously hoping to see a telltale twitch of flesh. But Edgar thought that if the girls moved, the spell would be broken. He remembered a striptease act that he had once watched with Max.

That had been a sad affair, as erotic as stripping for an army medical examination. But this, this had its own strange enchantment. It wasn't something he would say to Emma, of course.

He didn't go backstage in the interval. He didn't want to see Ruby and distract her and himself. He'd asked Max to tell her that he'd see her backstage when the show was over. The second half passed in a haze of anticipation at the thought of seeing her offstage. Hearing Max's music, that slow Saint-Saëns played here with real menace, made the hairs on Edgar's neck stand up. He waited with impatience for the moment when Ruby appeared in the spotlight, marvelling again at her grace and poise, her comic timing, her apparent lack of nerves. Edgar had been in the war, he had faced murderers and once carried a bomb in his bare hands, but he sometimes thought that he had never seen anything more courageous than a performer facing an audience.

Afterwards, he gave his name to the man at the pass, door and entered the world of backstage. There was the usual febrile after-show excitement in the air but Edgar thought that he also detected something else tonight, an undercurrent of fear and tension. He heard some shouts of congratulations but there was an undertone of "Did you hear? Is it true?" Outside Ruby's dressing room he saw two of Vic Cutler's girls deep in conversation, their feathered heads close together.

He knocked on the door. "Come in!" called Ruby.

168

She was at her dressing table, taking off her make-up, but turned at once to embrace him. "Ed!" Her cheek was cold and smelt of face cream.

"I brought you these."

The roses were rather battered but Ruby seemed pleased. Edgar wondered if flowers would now always remind him of Lily.

"You were brilliant," he said, thinking, as always, how inadequate his praise sounded.

She pulled a face. "I nearly messed up that business with the hat. You should have seen the look Max gave me."

Ruby always called her father Max. Dad was reserved for the stepfather who brought her up. Edgar didn't know how Max felt about this but he was always grateful not to be reminded of the relationship. It was difficult enough, being engaged to his best friend's daughter.

"I'm sorry I haven't seen much of you this week," he said, still standing awkwardly by the door. Ruby's dressing room was much smaller than Max's and there was nowhere to sit down.

"That's OK," said Ruby, taking her hair out of its bun and brushing it fiercely so that it flew around her face in a dark halo. Edgar could almost see sparks flying out from the brush. He'd never met anyone who created so much static electricity. Sometimes, when he touched her, he felt a shock that made his fingertips tingle.

"It's so awful," she said, "what happened to Vic."

"Who told you about it?"

"Max," said Ruby. "He told me to keep it to myself but everyone knows. All the dancers were talking about it in the break."

"Did you know Vic Cutler at all?"

"Not really. I came across him in the corridor a few times. He was a bit of a lech."

"In what way?" Edgar sometimes wished that he could stop any other man from looking at Ruby. A bit ridiculous, really, when she made her living appearing on stage. Soon, when she and Max had their television series, thousands — millions — of men would see her and fall in love with her.

"Oh, he wasn't a groper but he had this way of looking at you. He kept saying that I should join his stupid tableaux act. I can't think of anything worse than standing there on stage like a dummy. I'm a magician." She said this rather defensively. Edgar knew that Ruby constantly fought against the convention that made pretty girls assistants or backing dancers, never the main attraction.

"You're a wonderful magician," he said. "As good as Max." He wondered if he should have said "better" but she seemed delighted, giving him one of her most irresistible smiles.

"Thank you, Ed. You may be biased though."

"Never."

"Are we going out to dinner?" she asked, giving her face a final wipe with a tissue.

"If you'd like to. Shall we ask Max too?"

"No." Ruby stood up. "I'd like to have you to myself for a change."

170

Edgar had never had two thousand people cheering for him on stage but he thought that it must feel something like this.

CHAPTER
FOURTEEN

Thursday

Wednesday's edition of the *Evening Argus* had led with HORROR IN HOVE HOUSE so there was quite a crowd of reporters gathered outside Lansdowne Road when Emma and Bob arrived in the morning.

"Emma, Bob." Don from the *Argus* made use of his local knowledge. "What's the news? Is there any link with the Montpelier Crescent stabbing?"

"No comment," said Emma.

"We've got the nationals here today," said Don, with some pride. "I need a local exclusive."

"I've got chilblains," said Bob. "Will that do?"

"Can't see my editor holding the front page for that."

Emma knocked on the door and it was opened almost immediately by Norris. He must have been waiting for them, she thought. It couldn't be much fun being the landlord of a Horror House.

Edna was in the hall holding a feather duster like a prop. "Can you stop those newspaper men harassing us?" she said.

"We can ask them to give you some privacy," said Emma, "but we can't do anything unless they trespass or threaten you."

"I'm sure one of them stole a milk bottle," said Norris. "The milkman always leaves two on a Thursday."

"We're sorry to bother you again," said Emma, "but we've got a few more questions for you. We'd like to speak to Betty and Janette too, if possible."

"They'll still be in bed," said Edna, with a hint of a sniff. "They're not early risers."

Emma looked at her watch. It was nine-thirty. It seemed amazing that anyone was still asleep, especially with all the noise the reporters were making outside, but she supposed that show-business people went to bed late and got up late. The DI had been to see the show last night but he was already at his desk when she got in that morning. She couldn't tell from his face whether or not he'd had a good evening.

Edna went upstairs to knock on the girls' door while Norris ushered them into the snug and offered tea. He was rather an ineffectual man, thought Emma, but he was very good at making tea.

When Edna came back in, Bob said, "When I spoke to Mr Entwhistle yesterday, he mentioned seeing a man in the house last week, possibly on Wednesday or Thursday. We wondered if either of you had seen this man."

"I told you," said Edna. "There was no man here. Mr Entwhistle imagines things. It's a shame you people can't leave him alone."

Emma put a photograph on the table. "Have you seen this man?" she said. "Either in the house or waiting around outside."

They had borrowed the photograph from the flat in Montpelier Crescent where it had stood in a silver frame on the sideboard. It showed Cutler standing beside a gleaming Rolls Royce and had clearly been taken to showcase the car, and not the man, as Cutler was on the very edge of the picture. But then, thought Emma, he seemed to have been a man who preferred backstage power to centre stage.

Edna peered at the photograph. "That's Vic Cutler, isn't it?" she said.

"Do you know him?" said Emma.

Edna folded her arms. "I remember him from the old days. He was always here, sniffing around Cecily."

"Cecily? Lily's mother?"

"Yes, he was mad about her in the old days. I told her, don't fall for it. Men like that are only after one thing. I've seen a lot of it in my time. Thank goodness she came to her senses and married Burt."

"Burt Burtenshaw?" said Bob.

"Everyone called him Burt. I think his first name was something else."

Norris came into the room with the tea tray. He leant over to look at the photograph. "Vic Cutler."

"Did you know him too?"

"He used to come round when I was first courting Edna. I never trusted him." It was hard to imagine Norris doing anything as virile as courting, thought Emma, but she supposed that everyone has their day.

"So neither of you saw Mr Cutler in this house last week?" she said.

"Cutler here?" said Edna. "I should think not. He wouldn't come here. Why don't you ask him yourself?"

Edna and Norris clearly hadn't heard about Vic Cutler's murder. Should she tell them? They would know soon enough when Betty and Janette woke up and it would be in the papers tonight. It wasn't as if they would be exactly heartbroken, after all.

"Mr Cutler was found dead yesterday," she said. "We're treating his death as suspicious."

"Dead?" Edna put her hand to her heart. "Oh good heavens. Was he murdered like Lily?"

Interesting supposition, thought Emma. "I'm afraid I can't tell you any more at this moment," she said.

Norris was looking anxiously at his wife. "Can I get you some sal volatile, dear?"

"No, I'm all right. It's just the shock. What a wicked world we live in."

There was no answer to that. They drank their tea quickly and Bob asked if they could talk to Mr Entwhistle, "just to see if he recognises the picture".

"You can talk to him," said Edna, recovering slightly. "Whether you get any sense is another matter."

But, in fact, Peter Entwhistle seemed on rather good form. He put on a pair of half-moon glasses to look at the photograph.

"I think that's the man except that he looked a little older and a little fatter."

"So this was the man you saw in the house last week?" said Bob.

"I think so, yes."

"And it was Friday," prompted Bob, "at about four o'clock?"

"I think so, yes. We normally have a cup of tea at four, then supper at six-thirty. Not the theatricals, of course. They're at the theatre by then. That's when the night starts for theatrical types. I remember that from my own show-business days."

Emma and Bob looked at each other. "I thought you were a . . ." Bob flipped through his notepad, "a retired bookkeeper."

"Oh, I am," said Peter, "but before the first war I used to play the piano in the cinema. For the silent films," he added, as if afraid that they wouldn't understand. "It was a wonderful time," he continued reminiscently. "'Hearts and Flowers' for the romantic stuff, Handel's 'Water Music' whenever there was a boat, 'William Tell' for the chases. But I liked comedy best. Harold Lloyd, Ben Turpin and Buster Keaton. You have to be quick to play the music for someone falling down stairs or hanging off a skyscraper roof. Playing in the dark with just your pilot light on the score, you could be *there*, you could be anywhere."

He lapsed into silence and Emma felt almost sorry to break the spell, to bring Peter back to the present and the cramped single room.

"Do you still play?" she asked. She remembered the piano in the parlour and Edna saying, "No one really plays it now except Mr Entwhistle sometimes."

176

"The occasional tune on Edna's upright," said Peter, "Christmas carols and the like. But not seriously. I joined up when the war came because that's what you did. I was in my thirties but I was very fit, I was a runner in those days. We were at Ypres and my sergeant asked me to take a message to another trench because he knew I would get there quickly. I went off, leaving my mates playing cards. When I got back they were all dead, still playing cards, sitting there like statues. Blast, you see. After seeing that I couldn't just go back to playing the piano. And the talkies were in by then anyway. No, I settled down after the war and got a proper job. You can't muck around enjoying yourself for ever, can you? I went to a recital at St Peter's the other day. That pianist from the Hippodrome was playing. Tommy Watson. He's pretty good, a bit heavy on the bass, but good. I thought, that could have been me. But I don't regret it, not really."

Emma was sure that he regretted it every day, that he missed writhing on the tracks with damsels in distress, dancing minuets with girls in crinolines, swinging from the hands of a clock with Harold Lloyd. But there was nothing she could say. For her the war had been a welcome respite. Her school had been evacuated to the country and she'd known freedom for the first time. How could she ever understand the thoughts of a man who had seen his friends blasted to death in front of his eyes?

"So you're quite sure that this was the man you saw in the hall?" Bob's voice brought them back to the case in hand.

"As sure as I can be," said Peter. "Why?" He put a shaking hand up to his mouth. "You don't think he was the man who killed Lily?"

"It's just a line of enquiry." Bob looked worriedly at Emma. Peter Entwhistle was very pale now with a bluish tinge to his lips.

"Mr Entwhistle," said Emma. "Can I get you a glass of water?"

"Yes," said Peter faintly, "and one of my pills. Over there by the shepherdess."

There was a pillbox on a small table by the bed next to a couple of hardback books and a Dresden shepherdess holding a grinning lamb. Bob went to the sink to fill a toothmug of water and Emma fumbled for the pills, knocking over one of the books in her haste. After Peter had taken his medicine and reverted to a more normal colour, Emma retrieved the book and saw that something had fallen out from within its pages. She picked it up. It was a colour postcard showing a girl on a flower-garlanded swing.

Edgar was having an uncomfortable meeting with his boss, Superintendent Frank Hodges. He knew that Hodges was suspicious of him at the best of times. Hodges was, as he often said proudly, an old-fashioned policeman. He distrusted people like Edgar who had been to university and used words like "psychological". Edgar had tried to tell Hodges that he had only been at Oxford for two terms before the war came but it was no good. To Hodges, Edgar would always be "too clever by half", a phrase which reminded Edgar uneasily of his mother.

"Why haven't you arrested the fancy woman?" That had been Hodges' first question.

Edgar counted to ten silently. "We've interviewed Miss Jones. We have a witness that says she left the house at two o'clock, half an hour before Cutler got back."

"Who is this witness?"

"A man who spent the morning with her."

"Spent the morning with her?" Hodges' eyes bulged. "Spent the morning in her bed, you mean. Woman's little better than a prostitute. You can't take the word of people like that. Who was the man, anyway?"

Edgar didn't think he could avoid it any longer. "Max Mephisto. The magician."

"Mephisto? He's a friend of yours, isn't he?"

"I served with him in the war, yes."

Hodges always looked uncomfortable when the war was mentioned. Childhood polio had caused him to miss out on both wars. He tried to make up for it by being as brisk and military in his bearing as possible but he could never shake the suspicion that people like Edgar (who, despite being a captain in the war, was damn well near to being a *pacifist*) secretly despised him because of it.

"Seems to me damn suspicious that Mephisto was in at the death again," said Hodges, chewing the end of his moustache. "Wasn't he involved in that other affair? The Conjuror Killer?"

"Not really," said Edgar, although Max had been immersed so deeply in the case that it had nearly killed him.

"Get him in," urged Hodges, "question him. Can't have it said that the police went gently on him because of some old pals brigade nonsense."

"I have questioned him," said Edgar. "We've got no reason to suspect that he killed Cutler."

"Except that he was sleeping with his girlfriend," said Hodges. "Oldest motive in the book."

The super wasn't entirely wrong about that, thought Edgar when he had finally escaped back to his office. Passion and jealousy were two of the most likely motives for murder. The question was: who had felt passionately about Lily Burtenshaw?

Emma and Bob had a whispered conversation in the front parlour as they waited for Betty and Janette.

"I can't believe you just pocketed it," said Bob.

"I wanted to show it to the DI," said Emma. She knew that Bob was right. The postcard belonged to Peter Entwhistle and she had no right to take it from his room. It was just that she was sure that the DI had mentioned a variety performer who had an act with a swing. Was it Lily's mother?

Bob looked as if he wanted to say more. He often accused Emma of sucking up to the DI and he was probably right there too. But, before he could get into his stride, the door opened and Edna appeared.

"The girls are on their way down. Can I get you anything?"

On an impulse, Emma held out the postcard.

"Mrs Wright. Is this a picture of Cecily Burtenshaw?"

Edna looked, without much interest. "Yes. That's Cecily. I told you she had an act with a swing."

"Have you ever seen this picture before?"

Edna shrugged. "There were lots of them about at the time. Cecily was quite famous in her day."

"But it's not yours?"

"No. Where did you get it?"

Emma hesitated and was saved from answering by the appearance of Betty and Janette. Both girls looked pale and heavy-eyed. Betty, with her round face and curly hair, usually had the sort of cheerful prettiness that made you think of milkmaids or land-girls during the war. Janette, who had dark hair and high cheekbones, was both more striking and less attractive. Today, though, they both appeared distinctly lacking in glamour. Janette was still in her dressing gown but Betty was dressed in slacks and a sweater. Emma noticed that Betty had also put on some eye make-up, dark kohl that only emphasised her pallor. She wondered if this was for Bob's benefit.

Edna left the room with obvious reluctance and Emma asked the girls to sit down. "Sorry to bother you again. Mr Cutler's death must have been a terrible shock for you."

"I still can't believe it," said Betty, sitting on the sofa and smoothing down her hair. "He just didn't seem the sort."

"The sort to get murdered?" said Janette, taking the seat next to her. "I'd say he was just the sort."

"The sort to die," said Betty.

"Why do you say he was the sort to get murdered?" said Emma.

Janette looked slightly embarrassed. "Well, he wasn't a very nice person."

"In what way?"

"He shouted a lot," said Betty. "And he had favourites amongst the girls."

"Who were his favourites?" said Emma, knowing some of the answer.

"Florence Jones," said both girls. "And Rose," offered Betty.

"He liked you, Betty," said Janette. "That's why he made you the Lady of Shalott."

"We have a witness," said Emma, "who saw Mr Cutler at this house last week on Friday afternoon at about four. Could Mr Cutler have been waiting for you two?"

The girls looked at each other. "Mr Cutler wouldn't come here," said Betty, unconsciously echoing Edna. "He wouldn't come to our digs."

"Are you sure?" said Bob. He slid the photograph across the table. "Our witness identified him from this picture."

"That's Mr Cutler all right," said Janette. "His car too."

"But you didn't see him here last week?" said Emma.
"No."

"When did you see him last?" said Bob.

"It must have been Tuesday night after the show," said Betty. "That was the night you came," she said to Bob, who blushed.

182

"How did he seem that night?" said Emma.

"The same as usual," said Betty. "He always told us where we went wrong and all that. But he was quite mild on Tuesday. Maybe he was on good behaviour because you two were there."

"Did you hear him arguing with anyone?" asked Bob. "Maybe before the show?"

"No," said Betty. "Not really."

"I did," said Janette suddenly. "Just before we left on Tuesday night I went to the lav and I saw Mr Cutler talking to Florence in the corridor. He seemed quite upset."

"Did you hear what he said?" asked Emma.

"He said, 'If you leave me, you'll be sorry.'"

CHAPTER
FIFTEEN

At first Max thought that she wasn't coming. He'd chosen Susie's because that's where they had met the first time and because he didn't want to add to gossip that was already swirling around the theatre by meeting Florence there. But by ten past eleven she still hadn't appeared. Was she being questioned by Edgar at the police station? Edgar was determined when he was on a case, Max knew that he wouldn't lay off a witness just because she was having an affair with his best friend. Or maybe Florence had just thought better of their liaison. It didn't look good after all, being involved with another man when your lover had just been brutally murdered.

Max drank his coffee and wished he could smoke but a sign quaintly embroidered in cross-stitch asked him not to. Another reason to avoid coming to places like this. He'd once shared the bill with a comedian called Nosmo King. Nosmo King. No Smoking.

Was he taking a risk asking to meet Florence after what happened yesterday? It would probably be sensible to put some distance between them but, where Florence was concerned, Max was aware that he didn't feel very sensible. Also, in a strange way, he felt responsible for her. It couldn't be very pleasant to lose your lover and then become the prime suspect for their murder. Florence had seemed calm enough last night — and the act had apparently gone without a hitch — but she must be feeling rather frightened all the same. The killer would strike again, that's what Edgar said. Was Florence in danger? Was *he* in danger? Even during the war, Max had always found it hard to believe that he might be killed. It wasn't because he felt particularly lucky. It was more that he just didn't care enough. Surely the Grim Reaper would rather pick on someone else, someone who would take the news in a big way. Max pushed his cup away and felt in his pockets for change. Twenty past eleven. She obviously wasn't coming.

"Max! I'm so sorry. I had to go in to the police station. They wanted to take my prints. Hell on the nails."

She was as beautiful as ever. For some reason he had expected the events of last night to mute her glamour but, taking off her hat and shaking out her hair, Florence was almost dazzling. The little café with its flowered wallpaper and china ornaments seemed suddenly to blaze and sparkle. Even the waitress, a motherly woman whom Max thought of as Susie herself, blinked in a rather stupefied way.

"Tea, dear?" she asked Florence. "Or something to eat?"

"Tea please," said Florence. "But something to eat too." She turned to Max. "It's awful but I've been hungry all morning."

185

"Why's that awful?"

"Well, Victor's dead and everyone thinks I did it. Last night Rose, the girl I'm staying with, kept saying 'I couldn't eat a thing' and all I could think of was that I was dying for some toast."

"Eat," said Max. "It's probably nature's way of saying that you should keep your strength up."

"I'll have a Welsh rarebit," said Florence, smiling up at Susie. "It'll remind me of home."

"Where is home?" said Max, after Susie had bustled away.

"Maesteg. Glamorgan. It's a mining town. Well, it used to be. So many men lost their jobs in the thirties — my dad included — that it turned into a ghost town. Of course, the mines opened again in the war. My brother was a Bevin Boy; he went down the mine instead of going into the army. He hated it, people thought he was a conchie, shouted at him in the street. Now the war's over he's out of work again with nothing to show for it."

"Forgive me," said Max, "but you don't look like a miner's daughter."

"What does a miner's daughter look like?" said Florence. Then she smiled, relenting. "My mother's half Italian. I'm supposed to look like her. Her mother was from Florence. Hence the name."

"My mother was Italian too," said Max.

"I know. It accounts for the bond between us."

"Does it?" said Max. He felt jolted and uneasy. To cover the moment, he asked, rather abruptly, "What happened at the station? Did you see Edgar?"

186

"DI Stephens? No. I just saw a rather tongue-tied policeman who obviously thought I was a scarlet woman."

She laughed but looked slightly upset all the same. Max could just imagine all the PC Plods at the station staring at her, at someone so glamorous and exotic. Someone, furthermore, who might have blood on her hands. He felt angry with Edgar for leaving her at their mercy.

"Do you know what's happening now?"

"No. Apparently the police have contacted Victor's mother. I wanted to telephone her myself but then I thought, she probably doesn't want to hear from me. And, anyway, what would I say?"

"It's hard to imagine Vic having a mother," said Max.

"I know," said Florence, "but he did. He didn't talk much about his past but I think he had a very poor upbringing. His father died in the first war and his mother had to struggle to make ends meet, she took in washing and cleaned people's houses. Victor said once that the first thing he did when he made enough money was to buy her a house of her own and a washing machine. It was the first one in the street, he said."

So even Victor Cutler had loved his old mother, thought Max. The thing about clichés was that they were often true. For a moment he felt almost envious of Cutler, notwithstanding the fact that he was in the morgue with a knife wound in his chest. At least he'd still had his mother. It was like Edgar, always complaining about visiting his mother in Esher. He didn't know how lucky he was.

"How did you meet Cutler?" he asked.

"Like I told you, I answered an advertisement," said Florence. "Vic was interviewing girls in his office in Soho. Very sleazy, above a brothel. He made it clear almost immediately that he was interested in me and I thought, why not? No one at home is earning. If I've got a roof over my head I can send them money back and they'll never know."

This was said with a certain amount of bravado. Max wondered what Florence's parents had thought about the money that had come back to them. Perhaps they assumed that all variety performers were awash with spare cash. They wouldn't be the first people to have made that mistake. Susie arrived with the Welsh rarebit and Florence attacked it with relish. Max hated watching people eat but he was prepared to make an exception in Florence's case. All the same, it gave him a chance to ask a slightly unfair question, "Do you have any idea who could have lulled Vic?"

Florence went on eating, cutting the toasted cheese into squares and posting them into her mouth without ruining her lipstick.

"I don't know," she said at last. "He had enemies but who doesn't? He always insisted on his rights, closing the show, having the best dressing rooms, that sort of thing."

"He didn't close this show."

"No, but that was because you were on the bill. He didn't mind too much because you're a big draw."

"Very gracious of him. So there was nobody threatening him, blackmailing him? Nothing convenient like that?"

"Not that I knew of," said Florence. "He'd been in the business a long time and he actually seemed on quite good terms with some of the girls who'd been in his old troupes. I think he helped a few of them out occasionally."

Vic Cutler was turning into a real Santa Claus figure, thought Max. But someone had hated him enough to kill him. Could it have been the beautiful woman sitting in front of him? *I can take care of Vic.* That was what she had said. Strangely enough, this thought did not lessen his desire for her. It increased it, if anything.

"What are you going to do now?" he asked.

"I don't know. What I'd really like is to sleep for a few hours. I had to share a bed with Rose last night and she talked in her sleep. I can't go back to Montpelier Crescent but I keep thinking about the bed there."

Her green eyes met Max's.

"What if I booked a hotel room for the afternoon?" he said. "You could just sleep if you wanted to."

"Can I sleep with you?" she said.

"If you'd like to," said Max. "I promise I won't say a word."

Edgar was looking back through his notes. The murder of Vic Cutler had changed the case, widening the scope from the boarding house in Lansdowne Road to the more salubrious streets of Hove. Edgar had always been sure that Lily's killer would strike again. Too much planning had gone into her death, too much emotion and much detail. The murderer would not be satisfied with just one scene; he would want a sequel. But Edgar had not imagined that the next death would be that of a wealthy show-business impresario, or that it would involve a simple dagger to the heart. The dagger had been Cutler's own, a Japanese curio that, according to Norman the porter, normally resided in a glass-fronted cabinet. Had the killer known it was there? The knife would be dusted for prints which should clear things up a bit. They'd taken Florence's fingerprints that morning and, at some point, he'd have to take Max's too.

Edgar looked again at the photographs of Lily, the kneeling figure, the extended hand. Was it possible that they were looking at two different killers? But the links were too strong. Cutler had written to Lily and now he was dead. Could Cutler have been having an affair with Lily? He was older than her but powerful, attractive men didn't usually have difficulty in attracting younger women. Florence Jones was probably his junior by at least ten years. And what about Florence? Could she have killed Vic? Could she have killed Lily? Edgar thought of the watchful figure sitting by her dressing room mirror. Florence was certainly beautiful but she had a sort of fatal, operatic quality that made it quite possible to think of her with a knife in each hand, like Lady Macbeth. *Infirm of purpose! Give me the daggers.* It was, of course, extremely bad luck to mention Macbeth in a theatre. How did the rest of the quotation go? *The sleeping and the dead are but as pictures; 'tis the eye of childhood that fears a painted devil.*

But as pictures . . . He looked again at the painting of Lady Jane Grey. Why had the killer wanted to re-create this particular pose? Edgar had been reading up on the Tudors and the popular view seemed to be that Lady Jane had been the victim of her parents' machinations, an innocent girl forced to claim the throne in the name of the Protestant faction. When the people had rallied to the rightful heir, the Catholic Princess Mary, the Privy Council had switched their allegiance and abandoned Jane. Mary Tudor had at first been magnanimous but, when further rebellions followed, Jane had been condemned to death and was beheaded on 12 February 1554. Once blindfolded she had apparently been unable to find the block and her hands had been guided by the Lieutenant of the Tower. That had been the scene depicted by Delaroche. Jane's last words had echoed those of Jesus: "Into your hands I commend my spirit."

Queen Jane. Queen Mary. King Henry. King Edward. King Edward potatoes. What had the killer been trying to say with his carefully staged tableau? That Lily was innocent or that she had deserved to die? By all accounts, Lily certainly seemed to have lived a blameless life. She went to work, she went out with girlfriends, she sat in her room reading doctor/nurse romances. Could she also have been having a secret affair with Vic Cutler? That would certainly explain why he had been in the house that day. Except that Lily hadn't been there, she had still been at work. Was

Cutler visiting Betty and Janette? He didn't seem the sort of person to be making house calls somehow. And four o'clock was an odd time, too late for lunch, too early for supper. He wondered what time the theatricals needed to be at the theatre. Florence Jones claimed to have gone straight to the theatre yesterday, after leaving her flat at two. What had she been doing all that time? Staring at herself in the mirror?

Edgar looked again at the photograph of Lily. Her eyes were bound but her hand seemed to reach out to him. Help me, save me. But it was too late for that. He just had to prevent anyone else dying in the same way.

Max was tempted by the Grand but he was known too well there so, in the end, he booked a room at the Royal Albion, on the corner by the Palace Pier. Mr and Mrs Carboni, he wrote in the register. He thought Florence would appreciate him choosing the Italian word for coal. The concierge did not comment on their lack of luggage but bowed them to the lift with every appearance of civility. Max had paid extra for a sea view but, as soon as they had entered the room, he had drawn the curtains and they had fallen onto the bed, heedless of anything: propriety, contraception, suspicion, even murder.

The curtains were still closed but Max was not complaining about the view. He propped himself up on one elbow looking at Florence as she slept, the sheet tangled around her like a prop designed to appease the censor. She was a monochrome Madonna: black hair, white skin, shadows and lamplight.

192

Florence stirred, said something indistinct and opened her eyes.

"Now you're the one talking in your sleep," said Max.

"I'm sorry."

"I'm not complaining."

Florence sat up, pulled the sheet round her like a toga and announced her intention of having a bath. "The bathroom at Rose's was freezing and there was only one in the whole house."

Welcome to the world of theatrical digs, thought Max. Aloud, he said, over the sound of running water, "What are you going to do now?"

Florence appeared in the doorway. She had piled her hair on top of her head and looked suddenly much younger.

"I need to go back to Montpelier Crescent and get my belongings. I suppose the flat belongs to Victor's mother now. Anyway, I couldn't stay there. Not after what happened."

"Where will you go?"

"I'll stay with Rose until Saturday, then I suppose I'll go to London. Try to get more work."

Max thought of Florence answering more advertisements, meeting more Vic Cutlers. He said, "I could rent a flat in Brighton. Or London for that matter. You could stay with me."

Florence didn't answer for a moment. Then she said, "You hardly know me."

"Well, I know you in one sense," said Max. Florence's eyes flickered towards the rumpled bed but her expression didn't change. "Anyway," Max continued, "it could just be a temporary arrangement. Until you get established as a scriptwriter."

"Do you really think that might happen?"

"Yes," said Max, crossing his fingers behind his back. He hadn't read her scripts yet but he would do so, as soon as he'd sorted out the situation with Mrs M.

"Then I'd like that," said Florence, giving him one of her brilliant smiles. "I'd like that very much."

"Telephone for you, DI Stephens."

Edgar pulled his notepad nearer, thinking that the caller must be Emma or Bob with news from Lansdowne Road. Instead, a very different woman's voice answered him.

"Sorry to ring you at work but you haven't answered any of my letters."

Lucy. His sister. What letters? Guiltily he thought of the unopened pile in the hall of the Brunswick Square flat.

"Sorry," he said. "I've been a bit busy."

"Yes," said Lucy. "I read about that poor girl. The house of horror and all that."

"Sorry," he said again.

"I just wanted to know what you want to do for Christmas. I've invited Mum to us and I wanted to know if you're coming too. It's just that I need to order the turkey from the butcher."

Christmas. Edgar looked around the room as if searching for inspiration. Certainly there was nothing Christmassy in the incident room, no paper chains or

Yuletide greetings . . . though, now he came to think of it, he thought he remembered seeing a Christmas tree in reception. Was it really that near? He looked at the date on the board. Seventeenth of December. Christmas Day was just over a week away.

"I don't mind," Lucy was saying, in the voice that meant that she did mind, rather a lot. "It's just I need to know. Are you coming or not?"

Edgar thought of Christmas with his sister, her husband and their two sons. He thought of his mother being bravely disappointed when she looked at her presents, her palpable disapproval of Lucy's cooking, her inevitable bouts of late-night indigestion. Then he thought of sitting alone in his flat, going for a brisk walk by the sea, dining off a solitary chop. There was an alternative vision involving Ruby and a double bed but that stubbornly refused to come to life. Ruby would be with her parents anyway. What about Max? He had spent the last two Christmases with Mrs M and her merry family of lodgers. Would he still be able to sit at that table after what had happened with Florence? If he knew Max, he thought that his friend would be heading for a five-star hotel in London as fast as his famous Bentley could take him.

"I didn't know if you'd be with Ruby or not," said Lucy. She had met Ruby and approved of her, in her way. Lucy's most frequent comment was, "I can't think what a girl like that would see in you." Edgar's mother clearly thought the same. "Ruby's very glamorous" was her (damning) verdict.

"I'll come," said Edgar. He hoped that it didn't sound too much like a concession.

"Good," said Lucy. "Remember to get nice presents for the boys. It doesn't matter about me and David. Oh, and Mum said that the Morny soap you gave her last year brought her out in a rash, so don't get that again."

Where on earth would he find nice presents for his nephews whilst trying to solve two brutal murders? What did boys these days like anyway? Aeroplanes? Meccano? He'd have to ask Bob whom he was sure was in touch with his inner eight-year-old.

Footsteps on the stairs. Emma and Bob must be back.

"I've got to go," he told Lucy. "Sorry. Looking forward to seeing you on Christmas Day."

Lucy laughed. She had a nice line in dark humour. "Bye, Ed. Good luck with the house of horror."

He could tell at once that Emma had news. She was looking important and rather defensive. Bob had his "don't blame me" face on.

"I found this," she said, putting a postcard down on the table. "It was in Peter Entwhistle's Bible."

"You took it, you mean," said Bob.

Edgar looked at the picture. It was a black and white photograph that had been coloured at a later date; the girl's hair was an improbable yellow and her cheeks two spots of pink. She was in mid-swing, head tilted back, one foot forward. Despite the old-fashioned shingled hair and a frilly dress that looked like something from a child's dressing-up box, the woman was very pretty and very like Lily.

"I asked Edna," said Emma, "and she confirmed that it's a picture of Cecily, Lily's mother. She was famous for her act with a swing."

"How did that work then?" said Bob, as if working out the mechanics of her act would help him find Cecily's daughter's murderer.

"I think the swing was fixed onto the rafters somehow and it swung out over the audience," said Edgar. "Must have been quite spectacular."

"The question is, why did Peter Entwhistle have the picture?" said Emma.

"He could have stolen it," said Bob. "The Bible as well as the picture. Remember what Edna said about Peter? He takes things and squirrels them away in his room."

"The Bible had his name in it," said Emma. "I checked."

"I suppose Entwhistle could have had a crush on Cecily," said Edgar. "She was quite famous in her time. Entwhistle could have seen her act before the war."

"And he liked a bit of show business," said Bob. "He used to play the piano for silent films."

"Did he?" said Edgar. "That's interesting." His mother had tried to make him play the piano. She had seen it as the ultimate middle-class accomplishment. He'd had no aptitude for it unlike Jonathan, his younger brother, who had been quite musical. "We need to find out if Peter knew Cecily," he said. "And we need to know why Cutler was in the house that day."

"We only have Peter's word for it that he was," said Emma.

"But we know he wrote to Lily," said Edgar. "We need to know why. Could they have been having an affair? That would explain why he was in the house too."

"No," said Bob, as if keen to protect Lily's virtue. "Cutler was far too old for her. But what about the thing that Janette overheard? Vic Cutler threatening Florence Jones? Saying she'd be sorry if she left him. Surely that gives her a motive for killing him?"

"Was Florence planning to leave Vic?" said Edgar.

"Maybe she was planning to leave him for . . . someone else," said Bob, clearly trying to avoid saying Max's name. "Maybe Cutler tried to stop her and she killed him."

It was a scenario that made sense, thought Edgar.

There was a problem, though, which Emma voiced at once, "But Florence didn't have a motive for killing Lily."

"Unless Lily was having an affair with Cutler too," said Edgar.

"Why would Florence kill Lily over Cutler and then kill him herself?" said Emma. "It doesn't make sense. Also, if she loved Cutler enough to kill him out of jealousy, why was she two-timing him?"

Two-timing had an innocent, schoolgirlish ring to it, thought Edgar. A hundred miles away from what he thought must have happened in Montpelier Crescent yesterday.

198

"We need to ask some questions," he said. "Cutler may or may not have been in the house last Friday but we know he wrote to Lily. We need to find out what was in that letter. I've got a telephone number for Cecily Burtenshaw. Emma, you make the call. Ask Cecily if she knew Vic Cutler or Peter Entwhistle. Bob, we need to speak to Florence Jones again. She's staying with one of the other girls. If she's not there, she'll be at the theatre tonight. We have to get moving. There's a killer out there, maybe two. And my guess is that they'll strike again."

An uneasy peace descended on the incident room. Emma tried to telephone Cecily Burtenshaw but there was no reply. Probably out somewhere organising her daughter's funeral, thought Edgar. He remembered Carl's remarks about a horse-drawn hearse and a glass coffin. He hadn't taken to Lily's brother and he wondered why. Was it just that the man had seemed rather peevish, more concerned about early closing day at his shop than his sister's death? But grief takes people in different ways, he knew that. After Jonathan's death he had felt stunned, unable to think or feel, whereas Lucy had cried and stormed, railing against Hitler, the British army, the fools who had let their sensitive little brother fight and die on a beach in Dunkirk. For their mother, it had been the disaster that she always knew was awaiting her.

Bob had no luck contacting Florence either. Eventually he set out to walk to Rose's digs in Kemp Town. He said that he'd go to Montpelier Crescent and then to the Hippodrome if he couldn't find the girls there. That left Edgar and Emma in the underground room with the electric heater that always smelt slightly of burnt flex. After a while Edgar noticed that the area steps were white.

"It's snowing," he said. It seemed like a long time since either of them had spoken.

"Bob hasn't got his fisherman's coat on," said Emma, referring to the yellow sou'wester that Bob donned in extreme weather. "He'll get wet."

For some reason, Edgar couldn't think of any reply to this. He listened to Emma's pen scratching as she wrote up her notes. Why did he feel so tense, as if something momentous was about to happen? He wondered what Max was doing today. He thought that Max was more deeply involved with Florence than he wanted to admit and the thought made him slightly uneasy. It wasn't just that Max was two-timing Mrs M, to use Emma's phrase, it was more the feeling that he had had earlier when he'd imagined Florence as Lady Macbeth. Florence was the sort of woman who attracted trouble, like a siren or some fatal water sprite singing men to their death on the rocks. What a ridiculously overdramatic notion. He was glad that Emma couldn't see his thoughts. Her head was bent over her work. Her hair was falling forward over her eyes but he knew that she would be frowning in concentration. He'd never met anyone who could concentrate like Emma. What would Ruby be doing now? Last night he'd walked her home to her digs but she hadn't invited him in. Her landlady, if not as rigidly respectable as Edna, drew the line at men in the bedrooms. Ruby was probably chatting with the other lodgers, getting ready for the show tonight, hair in rollers, face shiny with cream (he'd never been privileged to witness these preparations so he was basing the image on glimpses of showgirls backstage). When they were married she would probably still never let him see her with her hair in rollers. He looked up at Emma, who suddenly stretched like a cat and smiled at him.

"Emma . . ." He wasn't sure what he was going to say but they both jumped when the telephone rang. Emma went to answer it. "Yes," he heard her say, "we're on our way."

"It was Norris," she said, putting the receiver down. "Betty's been attacked."

CHAPTER
SIXTEEN

Edgar and Emma flagged down a police car on the coast road. It was still snowing, a white flurry that made it impossible to see the sea.

"What did Norris say on the telephone?" asked Edgar, as the car made its way up Holland Road, windscreen wipers struggling.

"He said that Betty had been attacked on her way home from the shops. He said that she was in a state but not actually injured."

"And she didn't see her attacker?"

"Apparently not."

Would Lily's murderer really hang around the house in the hope of striking again? Edgar didn't think so. He had been sure of two things when he had seen the crime scene, so carefully staged with Lily's poor dead body roped into place. One was that the killer would strike again. Two, that his second murder would be as elaborate as the first. The flowers left outside Betty's door might point to her being identified as the next victim but an opportunist attack in the middle of the afternoon? It just didn't add up.

At Lansdowne Road they found Norris making yet another cup of tea. Betty was sitting on the sofa, holding a handkerchief to her face. There was a strong smell of ammonia in the room plus another scent that Edgar couldn't identify. Janette sat beside Betty, fanning her with a playbill.

Betty's first words were, "Where's Bob?"

"Sergeant Willis is pursuing another line of enquiry," said Edgar. "Do you feel up to telling us what happened?"

"I went out," said Betty. "I had to go to the chemist before closing time. I went to the one on Western Road. Then I came back here, it was snowing so I was hurrying. I stopped by the front door to get out my key and someone grabbed me by the neck. I shouted, yelled, I don't know what. I fell and hit my head. Next thing I know, Janette and Norris were there."

"She was lying on the path," said Norris. "I thought she'd just fallen over in the snow."

Had Betty just fallen over? wondered Edgar. The atmosphere in the house must be fearful at the best of times. Add to that the darkness and the falling snow, it would be easy to mistake, say, the tap of a branch for the grasp of an assailant.

"You shouldn't have taken our policeman away," said Janette, shooting Edgar a dark look.

Edgar did feel slightly guilty. That morning he had asked the local police to disperse the crowds of reporters but he hadn't replaced the PC standing guard by the door. The reporters had been nowhere to be seen when they arrived, probably holed up in a local café drinking tea. Had the attacker, if there was an attacker, known this?

"What time did this happen?" asked Edgar.

"About twenty minutes ago," said Norris. "I rang you immediately. I mean, we're not safe in our beds."

"Who else was in the house at the time?"

"Peggy and Brenda are at work," said Norris. "Edna's out at a townswomen's guild meeting. I think Mr Entwhistle is in his room."

Edgar looked at Emma. "I'll go and check on Mr Entwhistle," she said.

"Where were you when you heard Betty cry out?" Edgar addressed the question to both Norris and Janette.

"I was in our bedroom," said Janette, "painting my nails for tonight." She brandished a hand with two red nails. That had been the other smell in the room. Nail varnish. "I heard a shout and I went to the window but I couldn't see properly because of the porch. I ran downstairs and met Norris on the doorstep."

"I was in the kitchen," said Norris, "peeling potatoes for tonight. I heard a sound, like a high-pitched yelp. I thought it was one of the neighbour's cats at first. They're always yowling. I brought a pan of water to throw at them. It's still in the hall."

Emma came back into the room. "Mr Entwhistle was asleep in his chair," she said. "He said that he didn't hear anything. He's a bit confused so I didn't ask him to come down."

Edgar thought back to Bob's map of the house. Peter Entwhistle's room was at the back on the first floor. It was quite possible that Entwhistle, who was probably slightly deaf, hadn't heard Betty's cry for help.

"Can you remember anything else?" Edgar asked Betty, who was sitting up straighter now and attempting to tidy her hair. She was brave, Betty, no doubt about it. Pretty too. He could see why Bob liked her.

"Not really," said Betty. "I didn't see who grabbed me but they were strong. That's what made me think it was a man. I dropped my bag and fell over backwards."

"What was in the bag?" asked Edgar.

To his surprise, Betty blushed a deep red. "*That* sort of thing," she said, mystifyingly. "My auntie paid me a surprise visit. Women's things."

"Your auntie? Oh . . ." Now Edgar knew that he was blushing too.

"I picked your things up," said Janette reassuringly.

"Thank you, dear."

"Did you smell anything?" said Emma. "Sometimes men smell different."

"It's silly," said Betty, "but I thought I smelt rabbits."

Edgar and Emma looked at each other. Emma said, "Rabbits?"

"I don't know," said Betty. "Funny the things you think about. We used to keep rabbits in the war. Mum used to skin them. It turned my stomach."

"Is there anything else you remember? Anything? However odd."

"No. Just his hands round my neck."

"Is there a mark?" said Edgar. "Do you mind if my sergeant takes a look?"

"Be my guest." Betty pulled her crocheted top down over one shoulder. Emma leant over to look.

205

"There are fingermarks," she said to Edgar. "Definite fingermarks, sir."

This remark made Norris gasp and Janette squeal slightly. Edgar wondered whether neither of them had really believed in the mysterious assailant until now. But someone must have grasped Betty pretty hard round the neck to have left marks.

"You should have a doctor check you over," he said. "Just to make sure that you haven't got concussion."

"I'll telephone Dr O'Shea, ask him to call," said Norris.

"I'm going out to have a look outside," said Edgar. "Sergeant Holmes, will you stay with Betty and get a proper statement? Don't worry," he said to Betty and Janette, now hand in hand on the sofa, "I'll get a policeman to stand guard outside the house tonight."

"We need to be at the theatre in an hour," said Janette. Edgar looked at the cuckoo clock above the mantelpiece. It was almost four o'clock.

"I'll get a police car to take you there," he said.

"That's all very well . . ." began Norris. But they never knew how this sentence ended because, at that moment, there was a heavy pounding on the door.

"Who on earth?" said Norris. "It can't be Edna, she's got a key."

There was something ominous about the knock, whose echoes still seemed to reverberate through the house. Without quite knowing why, Edgar accompanied Norris to the front door. He did not at first recognise the wild-eyed young man outside as Bob.

"Sir, you have to come," said Bob, almost clutching Edgar's arm. "It's Florence. She's dead."

CHAPTER
SEVENTEEN

The barge she sat in, like a burnished throne, Burnt on the water . . .

The quotation came, unbidden, into Edgar's mind. Whether the killer had read *Antony and Cleopatra* he didn't know, but they had certainly had the Living Tableaux recreation of the heroine's death in mind. The drawing room of the Montpelier Crescent flat was lit only by a fringed standard lamp. Florence lay on the sofa, one arm above her head, the other brushing the floor. She was naked apart from a white feather boa artfully arranged across her breasts and pubic hair. There was a gold coronet in her black hair and a heavy bracelet on one wrist.

"Was she like this when you found her?" Edgar asked Bob.

"Yes," said Bob. He was calmer now but still very pale, his hair standing on end as if he'd just finished running his hands through it. Edgar thought that he looked very young all of a sudden.

"I went to Rose's digs in Kemp Town," he said. "She said that Florence had come here to pick up her things. I got here at about three-thirty. I couldn't get an answer when I knocked on the door. The porter let me in and

208

I found her ... like this. The light was on and everything."

The porter was sitting on an upright chair by the door, head in hands. Bob had left him to watch over the corpse while he ran to Lansdowne Road. Edgar thought that the man looked as if he'd never recover from the experience.

Edgar approached the sofa. Florence's skin was marble white, the bruising very obvious around her neck. He touched her shoulder. It was cold and unyielding. Like a statue's.

"When you found her, did you think she'd been dead long?" he asked Bob.

"No," said Bob. "I mean, I knew she was dead but her body was still quite warm."

It was icy now, as was the room. "Was that window open when you got here?" said Edgar.

"Yes."

So the killer had left the window open, presumably to speed up the cooling process, as he had with Lily. The modus operandi looked the same too. They'd know more when Solomon Carter got there. Edgar had called Carter from Lansdowne Road, then he had commandeered the police car to take him and Bob to Montpelier Crescent. Emma had obviously been irritated to be missing out on the action again but was too professional to show it. However, the way things were, Edgar hadn't wanted to leave Betty and Janette on their own.

Edgar turned to Norman, the porter. "I'm sorry," he said. "I know you've had a terrible shock. Just a few questions and then you can go back to your own quarters."

"This is a house of hell," said Norman, his voice quavering. "A house of hell."

"Had you seen Miss Jones today, before Sergeant Willis asked you to open the door?"

"No. But I was in one of the other flats most of the morning. They've got a problem with their plumbing."

From the smell of Norman's breath, he had also been fortifying himself fairly regularly during the day. Edgar decided not to mention this. The man still seemed lucid enough.

"What time did Sergeant Willis knock on the door?"

"It was about three-thirty. I remember because I was listening to the play on the wireless."

"And you hadn't seen Miss Jones come in earlier?"

"No."

"What happened next?"

"Your man, the sergeant, he asked me to open the door to the flat. Then we saw . . . we saw poor Miss Jones, lying there like that. Just like one of the scenes in the show. It just didn't seem real. I mean, yesterday, finding Mr Cutler like that. I never thought it would happen again."

Nor did any of us, thought Edgar. They had still all been fixated on Lansdowne Road, thinking that was the house of hell. He had never expected another murder in this cool, Regency terrace.

"The sergeant asked me to stay here while he ran to get help. Poor young man. He seemed as shocked as I was."

210

"Did you touch anything in the room?"

"No, the sergeant asked me not to."

"Did you see anyone else come into the flats today?"

"One or two of the residents, a couple of the cleaners. That's all. Nothing untoward."

"Thank you. You've been very helpful. We might have to talk to you again but you can go now."

The porter didn't need telling twice. They heard his footsteps fairly galloping down the stairs. Edgar turned to Bob. "Are you all right? It must have been horrible, finding her like this."

Bob moistened his lips. "I'm all right, sir. It was just . . . I mean, Emma and I only saw Florence in the show a few days ago. And now, to see her lying there . . ."

"Do you think this is meant to be the death of Cleopatra? Like in the show?"

"Yes. Don't you? Look at the way that feathery thing is lying on her, like a snake. And the way her arms are. And the crown. It's all staged, like with Lily. Even the porter said so. Like in the show, he said."

"Is the crown the one she wore in the show?" said Edgar. "I can't remember."

"I don't know." Bob clearly didn't want to approach the body again.

Edgar went closer. Florence's eyes were closed and she looked quite serene. Sleeping Beauty. Skin as white as snow, lips red as blood and hair black as ebony. The crown was, in fact, a choker-style necklace. Edgar wondered if it had belonged to Florence.

"It's the same," said Bob, in the background. "The open window, the body. It's the same killer. It has to be."

It did look that way, thought Edgar. There had been an awful inevitability about the scene that had awaited him in the elegant drawing room. But where did that leave Vic Cutler, killed in a very different way? And what could possibly link Florence Jones with Lily Burtenshaw, apart from a tenuous link with the theatre?

"Your friend," said Bob. "He'll take this hard. I mean, I think he was fond of her."

Had Max been fond of Florence? Bob, bless him, could not imagine being intimate with a woman without fondness coming into it. But Edgar knew that Max's love affairs rarely touched his heart. However, whatever Max's feelings for Florence, her death would be a terrible shock. And he, Edgar, had to be the one to tell him.

But Max proved elusive. Edgar rang Mrs M's house from Florence's apartment. "I haven't seen him all day, darling. I expect he's found a restaurant or a club somewhere." Mrs M sounded blithe and unconcerned. She understood Max all right. Edgar couldn't bring himself to say more than, "Can you ask him to ring me when he gets in?" "I will," said Mrs M, "but it might be after the show now."

The show. That was the only way you would ever be sure of seeing Max, to have tickets for a show with his name on the bill. Besides, Edgar needed to talk to the Living Tableaux, their name now blackly ironic. He left

212

Solomon Carter with Florence's body ("Another one! DI Stephens, you're spoiling me") and walked to the Hippodrome with Bob. He asked Emma to meet them there. She was escorting Betty and Janette.

Walking back along the seafront, heads down against the driving snow, Edgar told Bob about Betty being attacked. "Nothing serious, she's fine."

"Nothing serious!" Bob stopped still, snow gathering on his bare head. "She might have been killed."

"It might be nothing," said Edgar. "Keep walking or we'll freeze to death."

"Are you sure she's all right?"

"Yes. She asked for you though."

"She did?"

"It was the first thing she said to us. 'Where's Bob?'"

Edgar couldn't see Bob's face but he was willing to bet that, despite the horrors of the day, it bore an expression of deep satisfaction.

Dick Billings, the theatre manager, met them at the stage door. "Well, if it isn't the laughing policeman. Who's dead this time?"

"Is Max in?" asked Edgar, not answering the question. Billings would know soon enough.

"Yes, he's in his dressing room."

"Thank you." Edgar left Bob to wait for Emma and set off along the backstage corridors.

He was disconcerted to find that Max wasn't alone. Ruby was there, sitting on the table, swinging her legs and telling Max some long story about one of the other acts.

"And he said, 'Max Miller couldn't have told that joke better' and Mr Billings said, 'Son, you're no Max Miller, he's funny for one thing —' Ed! What are you doing here?"

"Hallo." Edgar came awkwardly into the room and kissed Ruby on the cheek.

"Ed." Max's voice was sharper, as if he knew something was wrong. "What's up?"

"Can I talk to you, Max?" He turned to Ruby. "I'm sorry. Could I have a few minutes alone with Max?"

Ruby showed a tendency to flounce but, when neither man took much notice, she left the room quietly enough.

"What is it, Ed?" said Max.

"It's Florence."

"What about her?" Max saw Edgar's face. "Dear God, don't tell me she's . . ."

"She's dead, Max. I'm so sorry."

Max put a hand over his eyes. Edgar looked away. Somehow, this was the hardest thing, seeing Max, who never let his guard down, affected like this. He thought back to their Magic Men days in Inverness. Edgar had been in love with Charis Parsons, their commanding officer. One evening in the Caledonian bar, Tony Mulholland, who loved breaking bad news, had joked about Charis being unfaithful to him. Edgar hadn't wanted to believe him but, when he'd looked at Max, he'd known it was true. He'd known that Max wouldn't lie to him. He had to be straight in his turn.

"Was she murdered?" said Max.

"Yes," said Edgar. "We found her body at the Montpelier Crescent flat."

"I wanted to go back to the flat with her," said Max with what was almost a groan. "But she wouldn't let me. Said it would look bad if I was with her. I walked her to the street corner and left her. I can't even remember what I said to her. 'See you later', something like that."

"What time was that?"

"Is this the police interrogation?"

"I have to ask. You know that."

Edgar saw Max pull himself together with an effort. "It was about two-thirty, I think."

"Had you been with Florence all morning?"

"I met her at a café at eleven. Then we went back to the Royal Albion. I took a room there."

"What time did you leave the hotel?"

"About two. She wanted to collect her clothes and take them to Rose's place. Rose was the girl she was staying with. I offered to wait, to carry her bags, but she wouldn't let me."

Why? thought Edgar. Why had Florence, who had been happy to go to a hotel with Max in the middle of the day, not wanted him to come into the Montpelier Crescent apartment? Was it just because she didn't want him to watch her doing a mundane domestic task like packing or was there something — or somebody — she didn't want him to see?

Max was regarding him intently. "How did she die?"

"She was strangled."

"Oh God. Like the other girl?"

"Like Lily, yes. There were other similarities too."

"What do you mean? The other girl's body was arranged to look like some painting, wasn't it?"

"Yes. Florence was . . . we think she was laid out to look like Cleopatra."

"Cleopatra. Oh God." Max put his head in his hands again. Edgar put a hand on his shoulder. "I'm sorry," he said again.

Max looked up at him. His eyes were wet. It was the first time Edgar had ever seen him cry. "She was such a beautiful girl, Ed."

"I know."

"We were . . . I hadn't known her long but I thought . . . Oh, what's the use of talking. She's gone."

"Do you know where her family live?" asked Edgar, after a pause.

"Wales. Maesteg, I think she said. She sent them money every month. Will you talk to them?"

"We usually ask the local police to go round and break the news in person. It seems more human than telephoning."

"If you get an address, can you give it to me? I'd like to write to them."

"Of course . . . Max, I'll have to ask you some questions at the station tomorrow. Nine o'clock? It's important. You were probably the last person to see her."

"Yes," said Max, standing up. "I understand."

"You should go home now. You've had a terrible shock."

"Go home?" Max looked at him as if he was mad. "I've got to be on stage in an hour."

Edgar didn't know what he had expected. For the show to be cancelled, for black-edged notices to go up outside the theatre. But, when he got to the Living Tableaux dressing room, it was to find Janette addressing the troops.

"We've got to carry on for Florence's sake," she was telling them. "I'll take over the part of Cleopatra."

Bob and Emma were watching from the doorway. Edgar had told Bob to break the news of Florence's death and to watch the girls for their reactions. If they had responded with delirious grief, it had clearly been short-lived. The girls looked variously shocked, stunned and disbelieving but they were all still carrying on with their preparations for the show. Only Betty, a silk scarf round her neck, looked tearful and anxious.

"You don't have to go on," Bob told her. "You've been the victim of a crime."

"Mr Billings said that if we didn't go on, we wouldn't get paid," said Betty. "That's what it's like in variety. I'd better get changed now."

That was obviously their cue to leave. They had a whispered conversation in the corridor.

"We need to find out where everyone was this afternoon," said Edgar. "We'll have to interview all the girls tomorrow morning. Max, Billings, everyone."

"It might not be someone connected to the show." That was Emma. "There might be something else that links Lily and Florence.

"Vic Cutler," said Bob, "but he's dead."

"Excuse me."

Edgar turned to see a man in white tie and tails addressing him. Emma said, "Mr Watson, isn't it? The musical director?"

"Yes," said the man. "I just wanted to ask, is it true? About Florence?"

Watson really did look shocked, thought Edgar. His face was as white as his shirt and his voice had a definite tremor.

"We're investigating the death of Florence Jones," he said.

"Florence. Oh my God. I can't believe it."

"Did you know her well?" asked Emma. "I'm sorry if this is painful for you."

"Yes, I knew her well," said Watson. "I can't . . ." He stopped and looked round, rather wildly. "I've got to go. We need to play the overture in a minute."

He hurried away and they heard him descending the steps that led to the pass door. A few minutes later a round of applause from the auditorium signalled the arrival of the conductor.

"We'd better go," said Edgar.

For the first time in his life Max had too much to drink before going on stage and it almost did for him. He didn't make a mistake but it was a close thing. He had to force himself to concentrate, to remind himself: "pocket, handkerchief, twist, reveal." Usually, once he was on stage, it was all instinctive, each part of the trick leading seamlessly to the next. Tonight it was staccato, awkward. He could see Ruby looking at him anxiously but she played up like a pro, making up for his lacklustre performance with more twirls and smiles and kisses to the gallery. When at last the final trick was over ("cabinet, swivel, wait, twist") he kissed her as the applause rang out. "Thank you." Ruby smiled and curtsied to him.

Backstage, she said, "Are you all right?"

"I'm fine. It's just . . . you know, I was quite friendly with Florence."

"I know," said Ruby. Of course she did; there were no secrets backstage. "What actually happened to her?"

"She was murdered," said Max. "I don't know the details." He certainly wasn't going to tell Ruby about the Cleopatra scenario.

"Oh my God," said Ruby. "Do you think it's the same person who killed Vic?"

"I don't know," said Max, "but it can't hurt to be extra careful. I'll walk you home tonight."

"It's all right. Mummy and Daddy were in the audience."

Mummy and Daddy. Emerald and her husband, the man who had brought Ruby up and to whom she owed her true daughterly affections. He felt childishly irritated that Emerald had witnessed a performance that was, while not exactly bad, not good either.

"Say hallo from me," he said. "I'm going straight home tonight."

Home. All the way back to Mrs M's house on Upper Rock Gardens he hoped that she wouldn't be up, waiting for him with a nightcap. He knew that he had to end their relationship. These last few days with Florence had told him that. But, at the moment he felt that, if he said her name, if he spoke at all, he might actually break down. All he wanted to do was go to bed on his own with a bottle of Scotch. If he drank enough he might forget Florence's face as she had told him about the mining town where she grew up, her shimmering body, her magical green eyes.

The snow had settled, making the pavements treacherous. Max walked down the middle of St James's Street. He must still be drunk because it was quite hard to walk in a straight line. He tried just to concentrate on putting one foot in front of the other. Everything was lighter than usual, illuminated by the strange whiteness on the ground and on the rooftops. It was like a stage effect. Max thought of the pageant lamp shining on the stage for the tableaux, Florence's outstretched body reflected in blue light, the "Grand March" from *Aida* playing. He prayed that Joyce would have gone to bed by the time he got in.

But, as he got closer, he saw that the light was on in the downstairs sitting room. Their room, where they usually sat in the evenings, chatting, drinking brandy, listening to the wireless. It had been a restful interlude with Mrs M, one of the few times in his life when he had felt, if not at home, at least at peace. He should have known really. He was clearly not cut out for peace.

He had his own key but Joyce called out, "In here, darling."

She was sitting by the gas fire, wearing a peach negligee. A decanter and two glasses waited on a tray.

"You look exhausted," Joyce said. "Difficult house?"

Max opened his mouth to say something innocuous like "It's always sticky on a Thursday night" but somehow he found himself telling her another story, about him and Florence, how he had really thought that he might be in love with her and how she had been killed, her lovely body arranged in death to represent some ghastly tableau. He didn't remember what Joyce said but, at some point, she put her arms round him. Then he was sobbing on her shoulder, saying all sorts of wild things, that he wanted to leave the stage, go abroad, never do magic again. She stroked his hair, "There, there." And, for a moment, he heard a different voice, softly accented Italian, and soothing words in a different language. And, for a moment, he let himself be comforted.

CHAPTER
EIGHTEEN

Friday

Edgar had asked Dick Billings to assemble all the artistes in the theatre at ten o'clock. He knew that this would be a shockingly early start for them but, by the time he got to the Hippodrome, he had already been at work for two hours. He had closed the flat at Montpelier Crescent and told the porter not to let anyone in. He had contacted the Welsh police who had agreed to break the news to Florence's family. And he had, by telephone, informed Superintendent Hodges of the latest development.

"Another one dead in the same flat? What's going on?"

"That's what I'm trying to find out, sir."

"Well try a bit harder. This girl was the mistress of the man who was stabbed, wasn't she?"

"Yes."

"Well, what about your friend, the magician, Mephisto? He was having an affair with her, wasn't he? Then he's your main suspect."

"It's not as simple as that. The murder of Florence Jones has similarities with the Lily Burtenshaw case.

There's no way that Max Mephisto was implicated in that."

He had said the wrong thing. "It's not simple, is it? Well, I'm a very simple man, DI Stephens. If a man dies, it's usually the wife or mistress or a rival. If a woman dies, it's usually the husband or boyfriend. Either way, your friend Mephisto has got a lot of answering to do. Are you going to interview him?"

"He's coming into the station at nine."

He'd half expected Max not to come but at nine o'clock sharp a rather awed-looking desk sergeant appeared at his office door accompanied by an immaculate figure in a dark overcoat, trilby hat in hand.

"A visitor to see you, DI Stephens. He says you're expecting him."

"Yes. Come in, Max. Thank you, er . . ." He'd forgotten the sergeant's name.

Max sat down, putting hat and gloves on the desk. He looked as suave as ever but Edgar, looking his friend in the face for the first time, was shocked at what he saw there. Max must have really cared for Florence to be looking like that. He wondered what Max had told Mrs M last night. Maybe he hadn't told her anything. Pros, Edgar knew, were experts at carrying on in the face of bad news (critical reviews, bombs falling outside the theatre). Maybe Max was just going to ride this blow and go on as usual.

"Can I get you a cup of tea?" he asked.

"No, thank you," said Max, with a hint of a shudder. "There's no chance of coffee?"

"No, sorry." said Edgar, "Max, I'm so sorry about Florence. If it's any comfort, I think I do understand a little of what you're going through." Even now, all this time after her death, he didn't like to say Charis's name but he thought that Max would know what he meant.

Max's expression seemed to soften a little. "I know you do."

"But I have to ask you what you were doing yesterday afternoon. It's better to do this immediately, while it's still fresh in your mind."

"It's fresh in my mind all right," said Max. "I met Florence at eleven in a café near here called Susie's. She said she hadn't slept much last night so I took a room at the Royal Albion. We went back there at about twelve and . . . er . . . slept. We left at two. Florence wanted to collect some clothes from the flat in Montpelier Crescent because she was going to spend the night with a girlfriend in Kemp Town. I walked Florence to the flat but she wouldn't let me go in with her."

"What time did you reach Montpelier Crescent?"

"About half past two, I suppose. We said goodbye on the street corner. I watched her go into the flat and then I walked away."

"Where did you go?"

"I went to a café I know, little Italian place. I had a coffee and an omelette. Then I went to the theatre. I got there at about half four."

Edgar exhaled silently. Max had probably been at the café when Florence was murdered. He might yet be very grateful for this alibi.

224

"How did Florence seem when you said goodbye?"

He hadn't expected this question to floor Max. So far he had answered everything in the same businesslike monotone but now he hesitated, putting a hand up to his eyes and rubbing hard. Then he said, not looking at Edgar, "She seemed . . . happy. We were happy together. Despite everything, we'd had a happy few hours."

"How do you think she felt about Cutler's death?"

"She was sorry. She said he'd been good to her in his way. But she wasn't heartbroken. She wasn't in love with him."

Was she in love with you? But Edgar knew this wasn't a question he could ask.

"Do you know of any reason why anyone would have wanted to hurt Florence? Anyone who had quarrelled with her? Was jealous of her?"

"No. Any girl that pretty attracts jealousy but she seemed on good terms with everyone in the theatre."

"What about the musical director, Tommy Watson? Was she on good terms with him?"

"Tommy Watson? Why are you asking about him?"

"I'd heard that he was close to Florence."

"Really?" Max looked surprised and not altogether pleased. "I never saw them together. Tommy seems a nice enough man. He's a good musician, too good for a show like the one at the Hippodrome really."

Edgar wrote "Tommy Watson?" in his notebook. Max watched him and then said, "Have you got any idea who could have done this thing, Ed?"

"I don't know," said Edgar. "The way Florence was killed, there were similarities with Lily's murder, but I can't find any link between the two women." Except Vic Cutler. But he kept this thought to himself.

"Do you think it could be someone connected with the show?"

"It's possible but, like I said, we don't have any definite leads. Emma, Bob and I are going to interview everyone individually at ten."

"Are you finished with me then?"

"Almost." Edgar found the next bit rather awkward. "It's just . . . we need to take your fingerprints. Just to eliminate them from the scene, you know."

To his relief, Max laughed. "I've never had my fingerprints taken before. It'll be an experience." Then his face clouded. "Florence said you took hers. Said it ruined her nails."

"We'll find the person who killed her," said Edgar. "I promise." If he said it enough, he might even come to believe it.

They were all there, sitting in the first few rows of the stalls. The showgirls wearing brightly coloured scarves over their hair, handbags defensively in laps. The musicians looking pale and scruffy, as if they never normally saw daylight. Tommy Watson, sitting on his own, studying scores. Jim Jones, strangely bereft without his dummy. Ditto Madame Mitzi without her canine entourage. Stew Stewart, bright-eyed and curious. The dancers, slightly apart from the Tableaux girls, as if to demonstrate their superiority. Max and

226

Ruby, sitting together at the back. Edgar gave Ruby a small wave when he stepped forward to speak and was encouraged to see that she waved back.

It felt strange standing in front of the professionals, flanked by Emma and Bob. Apart from a few scenes as Donalbain in a school production of *Macbeth*, Edgar didn't think he'd ever stood on a stage before. The auditorium, with its famous banked seats, seemed vast and threatening, a colosseum packed with Caesars about to extend a downward thumb. The house lights were on but, even so, the furthest rows were in shadow. Who knew if anyone else was listening, in the blackness of the circle and the Royal Box?

His voice sounded both echoey and insubstantial, as if the theatre recognised and resented an interloper.

"You'll all have heard by now about Miss Jones's death. I'm sorry, I know she was your friend and colleague but my job now is to find her killer. My officers and I need to talk to all of you today. If you know anything, anything at all, about the deaths of Miss Jones and Mr Cutler, please tell us. It might be a small thing, it might not seem relevant to you, but it could be a crucial piece of evidence. We'll be as quick as we can but need to interview each of you separately. Please be patient. Thank you."

When he had finished (for some reason he'd expected applause but there was just an eerie silence, broken by someone rustling sweet papers), Dick Billings stepped out from the wings.

"Performance as usual tonight," he said. "We're sold out, despite the snow. Some of the punters are probably ghouls coming to see if there's a murderer on stage. That's not our problem. Tomorrow's the last night. Let's do a good show for Florence's sake."

Edgar was rather pleased that Billings didn't get applause either.

Edgar had decided that he would interview the Living Tableaux. After all, they were the people who were most likely to have information about Florence or Vic. The rest of the acts were divided between Emma and Bob. He'd asked Emma to interview Ruby, thinking that this would absolve him of any accusations of bias. He'd been surprised that Emma had demurred slightly. "It's just that I know Ruby and it might be a bit awkward. Maybe Bob . . ." "I think it would be better if it was a woman," said Bob and Emma had subsided. All the same, Edgar wondered about her reluctance. Was it possible that Emma didn't like Ruby?

He couldn't quite work out whether the Tableaux girls liked Florence or not. Rose, the girl she had been going to stay with, seemed upset enough, sobbing quite hysterically at one point, but she also took pains to point out that she was the "number two girl in the act". Rose, a brunette who looked not unlike a cut-price version of Florence, also had a way of eying Edgar beadily through her tears. He wasn't convinced of her undying grief. "The thing is," said Fenella, a good-looking statuesque blonde, "people were jealous of Florence, swanning around in furs and designer clothes. It was obvious that she was Vic Cutler's blue-eyed girl. But, actually, when you talked to her she was pretty straightforward, with no side to her. She

228

wanted to write scripts, you know. I don't think she really wanted to be a showgirl at all. Well, none of us really want to be doing it. It's not much fun, standing about stock-still on a freezing stage while perverts train their opera glasses on you."

"Did you have much trouble from people like that?" asked Edgar.

Fenella shrugged. "A few men hanging about outside the stage door, poor saps. Nothing serious."

"The same men every night?"

"Some of the same men."

He'd have to send a PC to check the stage door tonight. "What about in the theatre?" he asked. "Was anyone here particularly attracted to Florence?"

Fenella crossed her long legs. "Apart from Vic, you mean? I think Billings fancied her. I mean, he's just a lech, but he seemed particularly lecherous to Florence. Toby, the ASM too. He's always watching us from the wings. And the musical director, Tommy Watson, obviously had a thing for Florence. She told me that he'd written a song for her. Imagine that! But the one Florence was after was Max Mephisto. That was obvious from the beginning."

"How was it obvious?"

"Well, she was always making eyes at him. I know they went out for lunch one time. I think Florence thought that Max could help with her career. He's pretty well-connected, you know. And he's gorgeous as well. I wouldn't say no."

Florence hadn't said no either, thought Edgar, but it sounded rather like she'd been the one asking the questions. He wondered whether Florence had been pursuing Max for professional advancement only or whether genuine attraction had come into it. Well, they'd never know now.

It was Betty who seemed the most distressed.

"I keep wondering if it was the same man who attacked me," she said. "I can't stop thinking about it."

Nor could Edgar. Specifically, he kept thinking that if Betty was attacked at roughly three-forty, could the same person have killed Florence at three o'clock? Lansdowne Road was only about fifteen minutes away from Montpelier Crescent but it still seemed a rather tall order.

"I never thought anything like this would happen," Betty was saying, "not to people I knew. It makes me want to give up the stage and go home to my mum."

Where was home? asked Edgar. "Billericay," was the answer but, as her mum had six children still living at home, Betty doubted that she'd be welcome there for long.

"I suppose I've got to do this until I get married," she said. Was it Edgar's imagination or did she give him the ghost of a wink when she said this?

Emma spoke to Tommy Watson first. She was curious about him after their encounter last night. Also, she wanted to put off interviewing Ruby. She had commandeered the props room for her interviews. Bob had a little alcove known as "wardrobe" and the DI had Dick Billings's office. There was just enough room for two chairs but it was rather disconcerting talking to people under the shadow of Max's magic cabinet — the vanishing box — while crammed up against the miniature carriage that was pulled by two poodles in Madame Mitzi's act. It was also freezing cold. Emma kept her duffel coat on and wished that she could write with her gloves on.

Tommy Watson came in and sat down, immediately knocking over a stepladder also used by the enterprising dogs.

"Oh no. Mitzi will kill me."

Emma helped him right it. In contrast to his poise on stage, the conductor was rather bumbling and nervous in person. He was wearing a grey jumper with a hole in one elbow and his ungreased hair flopped untidily over his face. He sat on the chair opposite, managing to knock over some more scenery as he did so.

"You told us last night that you knew Florence well," said Emma. "Can you tell me about your relationship?"

Tommy brushed a strand of hair out of his eyes.

"I first met her when she was a dancer. She was in a show in Leeds, I was playing the piano. She had an act with another girl, one of those Spanish affairs, lots of castanets and foot-stomping. I fell for her. You couldn't not. She was so beautiful in her red dress with her hair piled up. And she was clever too, clever and funny." He stopped and rubbed his eyes.

"Did you have an affair with her?" asked Emma.

"If you call it that," said Tommy. "We were together just for that week. We met up again in London but she was in Vic's troupe then and, I soon understood, under his protection."

"Did Vic tell you that?"

"In a way. I was waiting for Florence one night and Vic's driver came up. A Neanderthal of a man. He told me that if I carried on bothering Florence he'd beat me to a pulp. I stood up to him, idiot that I was. I said I needed to hear from Florence herself that she didn't want to see me again. Well, a few minutes later, Florence came out and told me just that."

"Why did she do that?"

"She told me later that she did it to save me from Vic's heavy. 'It would be terrible if you damaged your hands,' she said." He laughed, rather bitterly. "My heart, though, was another matter. Sorry, I'm being melodramatic."

"And did you see her again?"

"Not until she came here on this week's bill. I meant to be cool. After all, I assumed that she was still living with Vic. But no, I had to go scampering up to her with a song I'd written for her. She was nice about it but she must have thought that I was pathetic. And she would have been right."

There was no disguising the bitterness now.

"Did you spend any time alone with Florence this week?"

"No. She was always with the other girls or with Vic. Mind you, the story is that she was having a walk-out with Max Mephisto. Is that true?"

"I can't comment," said Emma. "What were you doing yesterday afternoon from two o'clock?"

"Oh, this is the elimination of suspects, is it? Well, from midday to about three I was here, in the theatre, practising. There's no piano in my digs, you see."

"Was anyone else here?"

"Two of the cleaners. Dick Billings popped in once or twice."

"And after three?"

"I went back to my digs in Rock Place. I had something to eat — my landlady always does what she calls high tea for the pros — and came back here for five. I didn't hear the news until I was almost ready to go on. I couldn't believe it."

"Is anyone else from this show at your digs?"

"Yes. Jim Jones, the ventriloquist. Nice enough chap. His dummy gives me the creeps though."

"Did you walk to the theatre with Jim?"

"Yes, we set off early because it was snowing."

That gave Tommy an alibi for most of the afternoon, thought Emma. Still, it was just possible that he could have finished his practice early, sprinted to Montpelier Crescent, murdered Florence, maddened by unrequited love, and got back to his digs in time for high tea. Possible but not that probable.

"Thank you," she said. "If you could just write your address here in case we need to contact you again."

Bob found himself liking Stew Stewart. He hadn't really enjoyed the comedian's stage act. Bob liked comics who told jokes, ones that you could remember and retell in the pub. Not that he was any good at that sort of thing. His brother Archie, the one who was in the RAF, was great at telling jokes, had them all in stitches at Christmas and family parties. But Bob could never remember the punchline and, even if he could, somehow the words just weren't funny in his mouth. Stew Stewart had just stood on stage chatting about his life, going to the barber's, talking to girls, trying to get served in bars. There had been no jokes at all. Emma had laughed a lot though. Maybe you needed to be posh to understand that sort of humour.

But now he was thinking that Stewart was quite a good bloke. There was no showbiz talk (one of the male dancers had actually called Bob "darling" earlier), no airs or affectation. Stew was straightforward, the sort of person you could have a beer with. Maybe being ordinary was what his act was all about but Bob couldn't see the point of that. What's so great about being ordinary?

"I didn't really know Florence Jones," said Stew, "but she was bloody good-looking. You couldn't help noticing her."

"Did anyone else notice her? Did she have any special admirer?"

"Special admirer. That's a new word for it. Everyone knew she was living with Vic but, if you want my opinion, I'd say Mephisto had the hots for her. I saw him watching her perform once. He looked like he'd like to make her disappear all right. I tried to have a joke with him about it but Mephisto can be very stuck-up when he likes. He's a lord, you know."

"I'd heard something like that. Where were you yesterday afternoon?"

It turned out that Stew was playing poker with three of the musicians. He'd gone back to his digs at four, changed and walked back to the theatre for the five o'clock call. A pretty good alibi, all things considered. Bob took Stewart's address and said that was all for now.

"Shall I send in the next victim?" said Stew. "My money's on the dummy. Or one of the poodles. One of them nearly had my hand off the other day."

Ruby looked nervous, thought Emma. She was as pretty as ever in a fluffy white jumper and slim-fitting blue trousers but she couldn't seem to sit still in her chair, crossing and recrossing her legs, fiddling with her hair.

"It's so awful," she said. "I mean, I didn't really know Florence but I saw her every day. To think that someone broke into her house and murdered her. It makes you feel cold inside."

More terrifying still, thought Emma, the killer hadn't broken into Florence's flat. They had somehow spirited themselves inside without anyone noticing. She didn't say this but contented herself with asking Ruby what she did yesterday.

"I went Christmas shopping with Joan, a girl from my digs. We met up with my mum for a cup of tea in Hanningtons, then I came back here for five. I was just chatting with Max in his dressing room when Edgar came bursting in."

"That's fine," said Emma, writing in her notebook. She was anxious to get the interview over.

"You'd think he'd talk to me himself," said Ruby. It took Emma a few minutes to realise that she was talking about the DI.

"DI Stephens is really busy at the moment," she said. "This is a massive case now. Three murders in a week. He's in charge. It's a big responsibility."

"You'd think he'd be worried about me," said Ruby, twisting a strand of hair round her finger.

"I'm sure he is."

"I haven't spoken to him since Wednesday."

It's only Friday now, thought Emma. She wondered what it would be like to be Ruby. To have nothing better to do than spend your days shopping and your evenings complaining that your boyfriend wasn't paying you enough attention. But then she forced herself to be fair. Ruby was actually a successful performer in her own right. She would probably out-earn Edgar when they got married. And she was potentially in danger. Maybe the DI should be taking more care of her. Certainly, sitting disconsolately in her chair with the vanishing box looming over her, Ruby looked very young and rather vulnerable.

"Was Miss Jones, Florence, particularly friendly with anyone on the bill?" she asked.

"Well, she was friendly with Max," said Ruby. "I'm sure you know that. Max and Edgar tell each other anything."

Emma looked at Ruby, feeling sorry for her again. What must it be like to have a father you called by his first name? And to have a fiancé who was close friends with that distant, romantic parent? Not easy, she was sure.

"What about Tommy Watson?" she asked. "Was he friendly with Florence?"

236

"I don't think so particularly," said Ruby. "I never saw them together."

"Apparently Tommy Watson wrote a song for Florence."

"I wouldn't take too much notice of that," said Ruby. "He wrote a song for me too."

Jim Jones looked older than he had on stage. He also had a rather high-pitched voice. Bob tried to remember what Reggie, the dummy, had sounded like. He'd been a rather more impressive presence, as he remembered it.

Jim had been in his digs yesterday afternoon. "I've had a bit of a cold, not sleeping well, I tried to catch a few extra hours. A head cold's no fun in my game, I can tell you. I had high tea at four-thirty and then walked to the theatre with Tommy, the conductor."

"How well did you know Florence Jones?"

"Not very well. I try to steer clear of the girls. One false move and they're accusing you of assault. 'Oh, officer! That man touched me where he shouldn't.' "

Bob had to stop himself crying out because, horrifyingly, the last voice had come, not from Jim's mouth, but from the other side of the tiny room.

"How the hell did you do that?"

"All part of the game," said Jones, shifting his voice down a register. Was he being Reggie now?

"Did you know if anyone was particularly friendly with Miss Jones?"

"I don't know if anyone was friendly with her but I did hear her having a row with someone."

"Really?" Bob leant forward. "Who was it?"

"I couldn't see them. It was during the interval. I was just passing the dressing room and I heard Florence say, 'You can't threaten me like that.' "

"Are you sure it was her?"

"Oh yes, you get good at voices in this game."

"Who was she talking to? Was it Vic Cutler?"

"No. This was only the night before last. Vic Cutler was already dead."

CHAPTER
NINETEEN

It was nearly two o'clock by the time they left the Hippodrome. They walked back through the Lanes, the shop windows twinkly and Dickensian with their frosting of snow. Emma concentrated hard on not falling over on the icy cobbles. She was wearing fur-lined boots which were lovely and warm but not ideal for walking. A present from her mother, of course. Who else would buy boots you couldn't walk in?

They didn't talk about the case. Bob went into a sweetshop and came out with a pennyworth of fudge. Emma realised that she was very hungry.

"I'll send out for some sandwiches when we get back," said the DI, reading her mind (or perhaps listening to her stomach rumbling). "We need to get all these interviews transcribed and work out a plan of action."

The incident room was more crowded than usual because the DI had called in specials from Hove and Shoreham. He briefed them quickly and efficiently. He was good at this, thought Emma. She knew that, whilst his own staff were devoted to him, some officers from other forces thought Edgar reserved and standoffish, ex-MI5 and all that. But he was good at putting a case in simple terms, assigning duties and assessing situations. Even Superintendent Hodges, standing in the doorway with his handlebar moustache aquiver, couldn't really find any fault with the briefing.

"We've got two women dead and the crime scenes are remarkably similar. A man linked to both women is also dead. I'm certain in my own mind that the killer will strike again. We need to interview all the neighbours in Montpelier Crescent and collate the results carefully. We also need to provide round the clock protection for the residents at number twelve Lansdowne Road and for the performers in Florence Jones's troupe."

Someone laughed and hastily turned it into a cough.

"Florence Jones may have been a showgirl," said the DI, "but she was still a woman who had a family that loved her. We owe it to them to find her murderer."

Emma kept a low profile throughout the meeting. The Brighton police were used to her now but neighbouring officers still thought it was funny to joke about "Sherlock Holmes" and "the blonde bombshell". She sat at the back trying to look inconspicuous and dark-haired.

Finally, when the specials filed out, collecting their briefing papers from Bob, the DI turned to her. "Come on, Emma, let's see if we've got anything from this morning."

It was almost cosy in the incident room now, blinds drawn, both bars of the electric fire glowing. A WPC brought in some sandwiches and Bob made tea without being asked. There was a sense of being alone in the

240

world, dangerously seductive as far as Emma was concerned. She thought of yesterday afternoon, working alone with the DI while the snow fell outside. She could have sworn that he was just about to ask her something, something unconcerned with the case, when Norris had rung with the story of the mysterious attacker.

"It might be worth looking more closely at Tommy Watson," she said now. "He admitted to having feelings for Florence and had a grudge against Vic Cutler."

"The musician bloke?" said Bob. "I can't see him as a killer."

"Killers come in all shapes and sizes," said Edgar. "And Watson certainly has a motive, of sorts. There's no link with Lily though."

"She came in to watch a rehearsal," said Emma. "She may have met him then."

"What's his background?" said Edgar.

"Studied at the Royal College of Music before the war," said Emma, looking through her notes. "Served in the Fusiliers."

"Probably saw a lot of action then," said Edgar. "Must have been a bit of a shock to come back to playing the piano in draughty theatres."

"That reminds me of something," said Bob. "I can't think what." He frowned, looking pained, as he always did when thinking hard.

"And if Watson really was obsessed with Florence . . ." the DI was saying.

Emma hesitated before saying, "Maybe we shouldn't put too much emphasis on Watson's feelings for

Florence. Ruby said that he'd written a song for her too."

"Really?" The DI's expression was hard to read. "That might have been Watson's technique with girls. It doesn't mean that he didn't have feelings for Florence."

"I thought he was a good pianist," said Emma, "not that I'm much of a judge."

"That's it!" Bob thumped the table, making them all jump. "Mr Entwhistle said that he'd heard Tommy Watson play in some church hall. He said that he thought he was a good player but heavy on the bass." He looked at them impressively. "On the piano you play the bass with your left hand. Tommy Watson's left-handed."

"Perhaps," said the DI slowly, "but Solomon Carter wasn't absolutely sure that the killer was left-handed. He said that you couldn't tell with Florence."

"What about the row that Jim Jones overheard?" said Bob. "'You can't threaten me like that.'" She could have been talking to Watson."

"Except that it was in her dressing room," said Emma.

"So?"

"Well, apart from Vic Cutler, no men were allowed in the dressing room. Vic was already dead. Florence must have been talking to one of the other girls."

Max didn't want to hang around at the theatre listening to people talk about Florence ("Have you heard? She was dressed up as the Queen of Sheba apparently"). But equally he didn't want to go back to Upper Rock

Gardens and see Joyce. Last night she had been amazing, she had comforted him over the death of the woman he had preferred to her. He had let his guard down as he had never done with any woman before. In some strange way, he now felt closer to Joyce than ever. They had slept in the same bed last night, for comfort and warmth as much as anything, but he could not imagine making love to Joyce with the memory of Florence still imprinted on his brain. It was over and he knew that Joyce knew that too. Only two more nights to go then he could escape to London, take a hotel room and get through Christmas somehow. All he had to do was spend as little time at the house as possible.

He walked towards the seafront with Ruby. "Where are you going now?" he asked. Perhaps he could take her to see a film or something, a suitably fatherly way of spending the afternoon.

"I'm going to Mum's," said Ruby. "I don't feel too well."

She did look a little peaky, thought Max. Florence's death had been a shock for everyone but last night Ruby had seemed her usual self, in fact she had carried their act. Today she seemed a little pale and wan, slouching next to him with her head down and her hands in her pockets.

"Will you be all right for tonight?" he asked.

"Oh, I'll be fine for the show," said Ruby, flaring up. "I know that's all that matters to you."

It wasn't all that mattered, thought Max, watching Ruby walk away towards Hove. In fact, Ruby would be shocked to know how little it mattered to him. He had only meant to show concern but clearly he'd said the wrong thing again. Was there no relationship that he couldn't mess up?

He walked briskly along the promenade, going nowhere in particular. The sea was a dark pewter colour and the sky was only a shade lighter, promising more snow to come. The merry-go-round was covered up for winter and the fishing boats were high on the beach. Max walked past the Fortune of War and the other slightly disreputable pubs under the arches. It would be tempting to go in and drink whisky and try to forget the horrors of the past few days but he didn't want to dull his reactions with drink. He had come close to making a mistake on stage last night and he didn't want it to happen again, especially if Ruby wasn't feeling well. As he walked towards Kemp Town, the lights on the Palace Pier seemed to beckon to him. He would go and have a cup of tea with Lou Abrahams who managed the end-of-the-pier theatre. Lou was a good sort and it would pass a couple of hours.

The domes and arcades of the pier were still white with snow but the walkways had been cleared. Billboards advertised a pantomime with the Flying Fantinis, performers Max knew quite well. If he met up with Ernesto Fantini they could drink coffee and talk Italian, which would be better still. Max often worried that he was forgetting the language that his mother had taught him. He walked along the slippery gangplanks, trying to remember the words of a nursery rhyme about the nativity. *Uno, uno bambino nella culla . . .* Then

244

there was something about the sun and the moon. *Due, due l'asino e il bue . . .*

"Mr Mephisto!"

Max stopped. He didn't recognise the voice and, at first, couldn't work out where it was coming from. A woman was hailing him from the other side of the latticed windbreak. She was bundled up in a thick coat and wearing a woolly hat but there was something about the energetic way she was walking and the tilt of her head . . .

"Miss Collins." He lifted his hat. "The intrepid reporter."

Sam Collins laughed, skirting the windbreak to join him at the railings. "Not very intrepid," she said. "I've been investigating the shocking case of a break-in at the penny arcade. Somebody has made off with several bags full of small change."

"I'm sure there's a joke in there somewhere," said Max.

"We've had them all in the newspaper office this morning," said Sam. "It's a copper-bottomed crime, et cetera." She paused, looking at him slightly speculatively. "I don't suppose you've got time for a cup of tea, have you? There's a nice café on the pier."

Max hesitated. He may have wanted to waste a few hours but spending time with a reporter was probably not a good idea under the circumstances. On the other hand, he did find Miss Collins strangely refreshing.

"I won't ask about the murders," she said. "Girl Guides honour."

"In that case . . ." he said and offered her his arm.

"I think it's worth looking at Dick Billings," said Bob. "He seems a seedy character to me."

Emma could imagine that Bob would not take kindly to Billings, with his coarse manners and casual bullying. On the other hand, there didn't seem any reason to suspect him. She said so.

"One of the girls, Fenella, said that Billings was attracted to Florence," said the DI. "We could do a bit of digging. Billings knew Vic Cutler from way back and didn't like him much. 'It couldn't have happened to a nicer bloke.' That's what he said when he heard that Cutler had been murdered. And they had argued about the Living Tableaux position on the bill. That's a motive of sorts. Incidentally, Billings said to me that he wasn't attracted to Florence because she was too tall."

"Billings told Betty that if she didn't go on last night she wouldn't get paid," said Bob. "What sort of a man says that?"

"A businessman, I suppose," said the DI. "I mean, he's not a very pleasant character but he's not running a charity."

"What motive would he have for killing Lily though?" said Emma.

"Like Watson, he could have seen her when she came in to watch the rehearsal," said Edgar, "but it's not much to go on. We have to keep an open mind on this. It may not be the same person who killed all three. Vic Cutler was stabbed. His body wasn't arranged in any special way. It was a very different crime. Even with the two women, we could be looking at two separate killers."

246

"I don't buy that," said Bob. He had his stubborn face on again. "The scenes were the same: the body, the window, all the little touches like the snake and the blindfold."

"It could have been a copycat," said Emma. She didn't really believe this but thought she should put up an argument. "It's possible that some of the details have leaked out."

"You didn't see them," said Bob. "They were the same, the feeling was the same."

Emma felt rather annoyed at this. It wasn't *her* fault that she hadn't seen either crime scene.

She said, "Tommy Watson said that he was frightened off by Vic's driver. 'A Neanderthal of a man' he called him. Might it be worth talking to him? If he was still employed by Vic? He might know some of his secrets."

"Good idea," said the DI. "You follow it up, Emma. Dick Billings should know where to find him."

The DI walked to the incident board and stood looking at the picture of Lily. Now it had been joined by a publicity photograph of Florence Jones, looking seductively over her shoulder, and the picture of Vic with his car.

"We need to find out who Florence was talking to in the dressing room," he said. "Bob, can you talk to Betty again? She might know if there was any bad feeling amongst the girls."

Emma didn't look at Bob but she knew he must be blushing. She thought she should be the one to talk to the girls (Bob could have the Neanderthal) and was about to say so when the telephone rang. Bob picked it up.

"It's for you, sir."

The DI spoke into the receiver. Emma watched his face and saw his eyes widen in surprise.

Edgar put the receiver down. "That was Mrs Burtenshaw," he said. "She's got something to tell me and she wants to tell me in person. I'm going to get a car and drive to London now." He looked at his watch. "I should be there by six. I'll talk to Cecily and come straight back. Emma, after you've spoken to Billings, can you keep watch at the theatre? There'll be a constable to help you. I'll make sure it's someone good. Bob, can you keep an eye on Lansdowne Road?"

"Nothing will happen tonight," said Bob.

Not for the first time, Emma wished that Bob hadn't spoken.

CHAPTER
TWENTY

Max had always liked the café on the Palace Pier. As with so many places in Brighton the grandeur of the past fought a losing battle with the practicalities of the present. The huge windows with their stained-glass panels harked back to the pier's original Victorian splendour but the tables and chairs were utility, chipped and stained. A magnificent tiled fireplace housed a tiny, modern electric fire and a silver Christmas tree sat forlornly on the wide, marble counter.

Sam ordered hot chocolate and a scone. Max, after one glance at the cakes under their spotted glass dome, asked for a black coffee. They sat near to the fire because the café was nearly empty and very cold. Paper chains hung limply over their heads.

"You could only be in England," said Max, looking out of the window. The sea and sky were almost the same colour now, sullen grey with streaks of white.

"I love Brighton," said Sam. "Try growing up in Southend. Brighton seems like the metropolis."

"I like Brighton too," said Max. "I suppose I'm not feeling full of *joie de vivre* at the moment."

"I don't suppose you are," said Sam. She looked at him inquisitively, head on one side, but obviously decided not to probe further. She had taken off her coat and underneath was wearing a thick fisherman's sweater. Max thought of Florence and her understated elegance and his heart twisted in pain. It still didn't seem possible that he would never see her again.

To stop Sam asking any difficult questions, he said, "How come you've ended up working on a newspaper in Brighton?"

Sam laughed. "Ended up? Yes, that's what it feels like sometimes. I studied English at London University. Afterwards, my dad wanted me to do a secretarial course so I'd have some useful skills. Until I got married, of course, and never did anything useful again. But I talked myself into a job on a local paper. It was mostly making tea but I did get to write up the births, deaths and marriages. Then the *Argus* job came up. Senior reporter, a step up. So I went for it. When they found out the awful truth — that I was female, I mean — they thought they'd got a permanent tea-maker. I had to put them right on that, of course."

She smiled when she said it. Max thought that Sam was one of life's improvers, not a complainer but someone who would cheerfully set out to make things fairer wherever she was. In a way, she reminded him of Emma Holmes.

"My friend Edgar says there's a lot of crime in Brighton," he said. "So you must be kept busy."

"Is that DI Edgar Stephens?" said Sam. "I heard you served with him in the army. He's a dark horse, isn't he?"

"He's a rarity," said Max. "A completely honest man. That makes him hard to read."

"You don't seem very likely friends."

"You mean, it doesn't seem likely that I would be friends with someone honest. That's very hurtful, Miss Collins."

"I mean, you're a magician, a star. He's a policeman."

"We met in the war," said Max. "We were part of a strange unit known as the Magic Men. Our aim was to use stage magic against the enemy."

"That's fascinating," said Sam. "Can I interview you about it?"

"No, you can't."

"What did you think of Vic Cutler?" she asked, idly stirring her hot chocolate.

"I thought we weren't going to talk about the murders."

"I didn't mention the murders. I wondered if he was another friend of yours."

"Certainly not."

"It's very hard to find anyone to say a good word for him. I'm not really surprised. After my review of the show, Cutler rang the paper and told the editor to sack me."

"You weren't a fan of the Living Tableaux, as I remember."

"I thought it was disgusting," said Sam, suddenly fierce. "Those girls just standing there for men to ogle them. I'm not surprised that it gave someone the idea for a murder."

"You weren't?" Max was aware of having to tread carefully. He didn't think that the press knew that the women's bodies had been arranged to resemble the tableaux.

"Well, one of the girls was killed, wasn't she?"

"Yes," said Max, "she was."

"The women on stage were just . . . *objects*," said Sam, "and people think they can do what they like with objects."

Was this what it had been like? thought Max. Had the killer thought Florence somehow less than human? He couldn't shake the suspicion that the solution was both simpler and more complicated.

"Do you have anyone in mind?" he asked. "I imagine you know a lot of the unsavoury characters around here."

"Yes, I do," said Sam cheerfully. "I know organised criminals and people who would kill your grandmother if you paid them enough. I don't know anyone who is obsessed with stationary women though."

"That's a shame," said Max. He meant it. He thought that, unless Edgar moved quickly, they might be about to watch another scene being enacted.

Dick Billings looked less than delighted to see Emma.

"I thought we'd seen the last of you lot for the day."

252

"Don't you want the murders solved?" countered Emma.

"Is that what you're doing?" said Billings. "Solving murders?" He was sitting at his desk with a large glass of whisky and what looked like a cheese sandwich to hand. Emma tried to look at the piece of paper in front of him. It was the running order for the show with numbers scribbled in the margin.

Billings saw her looking and pushed the paper towards her. "I'm just sorting out the timings for tonight. The girls were a bit under last night. Understandable in the circumstances but it can't happen again. I'll have to talk to Janette tonight."

Emma remembered Janette saying that her ambition was to manage her own troupe. Well, it looked as though that dream was coming true and that Janette was the de facto leader of the Living Tableaux.

"I came to ask if you knew anything about a man employed by Vic Cutler," said Emma. "He's been described as a driver and a heavy."

To her surprise, Billings smiled. "Nobby Coates. He's worked for Vic for years."

"Do you know where I can find him?"

"Yes. He lives in a mews in Kemp Town, above the garage where Vic kept his car. I've got the address somewhere."

Billings wrote the address on the back of another flyer, this one with different names on. *Tommy and Thomas: on laughter patrol. Eloise Hanley, the Croydon Nightingale. Soapy Syd, not quite himself.*

"Next week's show," explained the manager. "Can't say I'll be sorry to see the last of this lot."

Another week, another show, thought Emma as she made her way back through the shabby corridors. What must it be like to live in this transient world or, like Dick Billings, to be the still centre in a turning world? I've seen them come and I've seen them go. Who said that to her recently? Toby, the ASM, was on a stepladder outside the Living Tableaux changing room.

"Don't walk underneath," he said. "Bad luck."

Emma didn't believe in superstitions but she skirted the ladder carefully all the same.

Bob got a warmer reception at Lansdowne Road.

"Nice to see someone's looking after us," said Edna. "Cup of tea? I think Norris has made some mince pies."

"That would be great," said Bob. The walk had been a cold one. It was already dark and it felt as if more snow was in the air.

"I was wondering if I could speak to Betty," he said. "Or Janette." He thought he'd better add that. He didn't want Edna to think that he was committing the cardinal sin of becoming a "follower".

"I'll give them a call," said Edna. "They're probably getting ready for the show."

Bob thought about Peter Entwhistle's remark about show-business hours being different. It was only four o'clock but already Betty and Janette were thinking about the evening's show. And their night wouldn't end before midnight. No wonder they weren't early risers.

254

Of course, Peter had said that Edna always made a pot of tea at four. Good timing on his part. It had been at four o'clock that Vic Cutler had been spotted in the hall. Who or what had he been waiting for?

When Betty emerged, though, she looked comfortably normal in slacks and a pale pink sweater. Normally Bob didn't approve of women in trousers but he was prepared to make an exception in Betty's case.

"Sorry to disturb you when you're busy getting ready," he said.

"I'm just grateful you're here," said Betty. "Janette and I, we're so jumpy in the house now. I can't wait to get away on Sunday."

Bob felt a sudden panic at the thought that he had no idea where Betty was going on Sunday. He wondered if he could ask her, pretend that he needed to know for his files or something. But then he thought: if she wants me to know, she'll tell me.

"There'll be a PC outside the door all night," he said. "You'll be quite safe. I'll be here too, some of the time."

"I'll feel safe if you're here," said Betty, giving him a smile that showed her dimples. Bob found himself choking on a mince pie crumb.

"I wanted to ask you about something Jim Jones overheard in the changing room," he said, when his voice had returned to normal. "I think it would have been on Wednesday night."

"Jim Jones," said Betty. "He's ever so creepy. The way he makes his voice come from all directions. It's not natural."

255

"I know what you mean," said Bob. "Well, Jim heard Florence talking to someone and she said 'You can't threaten me like that'. Do you have any idea who she could have been speaking to?"

"When was this?"

"During the interval on Wednesday night."

"Wednesday." Betty furrowed her brow and absent-mindedly ate some of Bob's mince pie. "That was after Vic had been killed. Florence sort of took over. I don't think Janette was too happy about it but it just happened. After our spot, we came back to the changing room and Florence was telling us where we'd gone wrong, just like Vic used to. A few of the girls were a bit upset about it. I mean, none of us had really liked Vic but it was a big shock when he died. We felt that we should have been congratulating ourselves on getting through the night, not picking up on every little thing that went wrong. I remember Florence saying that I was breathing too loudly as the Lady of Shalott. I mean, a girl's got to breathe, hasn't she? 'But you're meant to be dead,' Florence said."

"Did anyone say anything to Florence that could have sounded like a threat?"

"No . . . unless . . ." Betty looked uncomfortable.

"Unless what?"

"Well, it was just that Janette said that no one had made Florence the manager. She said that she was going to ask Mr Billings to appoint a new leader. I think Florence might have said something like 'don't threaten me' but it wasn't a threat, not really. Janette's ever such a nice girl when you get to know her."

And she's now leader of the Living Tableaux, thought Bob.

The mews was in the back streets of Kemp Town, opposite the Catholic church where, earlier in the year, Emma had attended a lavish gypsy funeral. It was also near the council school attended by the two children who were murdered last christmas. These memories didn't make Emma feel exactly comfortable.

The mews still looked like the stables it had once been, except that now the steeds were shiny new cars, too big for their stalls sometimes. There was no sign of Vic Cutler's Rolls Royce but Nobby Coates told her that it was safely tucked away in its garage.

"Lovely car," he said. "Sweet as a nut. The boss loved that motor."

Emma was surprised to find herself liking Nobby. He was a giant of a man, broad-shouldered with the battered face of a boxer, but he greeted her with great politeness and invited her into his tiny, immaculately tidy, flat for a cup of tea.

"You have to be tidy when you live in close quarters," he said, seeing her looking around. "I learnt that in the navy."

"I'm so sorry about Mr Cutler," said Emma. "But, as you knew him so well, I wondered if you might know something that would help with our investigations."

"He was a gent, Vic," said Nobby. He had his back to her, busy with the kettle and teapot. His huge frame blocked out most of the light. "I know not everyone thought so but he was always straight with me. He'd had a hard upbringing and he didn't forget that. Not like some. He always treated me well, asked me about my little girl."

"You've got a daughter?"

"Yes. My Lilian. I'm divorced from her mother, she was always a cut above me, but I still see her regular. Look, here's the Christmas card she sent me."

He took the card down from the wall. It showed a snowman wearing a top hat and a disconcertingly wide grin. Inside was written, in careful copperplate, "Happy Christmas Dear Daddy with love from your little girl, Lilian." Emma was willing to bet that Lilian was being privately educated. It struck her as ominous that the name Lilian was so like Lily.

"Mr Cutler used to say that I was lucky to have a daughter. Treat her like a princess, he used to say." He put the tea cups in front of them. Bone china, Emma couldn't help noticing.

"A man like Mr Cutler must have had enemies," said Emma. "Can you think of anyone who might have wanted to hurt him?"

"He had enemies," said Nobby, "but mostly I scared them away." He gave her a sly grin, reminding her oddly of the snowman. "No, when he was killed, I knew at once who did it."

"You did?"

"Yes, it was that girl. Florence Jones. I never trusted her. Oh, the boss thought the world of her. Gave her everything, fur coats, jewels, the lot. But she was the sort of woman who was trouble, if you know what I mean. She came from nowhere, just like Vic, but she

258

behaved like she was a duchess. Gave herself airs like you wouldn't believe. All the men fell for her. That poor sap, the pianist, he was mad about her too. I had to warn him away. Gently, mind. I didn't hurt him. No, when a man is stabbed it's usually the wife. If not the wife, then the mistress."

Nobby would get on well with Solomon Carter, thought Emma.

"But if Florence killed Vic," she said, half to herself, "who killed her?"

"Someone else," said Nobby, as if stating the obvious.

It was pitch black when Emma left the mews. Half past four. Just time to get home and have something to eat before going back to the theatre. She headed towards the coast road, thinking of Edgar driving to London. "Go home quickly," Nobby had said when they said goodbye, "there's more snow on the way." She hoped that the DI wouldn't get stuck in London, that he'd make it back to Brighton tonight. For his own sake, she told herself. Edgar must be exhausted, they had all been working late for several nights. She was aware of feeling slightly floaty and unreal, as she always did when she was very tired. The snow had turned to slush during the day but was now icing over again. It was going to be a long slog home. Maybe she should catch a bus. The trouble was that they were few and far between and you were invariably stuck between stops when one lumbered into view.

She trudged along Marine Parade, hood up, hands in pockets. Twice she nearly slipped in the ridiculous boots. The third time she would have gone over completely if a passer-by hadn't put out a hand to save her.

"Careful there . . ." Then, "Emma!"

Emma pushed her hood back. A tall man was smiling down at her. He had black hair and sallow skin and, smile notwithstanding, there was something slightly dangerous about him.

"Tol. I was just thinking about you earlier."

"There you are. It must have been meant, as Astarte would say. Why don't you come in? You could have a cup of tea and warm up. I'll drive you home."

Emma knew that she should really go straight home but there was something seductive about the idea of being in the warm, chatting with friends. And, if Tol gave her a lift home, she wouldn't really lose any time.

"OK," she said. "Just a quick cup of tea." She would drown in tea soon, she thought.

Tol's house was just behind them. Emma remembered the shadowy staircase and the drawing room with its balcony and view over the sea. Today, though, the velvet curtains were drawn and Astarte was sitting by the fire, dealing cards. She looked up when Tol ushered Emma in.

"Emma!"

"Hello, Astarte." Emma felt rather awkward, awed as always by Astarte's extraordinary beauty, her silvery hair and her startling blue-green eyes. But Astarte showed no such reserve, jumping up and giving Emma a quick hug.

"I was thinking about you."

"I was thinking about you too," said Emma.

"As I said, it must be meant," said Tol. "Tea, Emma? Or would you like something stronger? Sherry? Glass of whisky?"

"I can't," said Emma. "I'm on duty tonight."

"Is it that murder in Hove?" said Astarte. "We were saying that you and DI Stephens must be involved."

"Yes," said Emma. Florence's death hadn't been in the paper yet but Emma was sure that it would be the lead story tonight. Of course, with Astarte's psychic powers she might know already.

Tol went downstairs to make the tea and Emma sat opposite Astarte. She saw that the cards on the table were actually from a tarot pack, the Thoth Tarot if she remembered rightly. She recalled some of the names: the Magus, the Priestess, Lust, Fortune, Adjustment.

Astarte saw her looking. "Shall I read the cards for you?"

"No thank you." Emma would have loved a reading but the trouble was that she wanted the cards to say that it was all going to work out between her and the DI and it wasn't. Astarte had already told her that.

"I could do with some help on this case, though," she said, only half joking.

"Have you got anything that belonged to the dead girl?" asked Astarte.

"No," said Emma. Then she remembered, she still had the postcard of Cecily, Lily's mother. She got it out of her bag and put it on the table.

"That was her mother."

Astarte looked at the photograph without touching it. "That's good," she said. "The mother's power linked to hers. Maternal love is very strong."

Astarte had lost her own mother when she was young, Emma knew. She had been brought up by her grandmother who was also dead now. Emma had investigated her murder.

Tol appeared with the tea tray, a surprisingly domestic image. Emma noticed that he had poured himself a whisky though.

"Readings cost five pounds," he said, straight-faced.

"Shut up, Dad," said Astarte. "This is a favour."

"Tol," said Emma. "When you were on the stage . . ."

Tol grinned. "When I had my famous knife-throwing act, you mean?"

"Yes. When you were a huge variety star, did you know a man called Vic Cutler? He had a tableaux act." She took a sip of her tea, it tasted strange and aromatic.

"Vic Cutler." Tol repeated the name, making the Cs very hard. "I think so. He used to have an act where girls acted out scenes from history, only scenes where they were half-clothed, naturally. Then, in the war, he combined patriotism with prurience. Semi-naked girls singing about England. It made me want to vomit." Emma knew that this would not have appealed to Tol, who always described himself as an anarchist. She

262

remembered Betty saying that she had been one of Vic's Victories, presumably one of the semi-naked patriots.

"The historical act," she said. "Do you remember which scenes they acted out?"

"Kings and queens," said Tol. "The usually monarchist garbage."

"The death of Lady Jane Grey?"

"I don't remember. Why? Is Lady Jane a relative of yours?" Tol liked to tease Emma about her supposedly aristocratic roots when the truth was that her father was a scrap metal merchant made good. Her mother was another story; she was the daughter of a lord and had been presented at court.

"I told you," she said, "I'm not posh. Just rich."

Tol grinned. "What's all this interest in Vic Cutler?"

"He's dead," said Emma.

"Murdered?"

"Yes." There was no point in denying it as this too would be in the papers.

"Good," said Tol. "Maybe one of the girls had their revenge."

Astarte made a shushing gesture with her hand. She was holding the photograph of Cecily Burtenshaw and breathing hard. "She was scared," she said. "There was a man she was scared of. She ran away but he will find her. His heart is black. He's swinging. I can see him swinging."

Emma looked at the postcard, the young Cecily, her head back, floating above the audience.

She ran away but he will find her. His heart is black.

CHAPTER
TWENTY-ONE

Most of the main roads to London had been cleared but, by the time Edgar got to the Croydon aerodrome, the ground was covered by a layer of ice and he skidded several times, once almost ending up in the beer garden of the Propeller pub. Eventually he got to Clapham, the common ghostly and white in the moonlight. It was only six o'clock but it felt like midnight.

He knocked on the door of the neat little house and, once more, Cecily greeted him, poised and frail in black. The front room was still full of flowers and Edgar wondered whether they were fresh bouquets; the smell of lilies was overpowering.

"Thank you so much for coming all this way," said Cecily. Close up, she looked very tired, with blue shadows under her eyes. This must be a horrible time for her, thought Edgar. Her daughter was dead but not buried, her killer had not been caught. The funeral was set for Monday. Edgar hoped that would give Cecily some relief, if not comfort. He was planning to attend, along with Emma and Bob.

"You said that you wanted to talk to me," said Edgar, trying to sound encouraging. He hoped that he could be back on the road by seven. He didn't like to think of

Emma — or Bob — being in the vicinity of a possible murderer.

"Yes." Cecily sat opposite him. "It's about Vic Cutler. You rang and told me he was dead."

It had seemed the right thing to do. The murders might not be connected but, if they were, Lily's family deserved to know the latest developments. Edgar had spoken to Carl, who had seemed rather odd on the phone. He was glad that he had passed the message on.

"What about Vic Cutler?"

"Years ago . . ." Cecily clasped her hands together, small white hands that didn't look as if they'd ever done any manual work. Lily's palms and fingertips had been calloused from twisting flower stems into wreaths. It had been mentioned in the post-mortem report. "Years ago I was in one of Vic's first tableaux acts. He took an interest in me. It was Vic who persuaded me to go solo. He had the idea about the swing and everything. Anyway, eventually we fell in love. We had an affair and I got pregnant. I didn't tell Vic. He was at the start of his career, he wouldn't have wanted to settle down. I couldn't stay in Brighton so I went to stay with my mum in London. I met Burt at the local market and married him. He knew but he was wonderful about it. 'I'll bring the little lad up as my own,' he said. And he did."

"Little lad?"

"Yes, Carl. My son Carl."

"So Carl is Vic's child, not Lily."

Cecily was silent for a moment longer, looking down at her hands. "The thing is," she said at last, "I think Lily thought that Vic was her father. I was clearing out her bedroom a few days ago. I didn't really want to touch her things but Carl thinks that I should take in a lodger. Anyway, she had this little box with a few precious bits in it, her confirmation certificate, cards from her friends, pressed flowers, that sort of thing. Anyway, there was a letter I had written to Vic. I never sent it. I never told Vic about Carl, I suppose because I thought that would be disloyal to Burt but, when Burt died, I decided to tell Vic that he had a child. But, when it came to it, I couldn't send the letter. I thought, Burt's still Carl's father, living or dead and, anyway, Vic won't want to hear from me after all these years. He's probably married himself by now. But I didn't throw the letter away. I don't know why. I kept it in my sewing box and Lily must have found it. In the letter I didn't name the child and I suppose she thought it must be her. I'd got Vic's address from a friend who was still in the business. She said that he had this really grand flat in Montpelier Crescent. I think that's why Lily decided to go to Brighton. To make contact with Vic. Lily is . . . Lily was . . . such an innocent but she could be very determined when she set her mind on something."

That certainly explained something that had been bothering Edgar all along: why quiet, shy Lily Burtenshaw left her home for Brighton. Had Lily actually contacted Vic? Was that why he was at Lansdowne Road that day?

"Could I possibly see it?" Edgar asked.

Cecily must have been expecting this request because the letter was face down on the coffee table. She handed it to Edgar.

The letter was written in blue pen on lilac paper and laid out as Cecily must have been taught at school: her address on the top right, recipient's address below left.

Flat 1, 20 Montpelier Crescent.

Dear Victor,

I know you'll be surprised to hear from me after all these years. I hope those years have been kind to you as they have to me. I married a wonderful man and we have two children. My dear husband passed away last year and so I thought it might be time to tell you what you must have suspected. My dear, one of those children is yours. I don't want anything from you, I'm comfortably off. I just thought you ought to know . . .

There the letter ended. Cecily was weeping quietly into her handkerchief. "If only I'd burnt the wretched thing. If Lily hadn't read that letter, she wouldn't have gone to Brighton. She'd still be alive today . . ."

"You can't think like that," said Edgar. "It's not your fault."

He looked at the letter, the careful, schoolgirlish handwriting. He couldn't help wishing that Cecily *had* burnt it.

"I don't understand," he said, "why Lily was so sure it was her. I mean, surely the oldest child . . ."

Cecily sighed and dabbed her eyes. "Like I say, Lily was an innocent but she was also quite selfish in a way. She would just assume that it was her, not Carl, because she was the special one, the pretty one, the one who was meant to be like me. She would assume that she was the one with the glamorous show-business father. Even though she was the apple of Burt's eye."

"Does Carl know?" asked Edgar.

"No," said Cecily. "And I want to keep it that way. Carl wouldn't want a show-business father. He's happy being a trader, like Burt. Funnily enough, though, I think Carl is a bit like Vic. He's got a lot of business sense, for one thing. He's very sharp."

Having met Carl, Edgar could believe this.

"I thought I should tell you," said Cecily, "since Vic was killed too. I thought there might be a link."

Oh, there's a link all right, thought Edgar, as he got into the car and pressed the button to activate the starter motor. The question was: what was it?

Max sat at his dressing room table putting on his makeup. It was something he had done for years so that now he looked at his face in an almost neutral fashion, the planes and contours nothing more than landscape. The fashion, amongst new acts like Stew Stewart, was for naturalism — no make-up, everyday clothes — but for Max it was part of the ritual to wear a dinner jacket and to apply greasepaint — nothing too obvious, though, he didn't want to look like a pantomime dame. He liked to be alone for this part of the evening, listening to the overture playing over the loudspeakers, playing patience, thinking through his act. Today, it felt even more important to concentrate only on getting through the next few hours. The last thing he wanted to do was to think about the past or the future. After leaving Sam on the pier he had eaten an early supper in an Italian restaurant. Now all he had to do was perform on stage, make his daughter disappear a few times, and go back to Mrs M's house. With any luck she would have the tact to pretend to be asleep.

He was annoyed, therefore, to have his pre-show reverie interrupted by a loud knock on the door. Who could it be? It wasn't the runner because Max wasn't due on until the second half. Even Ruby would think twice about disturbing him today.

"Yes?" he said, trying to sound as unhelpful as possible.

But the door was open and a Homburg hat had forced its way in.

"Maxie boy."

Oh dear God, not Joe Passolini. Today of all days.

"What do you want?" he said.

Joe sat, uninvited, on the sofa and laughed incredulously. "What do I want? I only want to make you a star, Maxie boy. That's all I want."

I am a star, thought Max. Or, at least, I was once. He wanted Joe to go away and to take his brashness and optimism with him.

But there was no stopping Joe now. He took off his hat and balanced it carefully on his knees. "I've only got a Hollywood agent to come and see you perform," he said. "That's all."

"A Hollywood agent? Tonight?"

"He's coming tomorrow," said Joe. "Harvey Broom. You've heard of him, of course."

"Vaguely."

"Well, he's in England looking for new faces for films. I heard that he was looking for a leading man type who could do magic and, of course, I thought of my old amigo Max."

"I'm not a leading man type. I'm forty-four."

"You don't look it, Maxie boy," said Joe earnestly. "Besides, they do clever things with lights these days."

"And Harvey Broom is coming to see the show tomorrow?"

"Yes. He's coming down from London specially. So make sure you're at your best. Well, you're always at your best. Ruby too. There might be something in this for her. A face like that should be in films."

What would Edgar think about that? Max wondered. He thought it was hard enough for Edgar to cope with Ruby being on television, much less twenty foot high on the silver screen. He was annoyed to find that he himself was not entirely immune to the lure of Hollywood. It would be a diversion and, God knows, he could do with one of those.

"There's a copper outside," said Joe, putting on his hat again and leaning forward to adjust it in Max's mirror. "What's going on?"

"There's been another murder."

"Bloody hell," said Joe. "You'll be safer in America. Toodle-pip."

And he was gone.

270

Tol dropped Emma at her parents' house at five-thirty. She changed into warmer clothes and shovelled down a hotpot at a rate that made Ada sigh and talk about indigestion. Even so, it was nearly seven o'clock when she arrived at the theatre. The curtain was going up but, backstage, performers were still wandering round in robes with their make-up half finished. The policeman stationed outside the dressing room of the Living Tableaux was in a state of high excitement.

"Half-naked, they are," he told Emma. "Just walking around in their underwear."

"Really?" said Emma coldly. "Remember you're on duty."

She had a quick word with Janette who was helping Betty put on her blonde wig.

"There's a policeman on patrol outside your lodgings," she told them. "Sergeant Willis should be there now."

"He's so brave," said Betty, her mascaraed eyes wide in the mirror.

Doesn't take much bravery to stand outside a house, thought Emma, but she didn't say so. If Emma wanted Bob to be her knight in shining armour, then he could be.

"What's it like doing the show without Mr Cutler?" she asked.

"It's much better," said Janette, giving the wig a final tweak. "We're going to carry on with the act, managing it ourselves."

271

Emma didn't ask who would be in charge; the answer was obvious.

Outside, she could hear the show being relayed over loudspeakers, Stew Stewart's brash London voice echoing in the low-ceilinged corridor, "So, I was just walking down the road, all on my ownsome . . ." If she remembered correctly, Madame Mitzi and her poodles would be next. She stopped outside Max's door. Should she go in and see how he was? Florence's death must have upset him, surely? But, although Emma liked Max, she shrank from the thought of discussing anything personal with him. Ruby had said that Max told Edgar everything. Emma wasn't sure that this was true, but she knew that the two men had a close bond, forged somewhere in their shadowy war experiences. If anyone was going to talk to Max, it should be the DI.

As she watched, though, Max's door opened and a man came out. He was wearing a pin-striped suit with very wide shoulders and looked vaguely familiar. He tipped his hat to Emma and gave her an appraising glance. She scowled back.

She had a sudden desire to see the show from backstage. After all, she was supposed to be keeping an eye on things. She descended the stairs until she saw a sign saying, "Wings. Silence." She pushed open the black door and she was there, right next to the stage, surrounded by pieces of scenery and shadowy figures who she assumed must be stagehands. No one took any notice of her. The stage looked very bright and unreal seen from this angle: you could see how it wasn't completely flat, how it raked downwards to face the audience. There were pieces of sticky tape all over the floorboards which she assumed were markers for scenery, but for Stew Stewart's act the set was bare. She could see the comedian's back, in his bright check jacket, facing the void that was the audience. What must it be like to stand in front of all these people and try to make them laugh? Stewart was working up to his punchline, the only one in the act as far as Emma could remember. "So my old ma, she turns to me and she says, 'Is this what you meant, son?'" A roar of applause and Stewart was bowing and walking off. He passed so close to Emma that she could smell his sweat.

"Fantastic house," he said to one of the stagehands. "Eating out of my hand."

Stewart went back for another bow and left the stage at a run. The stagehands rushed on and started putting up pedestals and hoops for the poodles. Emma heard shrill barks coming closer. Time to leave.

She went back upstairs to the dressing rooms. What should she be doing now? Checking on every door to make sure that no one was enacting a gruesome tableau within? The thought made her shiver. She wished that the DI were there.

"Excuse me, er . . . miss?"

Emma turned. It was the assistant stage manager. What was his name? Toby.

"I've got a call for you. In Mr Billings's office."

Emma followed Toby along the now silent corridor. She hoped that the call wouldn't be to say that Edgar was stuck in London.

Bob had a cup of tea and spaghetti on toast in a café off Western Road. It wasn't worth going back to his digs and, anyway, it was such a cheerless place that he avoided going there except to sleep. What would it be like to go back to a house where you actually felt at home? From what the DI said, his flat wasn't exactly comfortable, though he had moved recently. Emma, of course, lived in the lap of luxury. Bob didn't want luxury. He thought of the high ceilings and echoing stairwell of Montpelier Crescent with a shudder. He just wanted a place that was warm and friendly, where there was someone to greet him, not just Portslade Patsy demanding the rent. He sighed and reached in his pocket to pay the bill (he'd have to keep the receipt for expenses). Six o'clock. Time to get back on sentry duty.

The house in Lansdowne Road was in darkness. There was a policeman standing morosely by the porch and Bob recognised him as PC Barnes.

"Is anyone in?" he asked, opening the gate.

"Landlady's in the kitchen," said PC Barnes. "I've knocked twice to check that she's safe and she still hasn't offered me a cup of tea. I think the old boy's in but there's no light at his window. The girls are out. Christmas party at the bank, apparently."

Bob walked round the side of the house. He could see the light in the kitchen. Seen from the outside, it looked impossibly warm and cosy. Should he knock and see if he fared any better with the tea? He stood looking out over the snowy garden, the shrubs and rockery turned into mysterious mounds and hillocks.

274

Then he rubbed his eyes. A dark figure was forcing its way through a gap in the hedge. Bob flattened himself against the wall of the house. The figure grew closer, moving in a furtive fashion, bent almost double as it zig-zagged across the lawn. It was a man wearing a hat pulled down low over his face. Bob waited until he had almost reached the side passage.

"Looking for someone?"

The man jumped and swore. Barnes's torch shone a beam into the dark passageway.

"What's going on?"

Bob had the man by the arm. "I caught this gentleman paying a late-night visit." The man didn't resist, in fact he seemed to sag at the knees. "I wasn't doing anything wrong. Honest."

"Take off the hat," said Bob.

The man did so. He was youngish and dark, slimly built but with a wiry strength to him. He also looked vaguely familiar.

"What's your name and what are you doing here?" asked Bob.

"Steve Lewis," said the man. "I'm Peggy's fiancé."

Steve Lewis. The man who worked as a printer at the *Argus*. Bob had interviewed him earlier in the week. He had been nervous but not suspiciously so. He also had an alibi for Lily's murder.

"What are you doing here, Steve?"

In the light of Barnes's torch, Steve looked young and slightly sulky. "I've come to see Peggy. The old dragon — Mrs Wright — she won't let me go upstairs. If I so much as hold Peggy's hand on the sofa she looks at me as if I'm a monster. So, we've got a routine. I come through the garden and Peggy lets me in through the side door."

"Ingenious," said Bob. This probably explained the hole in the hedge that the search team had noticed on Tuesday.

"Peggy's out," said Barnes. "Some Christmas do at the bank."

"That's what she told Mrs Wright," said Steve. "Brenda's gone to the party but Peggy's upstairs. Watch." He put two fingers to his lips and produced a rather impressive owl impression. To-whit, to-whoo. There was a sound of a sash window opening and a woman's voice. "Steve? Is that you?"

"Can you come down a minute, miss?" said Bob. From inside the house he could hear martial music on the wireless. He hoped it would keep Edna and Norris occupied for a bit longer.

Peggy appeared a few minutes later. She was fully dressed and was obviously expecting a visitor. The scent of Californian Poppy floated on the night air.

"Steve? What's going on?"

"Let's go to the front," said Bob. They walked in procession round to the covered porch. Peggy was shivering in her thin dress and Steve put his arm round her.

"I understand that you were expecting Mr Lewis," said Bob.

"Yes," said Peggy. She sounded embarrassed. "You see, Edna won't ever let us be alone so we thought . . ."

276

"You're taking a risk," said Bob. "You know there's a murderer on the loose."

"I don't care," said Steve. "It's worth it to see Peggy."

He should have looked ridiculous, caught sneaking through a suburban garden at night, but Bob found the lovers rather touching.

"I can't let you in," he said. "I've been told to report anyone entering or leaving the house. Go home now and Barnes and I will forget that we've seen you. Won't we, Barnes?"

"Yes, Sergeant."

Steve hesitated. "Go round the side and kiss her goodnight," said Bob. "But be quick about it."

Peggy and Steve made a hasty exit, holding hands.

"Love's young dream," said Barnes. "We've all been there."

Bob hadn't been there but he hoped to visit one day.

The roads weren't bad until Edgar had almost left London. But, as he reached Purley Cross, it started to snow again. His car skidded on some black ice and he just missed a lamppost as he fought to right it. There were no other cars around, as if everyone knew something that he didn't. He drove slowly, not wanting to miss the signs for Brighton, windscreen wipers struggling. For some reason, he felt that, once he was on the Brighton Road, everything would be all right but, when he reached the long, straight road, the snow continued to fall, heavier and heavier. On Reigate Hill the streetlights disappeared and Edgar crawled on, alone in his circle of light. Broken words and phrases rushed past him like signposts, half glimpsed in the darkness.

Vic Cutler's Living Tableaux: scenes from the past brought to life.

She used to have a swing with flowers all round it.

Left is sinistra *in Italian.*

I used to do summer seasons at the Hippodrome.

It's a woman's crime.

It's a crime of passion.

The sleeping and the dead are but as pictures.

He skidded again but rode with it this time, not daring to put his foot on the brake. He thought of Evans, the soldier who had seen the angel, all those years ago in Norway. He had a sudden superstitious fear that, if he looked in the driving mirror, he would see it behind him, a monstrous figure made from snow and ice, its eyes aflame. He had to get back to Brighton. "Come on," he told the car, "you can do it." He leant forward, hands clenched on the wheel. He wished the car had a radio, like the Buick that he'd once driven in America. He could do with some company besides his own thoughts. He couldn't see the road now, the headlights reflecting only swirling snowflakes, dangerously mesmerising.

"Put something in the centre," Max had once told him, "create a space around it and it becomes important."

What was he missing? What was on the edge of his vision, significant but insignificant? Misdirection, that's what Max called it. Making the punter look the wrong way. Who was directing the trick this time?

The Living Tableaux. Lady Jane Grey, Cleopatra, Boadicea, the Lady of Shalott. He heard Diablo's voice, echoing down the years. The three of them in a drifting boat, Diablo with his eyes shut, reciting from memory.

> *And at the closing of the day*
> *She loosed the chain, and down she lay;*
> *The broad stream bore her far away*
> *The Lady of Shalott.*

Edgar drove on through the snow, trusting that he was going in the right direction, trusting that he knew what he was doing.

Bob and PC Barnes watched the snow fall as they stood in the porch.

"We'll freeze to death here," said Barnes, "just like those poor buggers at the South Pole. What did that bloke say? Captain Oates? 'I'm just going outside, I may be some time.' "

Bob pulled his coat round him. "I'll go and ask if we can wait inside."

"She won't let you," said Barnes. "She's a dragon, like our young Romeo said."

But before Bob could bring himself to knock on the door, it opened quietly behind them.

"You can't stay outside in this," said Edna. "Come into the kitchen for a cup of tea."

The two policemen were over the threshold before she could change her mind.

The Bolney Stage, an old highwayman's haunt, was like a lighthouse in a storm-tossed sea. Edgar aimed for it, hardly caring if he was driving on the road or across grass. He needed to telephone the station, to speak to Emma, to say that he was on his way. Finally he was in the car park, dark patches of ice gleaming evilly through the snow. His was the only car and he thought the pub might be shut but the door opened easily and inside there were people, lights, an open fire, gleaming brasses. It was as if he had entered a different world.

There was a public telephone in the passage, the barmaid told him. "I'll get you a brandy while you telephone," she said. Edgar couldn't bring himself to refuse.

He had expected the duty sergeant to sound bored, indifferent, surprised to hear from him. Instead, the man's voice was urgent, even — unbelievably — slightly frightened.

"DI Stephens! Where are you?"

"Bolney, On my way back from London."

"Get back as quickly as you can. We've just had a call from PC Hobbs at the Hippodrome. Sergeant Holmes has vanished."

CHAPTER
TWENTY-TWO

Edgar didn't even drink the brandy. He was back in his car and halfway to Hickstead before he had even caught his breath. Now all care was forgotten and he skidded and swerved, fighting to keep control of the wheel. He met no other traffic apart from a delivery van driving very slowly in the middle of the road. Edgar shot past in a blur of gritty snow. He had to get to Brighton. He had to get to Emma. Vanished, that's what PC Hobbs had said. He thought of Max and Ruby with their magic cabinet, the doors opening and shutting. The vanishing box. Now you see it, now you don't. But Emma hadn't vanished. Someone had taken her, someone who had already killed two women. Why did he ever let her go to the theatre? Emma wasn't just his sergeant, she was a woman, every bit as beautiful as Lily or Florence. If he ever saw her again, he would tell her so.

The snow was so heavy that he missed the Brighton gates altogether but, once near the centre of town, driving became a little easier. There were streetlights, for one thing, and some of the main roads had been cleared. He passed a group of youths throwing snowballs at the statue of the Prince Regent and realised with a shock that it was only ten o'clock. It felt like midnight. It felt as if he'd been away for years. He parked outside the Hippodrome, jumped out of the car and immediately fell flat on his face in a snowdrift. Cursing, he got to his feet. The theatre was in darkness, the solid façade expressionless. Edgar ran round to the stage door and hammered on it. He thought that he shouted too. The door was opened by the pimply assistant stage manager.

"Mr Billings is expecting you," he breathed.

There seemed to be a lot of people in Dick Billings's office and Edgar was relieved to see that one of them was Max. PC Hobbs was also there as well as the surprising, and not entirely welcome, figure of Ruby. She jumped up when he came in.

"Ed! What's happened to you?"

It was only then that he realised that he was dripping wet and covered in snow. The other people in the room were staring at him as if they'd seen an apparition.

"Never mind me," he said. "What happened to Emma?"

Billings was sitting behind his desk as if this gave him the illusion of being in control. Even so, Edgar thought that the theatre manager looked very shaken. His plump face was shiny with perspiration.

"There was a telephone call for the sergeant," he said. "I sent Toby to find her. She came in here to take the call and that was the last anyone saw of her."

Edgar turned to the ASM. "Are you Toby? What happened after Sergeant Holmes took the call?"

Toby now looked positively terrified. "I don't know. I had to go and call the performers for the second half. I just left her in Mr Billings's office."

"Where were you?" Edgar turned to Billings.

"I thought the young lady would want some privacy," said Billings. "So I went to talk to some of the artistes."

"Which ones?" said Edgar. Though he thought he could have guessed.

"The Living Tableaux," said Billings. "I wanted to check that they were all right to perform without Vic or Florence."

"Who was on the telephone?" said Edgar. "Man or woman? Did you recognise the voice?"

"A woman," said Billings. "I didn't recognise the voice."

"Have you searched the theatre?"

"From top to bottom," said Billings. "Ask the policeman here."

"We executed a very thorough search," said Hobbs. "At first I thought that Sergeant Holmes must be somewhere on the premises. The sergeant has her own way of doing things, we all know that. But we looked everywhere. The usherettes and stagehands helped. Even Mr Mephisto. There's no sign of her anywhere."

Edgar thought. His instinct was to tear the theatre apart with his bare hands but he knew it would do more good to try to use his brain, as he was sure Emma would do in the circumstances. Whose voice on the telephone would cause Emma to take off like that? He could only think of one answer, even though Billings had said the caller was a woman.

"Can I use your telephone?" he asked.

"Be my guest."

Edgar dialled the Lansdowne Road number. After a long pause, Edna came on the line.

"Brighton six four two."

"Mrs Wright. Edna. It's DCI Stephens here. Can I speak to Sergeant Willis?"

"He's not here," said Edna. "It was getting so cold, he and the other policemen went back. Betty and Janette are home though. Everyone's safe."

If only that were true, thought Edgar, putting down the receiver.

Emma was floating. She was on Hove Lagoon in a rowing boat, the DI was there too but she couldn't see his face. She was swimming at Coniston Water, lying on her back watching the clouds. She was in the bath at home, Ada calling from downstairs.

"This won't hurt," said a voice, "and then you'll sleep for ever."

Sleep for ever. It sounded lovely. *To die, to sleep; to sleep: perchance to dream.* Then she heard Astarte's voice. "Emma", she was saying, low and urgent, "Emma. Wake up."

She opened her eyes. There was blue all round her. She thought she saw goldfish, swimming round and round, their mouths opening and shutting. Was she drowning? She could smell flowers: lilies, roses, the pungent scent of evergreens. *We talked about making her a Christmas wreath. I'm famous for my wreaths.*

284

Dust to dust, ashes to ashes. Fear no more the heat of the sun.

"Beautiful," said the voice. "Just like the others. As still as death."

That wasn't right. She had to stay alive. She had a job to do. Edgar needed her. But then there were hands around her neck and it was darkness again.

Edgar rang the station and was told that Sergeant Willis wasn't back yet.

"He must be on his way," he said to Max, who had come to stand next to him. "I'll go back to the station and start organising a search party."

"I'll walk Ruby home," said Max, "and then I'll join you."

"I want to help," said Ruby. She put her hand on Edgar's arm, her eyes wide with sympathy. "I want to help find Emma."

"No." Edgar spoke with difficulty. "It's too dangerous. Max will take you home."

"Come on, sweetheart." Max turned to his daughter. "Let's go." To Edgar, "I'll meet you at the station. Don't do anything stupid."

Edgar hardly heard him. Calling to Hobbs to follow him, he was already at the door.

"Can we do anything?" asked Billings.

"Stay here," shouted Edgar over his shoulder, "just in case she comes back."

Outside, the snow had stopped but it lay smooth and white in all directions, giving the night an eerie lightness. Edgar's car was a moulded hillock and other similar shapes blocked the road in both directions.

"We'll be quicker walking," he said to Hobbs. "Come on."

They went through the Lanes. The snow wasn't as thick in the narrow streets but it was still icy and treacherous. Edgar was half running, slipping and sliding, holding on to railings and door handles. PC Hobbs followed more ponderously. "Steady," Edgar heard him saying to himself, "steady now." But he couldn't go steadily. He had to find Emma. Even now she could be . . . But he couldn't let himself think like that. He had to use his brain. "What would Sherlock Holmes do?" That was a running joke at the station, an allusion to Emma's unfortunate last name. What would the famous detective do? What was his famous saying? *When you have eliminated the impossible, whatever remains,* however improbable, *must be the truth.*

Lily had been killed. Someone had left her flowers. She believed that Vic Cutler was her father. Vic had been killed, stabbed as he sat in his smart apartment. Taken unawares. Florence had been killed and the scene arranged to look like the death of Cleopatra. The two women were linked only by Vic Cutler. Who else had links to the impresario? Dick Billings, who had quarrelled with him. Tommy Watson, who had been his rival in love. Cecily Burtenshaw, who had loved him and borne his child. Why hadn't Cecily told Vic that she was pregnant? Why had she left Brighton?

286

Then, clear as a Christmas bell, he heard Cecily's voice. He could even smell the flowers in the funeral bouquets.

We had some fun in those days. Then Edna got married so I couldn't stay with her any more.

Why couldn't Cecily stay with Edna once she got married? She ran a boarding house, after all. He thought of the picture of Cecily on her swing. It had been found in Peter Entwhistle's Bible but where had the old man found it first? Who else in the boarding house might have had a picture of Cecily in her prime?

He stopped. They were at the corner by the Bath Arms. Like the Bolney Stage, the pub was seemingly undeterred by the weather conditions. The lights were on and Edgar could hear laughter and shouted conversations, the sound of pool cue against ball. They were like echoes from another life, voices from the dead.

"Hobbs." The policeman was right behind him, red-faced from his exertions. "Go back to the station. Get all the men you can and meet me at number twelve Lansdowne Road. I'm going there now. Be as quick as you can."

Hobbs stared at him, his face ghostly in the light from the saloon bar.

"Hurry!" said Edgar. "Don't forget. Number twelve Lansdowne Road. Go on!" And he turned and headed off in the opposite direction.

Darkness. Silence. The ticking of a clock far away. Astarte's voice, "He is swinging." Peter Entwhistle:

" 'Hearts and Flowers' for the romantic stuff, Handel's 'Water Music' whenever there was a boat, 'William Tell' for the chases." Curtains opening and closing. "The Grand March" from Aida. Is this what it is like, sliding into another world? Voices, colours, shapes merging into one another. The DI's voice, "Hold on, Emma. I'm coming for you."

Edgar had hoped to be able to flag down a passing police patrol car but the streets were deserted. He toiled past the Clock Tower and along Western Road. His coat was still wet and his shoes quite inadequate for trekking through snow. He remembered Norway and the fight amongst the troops for a pair of boots that didn't let in water. He had once seen two men pulling the snow boots off a dead soldier. Edgar had lost a toe to frostbite and that foot ached now. His face was numb with cold and he thought longingly of the Russian fur hat, a present from Diablo, sitting on top of his wardrobe at home, The road seemed endless, shops with their shutters down, a sad-looking Christmas tree outside Woolworths. He had to get to Emma. "I'm coming for you," he told her silently, "hold on." Sending thought messages, it was something that gypsy-girl, Astarte, would do. Tony Mulholland, another member of the Magic Men, had claimed to be able to read people's minds. Well, that hadn't done Tony any good in the end. He thought of Emma, her white-blonde hair, her smile, her blazing intelligence. Somehow he had to reach her, across the snowy rooftops of Brighton, whatever evil creature lay in their path. Hold on, I'm coming for you.

At last he was at the bottom of Lansdowne Road, a glittering white slope in the moonlight. He had to pull himself up the hill by garden railings, falling over again and again. He would tell Emma one day. "I crawled on my hands and knees to save you." Please God, let him be in time.

He hammered on the door of number twelve. After a long wait it was opened by Edna, massive in a flowery dressing gown and curlers. Norris, in striped pyjamas, was in the background.

"What do you want?" Edna seemed to swell even larger. "Breaking into people's houses in the middle of the night."

Edgar barged his way in. "Where's Sergeant Willis?"

"I told you. He went back to the police station. He and that other no-good copper. Always hanging around trying to scrounge cups of tea. It's not right. This is a respectable house. I'm complaining to the council."

Edgar ignored her. He pushed open the door to the front room. The decorated piano loomed in the background. The gas fire was still glowing. Edna hadn't been in bed long.

"What's going on?" A quavering voice at the top of the stairs. It was Peter Entwhistle, wearing a coat over his pyjamas. Betty and Janette appeared at his side.

"What is it, DI Stephens?" Betty called. "Is Bob all right?"

Edgar looked up. "Betty. Have you seen Bob this evening?"

"No," said Betty. "He wasn't here when we got back from the theatre."

The show finished at nine-thirty. That was two hours ago. If Bob had left then he would have been safely back at the station by now.

Edgar crossed the hall. The dining room was empty, as was the kitchen. Edgar put his hand on the door of the snug.

"You can't go in there," said Edna. "It's private."

Edgar pushed open the door. Bob and PC Barnes were sitting in the armchairs, apparently asleep.

"Bob!" Edgar took Bob's arm and felt his pulse. It was beating sluggishly. Edgar shook him. "Bob, wake up!"

"He won't wake up," said Edna from the doorway.

"What have you done to him?"

"Sleeping pill in his tea. He won't give us any more trouble."

Edgar grabbed the landlady by the shoulders. "Where's Emma? What have you done to her?"

It was Norris who spoke.

"I killed her," he said. "Just like the others."

CHAPTER
TWENTY-THREE

Ruby was very quiet on the walk home. She held on to Max's arm as they crossed the icy coast road but her head was down and all he could see was the top of her furry hat. It made him feel very protective. Florence had worn a fur hat too but she had been tall, able to look him in the eye. He still found it almost impossible to believe that he'd never see her again.

"Are you all right?" he said to Ruby, when a few more minutes had passed in silence. The moon was high over the sea and black waves were breaking on the white beach.

"I'm just tired," said Ruby. Max remembered that she hadn't felt well earlier. You wouldn't have known it during their act though, she had laughed and bantered with him and performed her tricks with aplomb. She was a pro all right, he thought.

"Do you think they'll find her?" she said suddenly. "Emma, I mean."

"I'm sure they will," said Max. Though he was, in fact, far from sure. "Emma's a policewoman. She can look after herself."

"Edgar's very worried about her," said Ruby, after a pause.

"Well, yes," said Max carefully. "She works for him. She's his responsibility. That's how he'd see it anyway."

Another silence. They passed the peace statue, the angel garlanded in snow. Max walked quickly, wanting to get Ruby back to her lodgings so that he could help Edgar. After a while, Ruby started to pull back. Eventually she stopped altogether.

"Come on," said Max. "Not far now. You'll be in the warm soon."

"Max," said Ruby, looking up at him, her face pale in the moonlight. "Are you sad about Florence?"

Max looked down at her, wondering what had prompted this question. "Yes," he said eventually. "I do feel sad. I didn't know her very well but I liked her. I feel sad and I feel angry and I feel guilty."

"Why would you feel guilty?"

"Because I wasn't able to save her, I suppose."

"What about Mrs M? Do you feel guilty about her?"

"What is this?" Max tried to make his voice light. "The Spanish Inquisition? Mrs M is my business."

"Do you think Edgar feels guilty?" asked Ruby.

"About what?"

"About Emma."

"I don't know," said Max. "Come on. You'll freeze if you keep standing there."

Ruby said nothing but she put her arm in his and they carried on along the coast road until they reached Grand Avenue and her lodging house. Max saw her safely in and kissed her on the cheek.

"Don't worry," he said. "Everything will turn out all right."

That's the thing about becoming a parent, he thought, hurrying back along the snowy road. It turns you into an awful liar.

Edgar was shaking Norris by the throat. "What have you done to her? Where is she?"

Edna was pulling him away. She was very strong, probably far stronger than her husband. "Where's Emma?" Edgar shouted at her. He was starting to realise that he was outnumbered. Behind him Bob groaned gently. He was clearly not going to be any help. When would Hobbs get there with the reinforcements?

"I killed her," said Norris from behind his wife. "She's in the water."

"In the water?" Had the man thrown her into the sea? If so, he, Edgar, would soon be committing a murder of his own. He advanced on the cringing man.

"Tell me what you've done with her."

"She's in the water. With the flowers."

Flowers. Edgar thought of Cecily Burtenshaw surrounded by funeral wreaths. Red and white roses meant bad luck, that's what Emma had said. *The broad stream bore her far away, The Lady of Shalott.*

"I think I know," said a new voice. It was Peter Entwhistle, looking frail and scared with his striped pyjamas and bare feet appearing below his heavy coat.

"I think he's taken her to Montpelier Crescent. That was the address on the letter."

"You old fool!" Edna turned on him. "You'll be out on the streets tomorrow. You're a thief and a liar."

But Edgar had a lead now and he was going to follow it. "Thank you," he said to Peter. "Go back upstairs and lock yourself in a room with Betty and Janette. All of you in the same room. The police will be here in a minute. Betty?"

"Yes?" Betty was holding Peter's arm, looking with horror at Bob's recumbent form.

"Can you tell the policeman that comes here that I've gone to number twenty Montpelier Crescent. Can you remember that?"

"Yes."

"And tell them I said to arrest Mr and Mrs Wright. Now, go up to your room and lock the door. And, please, take Mr Entwhistle with you. Look after him."

Betty ushered the old man out. In the hall were two other terrified women. Peggy and Brenda, the bank clerks. Edgar told them to go into their room and lock the door.

"Inspector?" One of the bank women. Brenda, he thought.

"Yes?" He was already by the door. If Emma was dead, he would come straight back and kill Norris with his bare. hands.

"You can take my bike. It's in the front garden. It should be a bit quicker than walking."

"Thank you."

And, in a few minutes, he was freewheeling down the frozen road, faster than he would have thought possible, trying not to think about what lay ahead.

Max was almost at the pier when he stopped. What was the point of heading back to the police station with all the flat-footed coppers? He had to think. He lit a cigarette, his hands numb as he fumbled for the lighter. He always thought better whilst smoking. If someone had taken Emma, what would they do next? This man is a showman, that's what he told Edgar. And a showman needed a stage. Lily had been killed in her bedroom, her body arranged to resemble an old painting. Florence had been murdered in her own sitting room, or rather her lover's sitting room. She had apparently been posed to look like Cleopatra. Emma, he knew, lived with her wealthy parents in Roedean. The killer was hardly going to barge in there and start moving the furniture. But he needed an indoor space, somewhere where he could let his horrible imagination run wild.

Max ground the cigarette into the snow. He started to head back towards the town, slipping in his expensive Italian leather shoes. He thought he knew where there was an empty stage.

Number twenty was dark. For what felt like the hundredth time that night, Edgar hammered on a door. A sash window went up somewhere in the square and an expensive voice called out, "I say! What's going on?"

"Let me in!" shouted Edgar.

He was just about to barge the door when it opened and Norman the porter stood there, scrawny in an old-fashioned nightshirt.

"Let me into flat one," panted Edgar.

"There's no one there."

"Just let me in."

He'd flown across town like a fury only to be delayed by this gnome in a nightshirt fumbling with his keys. "Hurry up, damn you."

"All right, all right." The porter's voice was slightly slurred. "Just let me get the right key. Ah, there we are . . ."

Edgar threw himself through the door. All at once he was assailed by the scent of lilies, that terrible, sickly, ominous aroma. The sitting room was empty but the fragrance drew him on. Through a bedroom with a huge, decadent bed and gold mirrors and into the adjoining bathroom.

Emma lay in the bath which was filled with flowers. She was naked and her blonde hair streamed down on either side of her floating body. There were black marks round her neck.

"Emma!" He lifted her out of the bath and held her in his arms. He pressed his lips against hers and thought he felt a faint intake of breath. "Emma. Don't die. I love you. Please don't die."

He carried her, wet and dripping, into the bedroom and put her on the bed.

"Call an ambulance!" he shouted to the hovering shape that was Norman. "Hurry!"

How did you perform the kiss of life? He was back in a draughty Nissen hut having his basic training. Check the airway is clear, tilt the head back slightly, place your mouth tightly over the nose and mouth. Quick, shallow breaths. Don't die, he told her, trying to keep up the rhythm. Don't die, don't die. He was in a strange fugue state, as if he was somewhere up above looking down on the figures on the bed, a macabre parody of passion. His mouth against hers, one hand on her breast, hoping to feel her chest rise.

"Ed!" A new voice, one that seemed to come from a long way away. "Ed. She's breathing."

Edgar looked up. Max was standing in the doorway. Emma gave a faint moan.

"Turn her on her side," said Max.

Edgar did so, trying to cover her with the sheet at the same time. Max went into the bathroom and came back with a large towel which he put over Emma.

"The ambulance is on its way," he said.

"Will it get through the snow?" said Edgar.

"Of course it will. They're tough, those things. Remember in the war?"

Emma said, "Edgar?"

Edgar bent over her. "It's all right. You're safe. The ambulance is coming."

Emma looked up at him, her blue eyes troubled. "What happened? Where did Norris go?"

"He's under arrest," said Edgar, hoping this was true. "Don't worry about anything."

"Norris," said Max from the doorway. "The landlord?"

"Yes. He and his wife must have been in it together."

"God. Why?"

"Norris was in love with Lily's mother. He must have also become obsessed with the daughter. Seeing Vic

Cutler hanging around the house must have been the final straw. Norris killed him too."

Emma murmured but Edgar couldn't catch the words. "It's all right," he said again. "You're safe now."

Max was looking out of the window, checking for the ambulance. "I saw the bath and the flowers," he said, over his shoulder. "The Lady of Shalott?"

"I think so. I hate that bloody poem."

"What about Florence? Why did Norris kill her?"

"I hate to say so but I think she was killed to take our attention away from Lansdowne Road. They knew we were focusing on the tableaux and decided to act one out. I actually think that Edna might have killed Florence. She came round here, probably disguised as a cleaner, killed Florence and arranged the scene. At the same time, Norris was on the telephone to us saying that some mysterious assailant had attacked Betty. Norris probably did that himself. He seems to enjoy strangling women."

"Good God. So Florence was just misdirection."

"I'm afraid so."

Max was about to say more but a blue light was suddenly reflected into the bedroom.

"The ambulance is here."

Edgar gathered Emma into his arms, tucking the sheet and towel round her. Max watched him without expression. "What are you doing now?"

"Going to the hospital with her."

"You can't. You've got to catch these bastards."

"You're right." They faced each other with Emma between them. Edgar thought Max was going to say something about Ruby. He had no idea how much Max had seen and heard earlier. But Max just sighed and said, "I'll go to the hospital with Emma. You go and arrest people."

CHAPTER
TWENTY-FOUR

Saturday

It was past midnight by the time that Edgar had wearily cycled back to Lansdowne Road. He found Betty in the snug feeding black coffee to a groaning Bob. PC Barnes was still asleep in the chair.

"Sir." Bob tried to get to his feet. "What's happening? Betty said something about Emma."

"They tried to kill her," said Edgar. "But she's alive. She's going to be all right."

"They? Edna and Norris?"

"Yes."

"She invited me in for a cup of tea," said Bob. "That's the last thing I remember."

"It was drugged," said Edgar. "Where are Edna and Norris now?"

"In the front parlour," said Betty. She was pale and obviously frightened but otherwise in control. She had even found time to dress and tie her hair back in a red scarf. A resourceful girl, thought Edgar, and one who might do very well for Bob.

"Are the police here? They didn't try to escape?"

"No. They let the policemen in just like they were visitors. Norris even offered them a cup of tea." Betty shuddered. "I always thought they were a bit odd but . . ."

A bit odd doesn't begin to cover it, thought Edgar. Norris had killed Lily because he was obsessed with her, as he had been with Cecily. He'd put the flowers outside her door and, when Vic Cutler appeared, he must have thought that, once again, Vic was about to steal the girl he loved. That's why he had killed them both. Edgar just wasn't clear exactly when Norris's wife had started helping him. Leaving Betty ministering to Bob, he went into the sitting room. Edna and Norris were sitting side by side on the sofa. PC Hobbs and Sergeant McGuire from Bartholomew Square were standing by the door like sentries.

"Norris Wright," said Edgar, "I'm arresting you for the murders of Lily Burtenshaw and Vic Cutler and for the attempted murder of Emma Holmes. Edna Wright, I'm arresting you for the murder of Florence Jones. Do you have anything to say?"

"I loved Lily," said Norris. "I was saving her. Keeping her pure. It was only a matter of time before those showgirls corrupted her and she became like her mother. Then Vic Cutler started sniffing round her. I had to kill her. To save her from him. I couldn't let him defile her as he did Cecily."

Corrupt, defile. Norris's father was a vicar, remembered Edgar. Was this where he got this Old Testament language? Edna, at any rate, thought he was saying too much.

"Shut up, Norris," she said, "don't tell them anything." With her arms crossed over her chest she was still every bit the respectable landlady, horrified at this intrusion into her home.

The first thing he would do back at the station, thought Edgar, would be to put the Wrights in separate cells. He had a feeling that Norris would soon be singing to the rafters.

"Is a squad car on its way?" he asked Sergeant McGuire.

"Couldn't get through the snow," said McGuire, "so I radioed for a jeep from the army depot on Dyke Road."

"Well done."

"I had to kill her," said Norris earnestly, "to save her."

"Shut up, Norris."

When the jeep had taken the Wrights away, handcuffed to McGuire and Hobbs, Edgar called an ambulance to take Bob and PC Barnes to the hospital.

"I don't need to go to the hospital," said Bob. "I'm fine. I want to help."

"You've been drugged," said Edgar. "They need to check you out. If they say you're all right, you can come back to the station. Barnes is still out for the count."

Barnes groaned and muttered something about baiting the lines.

"He keeps talking about fishing," said Betty.

"What did I talk about?" said Bob.

Betty blushed. "Nothing much."

"Thank you for your help," Edgar said to Betty. "Try to get some sleep now. You're quite safe. Edna and Norris won't be coming back."

"What about this house?" said Betty. "It's all right for me and Janette. Tomorrow's our last night. But what about Peggy and Brenda and Mr Entwhistle? This is their home."

"I don't know," said Edgar. "They'll have to find new digs, I suppose. I'll see what I can do for Mr Entwhistle. I know a theatrical landlady who might be able to help. Where is Mr Entwhistle now?"

"In his room. Janette's with him."

Edgar climbed the stairs to the first floor. Peter Entwhistle was dozing in his chair, Janette was sitting on the bed knitting. Edgar thought how kind both the showgirls had r been. Brenda too, lending him her bike which may have given him the precious extra minutes with which to save Emma's life. It looked odd seeing Janette doing something as homely as knitting but there was also something almost ageless about her pose, sitting very upright with needles poised and the yarn beside her. Edgar thought of the women knitting at the foot of the guillotine, of the Goddess Frigg spinning the threads of life.

He leant over the sleeping man. "Mr Entwhistle?"

"What is it?" Peter looked at him blurrily. "Is it time to play the finale?"

"It's DI Stephens, Mr Entwhistle. We met the other day."

"Oh yes. There's been some bad business going on here. A girl was killed."

"I know," said Edgar, "but we caught the man who did it."

"I hope you hang him."

Edgar was against capital punishment but he couldn't bring himself to feel any pity for Norris and Edna. In any case, Norris would probably plead insanity and escape the gallows.

"Mr Entwhistle," said Edgar. "Would you mind if I had a look in your Bible?"

Peter did not seem to find this a strange request and, with Janette's help, they located the book on his bedside table. Edgar flipped through the close-written pages, discovering prayer cards, lucky pieces of heather and other, slightly odder, keepsakes, including a bacon rind. Eventually, though, he found what he was looking for. A letter headed Montpelier Crescent and beginning, "Dear Lily . . ."

"Can I borrow this for a bit?" he said.

Max waited until Emma was admitted to a ward and then left. As he walked through the main entrance he saw an ambulance draw up and Edgar's sergeant Bob get out, supporting a uniformed policeman who seemed distinctly unsteady on his feet. So both Edgar's lieutenants had been in the wars tonight. Max pulled his hat down over his face but Bob wasn't paying him any attention anyway. The policemen hurried through the double doors and the hospital swallowed them up.

Max walked along Eastern Road towards Upper Rock Gardens. The hospital had been an oasis of light and activity but the rest of the town was still asleep, the snow on the pavements unblemished apart from the occasional footprints of some night creature. The road had been partially cleared, presumably for ambulances, and he walked along the centre line, feeling as if he was the only man left alive in the world. Even so, it was hard going in places. His shoes, he thought with resignation, were ruined. There was a certain beauty to the night, though; the moon on the snow, the shadows deep and blue, the faded terraces transformed into a Tyrolean mountain scene.

He thought about what he had learnt tonight. Florence had been killed only to divert attention from the real murderer and his motive. That beautiful, brilliant woman had died for nothing. He had also learnt what he had long suspected; that Edgar was in love with Emma and not Ruby. His heart ached for his daughter. She had looked so sad tonight. She knew that something was wrong but just wasn't sure what it was. Max hadn't wanted Edgar to marry Ruby — in his view, the two were totally unsuited — but he wanted, more than anything, to save Ruby from heartbreak. Even though he knew it wasn't possible.

Mrs M's house was in darkness but, in the front room, there was a whisky decanter and a note.

Dear Max,
You might want to sleep in the first-floor front bedroom tonight. I've put a hot water bottle in the bed.
Love Joyce.

Max poured himself a triple whisky. Joyce was a wonderful woman, he thought. And, after tomorrow, he didn't think that he would ever see her again.

CHAPTER
TWENTY-FIVE

Visiting started at eleven and Edgar was there at five past. Even so, he wasn't Emma's first visitor. As he looked through the door of the ward he saw two familiar figures by Emma's bed — a woman in a fur coat and a man who, even from a distance, looked as if he wanted to shout at someone. Edgar pushed open the door and the man's dream was realised.

"You!" yelled Archie Holmes. "I've got a bone to pick with you."

A nurse materialised at his side. "Please keep your voice down," she said. "There are sick people in here."

"Stephens." Archie's face was alarmingly red. "A word in private please."

Edgar followed Emma's father into a waiting room. He didn't want to give the man a heart attack, after all. In the early hours of the morning, when he'd rung Emma's parents to say that she was in hospital, they had been too shocked to ask him many questions. Archie was certainly making up for that now.

"What's been going on? The matron says that someone tried to strangle Emma."

"Yes," said Edgar. He was trying to think of the least upsetting way to put it. "She was . . . er . . . attacked but not seriously hurt."

"Not seriously hurt? The man left her for dead, apparently."

Damn the matron and her all-too-accurate explanations. Norris had, almost certainly, left Emma for dead. But, as Solomon Carter was always saying, it was surprisingly difficult to strangle someone. Norris had managed it before, of course, but this time something, maybe the warm bath, had kept Emma alive.

"I reached her in time," he said, trying to sound soothing. "And was able to give her first aid."

"First aid? The kiss of life?"

"Yes."

Archie was silent, a lion deprived of its prey. Or rather, a lion who discovers that the wildebeest he is about to devour has just saved one of his cubs.

"All the same," he growled, "she shouldn't have been in danger like that. A young woman on her own. It's not right. I'm writing to your superintendent."

Frank Hodges would love that, thought Edgar. He had debriefed his boss earlier that morning. Hodges, as ever, torn between relief that the killers had been caught and annoyance that Edgar hadn't done it earlier.

"Mr Holmes," he said. "I'm so sorry that Emma was in danger. She's a brilliant police officer. The best I've ever worked with. And I'm sorry to ask this now, but could I have a word with her in private?"

Archie regarded him under lowered brows. "I'll see what her mother thinks," he said at last. Edgar crossed his fingers. He had a faint hope that Sybil Holmes might be on his side.

Sure enough, after a few minutes, Archie came back into the waiting room accompanied by his wife. "Five minutes," he said, "that's all."

Sybil put her hand on Edgar's arm. Even tired and distraught, she looked and smelt wonderful. "Thank you so much, Detective Inspector," she said. "Archie says that you saved Emma's life."

"After he'd put it in danger in the first place," said Archie.

"Thank you," said Sybil again. And she kissed him on the cheek.

Emma was sitting up in bed. There was a surgical collar round her neck and both her hands were bandaged. She saw Edgar looking at them.

"Apparently I tried to fight him off."

Edgar sat next to the bed. "Can you remember anything that happened?"

Emma frowned, as she always did when trying to think. "I got a telephone call at the theatre. It was Edna. She said that Bob needed me there urgently. I didn't think twice. I didn't even tell Hobbs where I was going. So stupid of me. Norris was waiting outside the stage door with a car. He said he'd give me a lift to Lansdowne Road. I got into the car and I don't remember anything else."

"He chloroformed you," said Edgar, "like he did the others."

"The next thing I remember, I was floating. He had his hands round my neck . . ." Emma was silent for a few minutes, looking up at the ceiling, where paper chains snaked between the light fittings. "I thought all sorts of stupid things. I heard voices. Astarte. You. My parents. I thought I was swimming at Coniston Water. In the Lake District. Where I was evacuated."

"That was the chloroform," said Edgar. It gave him a jolt to learn that Emma had also been thinking of Astarte.

"I was almost dead," said Emma. "That's what they told me in here. You saved my life."

"All part of the job," said Edgar, trying for a lighter tone.

Emma looked at him, her gaze blue and unflinching.

"I thought I heard you say that you loved me," she said. "Did I dream that too?"

"No," said Edgar. "I meant that."

Max was packing. Mrs M had thoughtfully moved his things into the front bedroom and he wanted to keep his side of the bargain by getting out of her hair as quickly as possible. He would do the last show tonight and leave first thing on Sunday morning. His car was parked in an underground garage in Kemp Town. He could be on the road by eight. He'd already booked a room at the Strand Palace hotel. He'd have a solitary Christmas, eating at Italian restaurants, walking in Hyde Park, reading Dickens or Tolstoy, practising his card tricks in the bar late at night.

He packed carefully. He was meticulous about his shirts, having them hand-laundered and pressed. His suits went in special bags, apart from his stage suit which was hanging on the back of the door. His shoes went in special containers too but the ones he had been wearing last night sat by the door, damp and misshapen. He'd have to throw them away.

As well as his suitcase he had an attaché case which contained his band music, playing cards and a few portable props. Looking through it now he found an envelope addressed, in a bold flowing hand, to "Max Mephisto". He opened it and found several typewritten pages.

Porter: We don't get much call for mummers, not at this time of the year.
Caller: Why not hear us mum? Live a little.
Porter: I don't like to. Not after the incident in West Riding.

It was Florence's radio script. Max sat on the bed amongst his folded shirts and started to read. Florence had been beautiful in such a serious, operatic way that it was hard to imagine that she could be funny too, but she was. The scripts were strange and surreal, no jokes, just unusual rhythms and catchphrases. Despite everything, Max found himself laughing aloud as he read them. Had the porter, a recurring character, been based on Norman? Was the greengrocer, Mick, always talking about his wares in nonsensical rhyming slang, a version of Vic Cutler? There were a few songs too. Was

Florence musical as Welsh people were supposed to be? He didn't know and now he would never know. She was half-Italian too, of course, a potentially explosive mixture. If she and Max had lived together, he was pretty sure that there would have been some impressive rows. He was sorry to miss them. It was a long time since he'd felt strongly enough to row with anyone.

Max put the scripts away in their envelope. He would show them to Joe. Perhaps they would be performed and earn Florence some posthumous fame, maybe even make some money for her family (not much, though, if Max knew anything about writing for the radio). Thinking of Joe made him remember Harvey Broom, the Hollywood scout who was coming to the show tonight. He was glad to discover that a small flame of ambition was still burning, deep down inside. He'd like to go to America, become seriously rich and leave variety behind him. The way he felt now he would be glad to leave everything behind him. Apart from Ruby and Edgar, of course.

Max started to pile the shirts into his suitcase.

Back at the station, Edgar started to wilt. He'd gone home at three a.m., slept for a couple of hours, showered and changed. He'd arrived at the station at six, fresh and revitalised. But now the manic energy was wearing off and the words on his incident report started to blur into each other.

For a few moments he stared blankly at the stenographer's notes from last night's interviews. The poor woman had been roused from her bed to take dictation so it was no wonder that the writing was a little shaky in places.

DI Stephens: Did you kill Lily Burtenshaw?

Norris Wright: She was so beautiful. Like her mother. I couldn't let her be defiled.

DI Stephens: Did you kill her? Yes or no?

Norris Wright: Yes. I had to kill her to save her. I knew she was in contact with Cutler. The same man who had ruined her mother. I saw a letter to him on the hall table and then, a few days later, he was actually in our house. I knew I had to kill her then. To keep her young and beautiful. Unchanging, like the tableau.

DI Stephens: How did you kill Lily?

Norris Wright: I drugged her cocoa on Friday night, then I went into her room and strangled her. I made her look like the painting. It was a famous pose of Cecily's.

DI Stephens: Did Edna know you were going to kill her?

Norris Wright: No. She didn't know until she saw the body. She guessed it was me though. She knew how I felt about Cecily. She forgave me. She's a wonderful woman, Edna.

DI Stephens: Who killed Vic Cutler? You or Edna?

Norris Wright: That was me. I was putting flowers outside Lily's door one day and he saw me. He must have been coming to see her. I told him that no followers were allowed in the house. He pretended that he was there to collect Betty and Janette but I knew better. He wanted to defile Lily. When I told Edna she

said that we had to kill him. He knew too much. So I
went over to his flat and stabbed him as he sat on the
sofa. It was as easy as that.
DI Stephens: How did you get into the flat?
Norris Wright: I dressed up as a cleaning lady. That
drunken sot of a porter would let anyone in.
DI Stephens: Is that how you killed Florence Jones too?
Norris Wright: I didn't kill her. You can't prove I did.
DI Stephens: Was that Edna then?
Norris Wright: [unintelligible] I didn't . . . I can't . . .
no more questions.

Norris has signed his confession quite readily, using his left hand. Edna was a harder nut to crack. At first she refused to answer any of Edgar's questions, sitting tight-lipped and immovable, like an Easter Island statue in a heather-mixture cardigan. Edgar left her to stew in the cells for the morning then went back in the early afternoon. Bob, who had just been discharged from the hospital, came with him. And it was Bob who had the breakthrough. He happened to remark on finding the photograph of Lily in Peter Entwhistle's room. "Was that Norris's?" he asked. "He must have loved Cecily a lot."

Edna gave him a look of pure contempt. "Cecily led him on," she said. "Norris was always weak."

"Yes, you're definitely the strong one," said Edgar, trying to sound admiring. "I'm sure Norris relies on you a lot."

"Someone has to take charge," said Edna.

314

"When did you take charge? When Norris killed Lily?"

"Yes. Norris would have gone to pieces then without me. We had to cover it up. Make it look like someone was killing off girls connected to the Tableaux. Vic Cutler had to die. He saw Norris putting flowers outside Lily's door. He knew. He was always a cunning one, Vic Cutler. I told Norris he had to kill him. He didn't mind. He'd always hated Vic."

"What about Florence Jones?" said Edgar.

"We had to make you think it was all about the Tableaux, you see," said Edna, becoming quite expansive, almost smiling. "I told Norris to put flowers outside Betty's door, so that you might think she was next. But I had to get you away from the house. That's why we staged that little scene with Betty. While you were busy at the house I went to Montpelier Crescent."

"You went to Montpelier Crescent," said Edgar, "to kill Florence?"

Now Edna turned on him with something like fury. "She was no loss. She was a tart like all the rest of them. Like Cecily and Lily. Like Betty and Janette and all the other showgirls. Prancing about on stage thinking that all the men were looking at them. I went to see the show with Norris and I saw that Florence lying there, almost naked, being Cleopatra. It was disgusting. Easy enough to make her look like Cleopatra again. After I'd killed her."

Edna had looked quite triumphant. The only time she had looked at all remorseful was when she had mentioned Lily. "I couldn't believe it when Cecily wanted to send her daughter to us. And then when she looked so much like Cecily. You couldn't blame Norris for getting confused."

Confused was one way of putting it, thought Edgar. Cecily had never dreamed that Norris's obsession would pass on to the next generation, even though Lily had looked so much like her. Norris had hoarded pictures of Cecily in her prime and one had found its way into Peter Entwhistle's room. Seeing Lily, looking so much like his idealised image of Cecily, had clearly driven Norris over the edge. The fact that Lily worked in a flower shop probably hadn't helped either, considering the famous pose of Cecily on the flower-garlanded swing. Norris had put flowers outside Lily's room, a murderous stage-door Johnnie. He had filled the bath with flowers before he had tried to kill Emma too. Unconsciously, Edgar clenched his fists. Emma's crime had been asking too many questions about Cecily. She'd found the photograph of Cecily, which must have belonged to Norris. She was obviously getting too close to the truth. And she'd been blonde too, which had obviously enflamed Norris. Edgar was a rational man and a police officer but, just for a second, he had the urge to go down to the cells and beat Norris Wright to a pulp.

He thought of Lily who had only wanted to come to Brighton to find the man she thought was her father. For the second time Edgar smoothed out the letter that he had found in Peter Entwhistle's Bible. The letter from Vic Cutler.

Dear Lily,

Thank you for your letter. I'm always happy to hear from any relative of Cecily's. I have to tell you, though, that I'm not your father. I haven't seen Cecily for twenty-one years and you say that you are nineteen. It sounds to me that your father was a good man and you should be proud of him. Your mother too. Cecily is a wonderful woman and I'm sure she is a wonderful mother to both her children. I hope to call on you on Friday afternoon to pass on my best wishes in person.

Yours very sincerely,
Victor Cutler

For a man variously described as a tough guy with many enemies, "a cunning one", "not a very nice person", it was a kind letter, thought Edgar. Vic Cutler had obviously had his redeeming features, after all. Had he known that he was the father of Cecily's older child? The reference to "both her children" made Edgar think that he had suspected. Sad that it was Vic's desire to see Cecily's daughter for himself that had led to his death.

"DI Stephens?"

Edgar looked up. A nervous-looking WPC was at the door. Edgar tried to think of her name.

"A visitor to see you, DI Stephens."

"I can't see anyone now."

"I'm afraid I muscled my way in," said another voice. It was Ruby, gorgeous as ever in a fur hat and fur-trimmed coat. Her cheeks were pink from cold and she seemed to bring colour and glamour into the dingy underground office. It was as if someone had switched on the Christmas lights.

"Have you time for a quick walk?" said Ruby. "There's something I want to say to you."

Edgar didn't have time but he'd already spent most of the morning feeling guilty about Ruby. He couldn't turn her away now.

"I'm afraid it will have to be quick," he said.

"Just round the block."

Outside, a bright winter sun was already melting the snow. Some children were building a snowman in the square and they could hear the shouts of tobogganists taking advantage of the car-free roads. Ruby led Edgar in the direction of the sea. When they reached the coast road she put her hand in his.

"I think you'd better have this," she said.

Edgar looked at his palm which now contained Ruby's engagement ring. Max himself couldn't have performed better sleight-of-hand.

"We aren't suited, Edgar," said Ruby. "We both know that."

"You're too good for me," said Edgar at last.

Ruby smiled, her enchanting grin that showed slightly crossed front teeth.

"No, you're the good one but I'm going to be a star and I don't think you're ready for that."

"I'd hold you back," said Edgar.

"Yes," said Ruby, "you would. And from now on, no one is going to hold me back."

She reached up to kiss him on the cheek and, without another word, turned and strode away in the direction of the sea.

Just keep walking, Ruby told herself. Keep walking, even if he calls you back. But he wouldn't call; she knew that. He would be surprised, even shocked, but, deep down, she knew that Edgar's primary emotion would be one of relief. Now he would be free to propose to the boring blonde policewoman. She hoped they would be very happy together, she really did.

The sky was bright blue and the sea almost white. Waves crashed against the shingle, carving stony rivulets on the snowy beach. Ruby remembered one of the first times she had spoken to Edgar. They had walked along the seafront together and she'd thought how safe she felt in his company. He was so tall and dependable, unlike Max who would always be slightly unpredictable and dangerous. Maybe that was all Edgar was, a father substitute. After all, she had met him when she was searching for her real father. But then she thought: how ridiculous. She had a perfectly good stepfather. She had been in love with Edgar and she still was. The most important thing now was that he should never, ever know that. He must always think that she'd grown tired of him, that he didn't fit in with her glittering future. Dignity was all she had now.

She walked quickly towards Hove. The promenade seemed to be full of people enjoying the sun and the snow. A few young men looked admiringly at her and one asked if she was going his way. "I doubt it," said

Ruby. She would never be short of admirers, she knew that and, even today, the attention from these strangers brought a small, but very welcome, ray of comfort. She thought of Florence Jones, whom she'd rather disliked, thinking her affected and ambitious. Florence had her eye on Max from the first and Ruby hadn't fancied the thought of Florence as her stepmother. But being beautiful hadn't done Florence any good in the long run. You had to have more, thought Ruby. You had to have talent and good looks and luck. Loads of luck. Well, she had the first two. She just had to make sure that the third came her way. Ruby squared her shoulders, tossed back her hair and prepared to be lucky.

CHAPTER
TWENTY-SIX

The theatre was full for the last night of the variety show. Box office receipts hadn't been harmed by the snow or by the publicity surrounding the case. HOUSE OF HORRORS KILLER CAUGHT screamed the *Evening Argus* billboards. Sam Collins had dropped off an early copy for Max. "Looks like your friend did the trick," she wrote over the front cover which included a grainy photograph of number 12 Lansdowne Road. Underneath, Sam had included a telephone number. "Ring me when you're next in Brighton." Max had thrown the newspaper in the bin. Later he would retrieve it and tear off the section with Sam's number.

Tommy Watson was whipping the orchestra into a lather for the overture. Backstage, Toby and his team moved the scenery into place and checked that the pageant lamp was ready for the tableaux. Stew Stewart stood in the wings, sweating gently into his loud check suit. He'd heard that Joe Passolini was in the audience with a real Hollywood agent. This could be his big break. America was the future, everyone knew that. Variety was dying. Soon comedians would no longer have to share the stage with performing poodles and dead-eyed ventriloquists' dummies. They would have their own television shows, maybe even appear on films. Oh God, prayed Stew, please let me be funny tonight.

Bob was watching from stage right. Betty had asked if he could have a complimentary ticket but, to Dick Billings's satisfaction, there wasn't a spare seat in the house. This obviously put Billings into a benign mood because he allowed Bob to watch the show from the wings. Bob's eyes were round as he saw the red light come on, the curtains draw apart and the stage fill with light. Then Stew Stewart strode into the spotlight. "Good evening, folks." Bob's admiration for the comic knew no bounds. He couldn't have faced that audience for a million pounds.

Was he mad to think that Betty, who belonged in this world, would ever be interested in him? But Betty had agreed to meet him after the show tonight. She was in Essex for Christmas but they planned to meet when she did a week in Worthing in January. The Living Tableaux would be continuing without Vic. The girls were going to manage themselves, apparently. "Even so," Betty had said to him sometime during those confused hours when Bob struggled against the sleeping pills, watching Betty slip in and out of focus, her voice seeming to come from the end of a long, dark tunnel. "Even so, I don't want to be in a tableaux act for ever. I'd like to settle down and have a family one day." Did she really say that? Did she mean that she would consider settling down with him? Bob didn't know but the possibility gave him a wonderful secret to hug to himself over Christmas when his mother asked him if he was ever going to meet a nice girl and become a respectable citizen like his brother, Archie.

Not that he'd have much time off at Christmas. They'd be short-handed at the station without Emma and there was always so much paperwork when a case finished. "Emma will be back at work before we know it," the DI had said that morning. "You know what she's like." He'd looked slightly odd when he'd said it though. What had happened when the DI had gone racing round to Montpelier Crescent and wrested Emma from the jaws of death? Rumours were already rife at the station. That Emma had been dead and the DI had brought her back to life. That Max Mephisto had been there and performed some secret black magic spell on her. That Emma had been naked, stretched out on the bed surrounded by flowers. That the DI had knelt by her side and wept. That the DI had fought with Norris, finally subduing him with techniques learnt during his shadowy secret service training. But this last wasn't true because Norris had been at Lansdowne Road at the time, locked in the front room with PC Hobbs and Sergeant McGuire, while Bob had sat dopily in the snug, not knowing if he was awake or asleep.

"He left her for dead," the DI told Bob. "Wright thought that she was dead but she wasn't. I arrived just in time."

Bob thought of Edna talking about the showgirls. *Prancing about on stage thinking that all the men were looking at them.* She'd talked as if Florence had deserved to be killed. Lily too. Just for being young and beautiful. And Norris had apparently killed Lily to keep her beautiful for ever. Bob did not share the DI's modern, liberal views. He thought that the Wrights deserved to hang.

Stew Stewart was coming off stage now. He returned to take another bow and then the stagehands were putting the scenery in place for the dogs. Bob watched, entranced, as the animals ran into their places and waited for their cues. They were so clever, skipping over ropes, jumping through hoops, pulling a carriage, climbing a stepladder. One little white dog could even count to ten although, from where Bob was sitting, he could see Madame Mitzi tapping her foot on the floor to give him the cues. But at least she seemed fond of her dogs, hugging and kissing them when they returned to their stools, slipping them treats from a sequinned bag tied to her waist. Bob would like a dog one day. Not a poodle though, something bigger and more manly, an Alsatian perhaps or a Labrador. He wondered if Betty liked dogs . . .

The dancers were next. Bob felt quite embarrassed because, from where he stood, he could almost see through their gauzy frocks. It was nothing to what he'd see when Betty and co. came on stage, of course, but somehow that was different. With a shock, he realised that he didn't like Betty because she appeared on stage wearing nothing but a long, blonde wig, but despite it. The dancers teetered off and the music changed. The girls were on next. Bob felt himself becoming quite breathless. "Break a leg", that's what Betty had told him to say, and he whispered it now. But he didn't want her to break a leg. He wanted her to remain exactly as she was.

Edgar and Emma had even better seats. They were looking out from a covered balcony on the fifth floor of the Royal Sussex Hospital. Visiting hours were over but a romantically inclined nurse had allowed Edgar to remain. What's more, she had ushered Edgar and Emma out onto the balcony and pulled the curtains behind them. From their vantage point, they could see all of Brighton spread out below them, the Christmas lights along the coast road, the piers two glittering arrows pointing into the dark sea.

"It reminds me of the time when we watched the fireworks on Coronation night," said Edgar. "Do you remember?"

"Well, considering we watched from the roof of a hotel, I'm not likely to forget," said Emma. "I think that was also the day we defused a bomb and caught a murderer."

"Just another day at the office," said Edgar.

The bandages had been taken off Emma's hands but she still had gauze wrapped round her throat.

"I look ridiculous," she complained. "Like Isadora Duncan."

"You look beautiful," said Edgar, and leant forward to kiss her.

His earlier declaration had been cut short by Emma's parents returning and by his own guilt about Ruby. However, when he returned to the hospital at six, Ruby had miraculously set him free and Emma was actually alone. There was enough time for him to tell her again that he loved her and for Emma to inform him, rather crossly, that she had loved him "for ages".

It seemed almost impossible that he could now kiss her and hold her hand and talk to her like this. Impossible but also oddly right, as if they had been in love for years instead of — officially — just for a few hours. Maybe it was tiredness, maybe it was the snow or the night or their private balcony overlooking the houses and the sea, but the whole thing seemed like one of those dreams that are more real than reality.

But Emma, being Emma, couldn't leave the job behind for long.

"Has Edna admitted killing Florence?" she asked.

"Yes," said Edgar. "Norris attacked Betty to distract us and Edna went to Montpelier Crescent and killed Florence to make us think that someone was murdering the showgirls and to stop us concentrating on Lansdowne Road. Norris had probably taken a key when he murdered Vic. I believe Norris when he said he got in earlier dressed as a charwoman. And I think he left wearing a fur coat and a black wig, pretending to be Florence."

"Edna had a fur coat," said Emma. "I saw it hanging in the hall."

"People notice clothes," said Edgar. "I remember thinking that, watching the performers arrive at the theatre. The women were all wearing heavy coats with scarves round their hair. You couldn't tell the artistes from the cleaners. I'm sure you wouldn't be able to tell a man from a woman."

"Well, the porter at Montpelier Crescent wouldn't anyway," said Emma. "I think he has a bit of a drink problem."

"He's a dipsomaniac," said Edgar. "Anyone could have turned up at those flats and asked to come in. Besides, Norris is a small man. He'd make a convincing woman."

Emma was frowning. "I should have guessed that it was Norris who attacked Betty that time," she said. "Remember that she said that she'd smelt rabbits? Well, Norris had been peeling potatoes. That was what made her think of rabbits. Betty's rabbits probably ate vegetable peelings."

"It was all misdirection," said Edgar. "Making us think that Betty was in danger or that the murderer must have had some link with Florence. Really it was only ever about Lily. Cecily and Lily."

"Did you talk to Cecily today?" asked Emma.

Edgar was silent for a moment, watching the lights of a car snake their way down through Kemp Town towards the sea. The snow had been cleared from most of the roads now, cars had been dug out and, tomorrow, life would go on as normal. Earlier in the afternoon, Edgar had sent one of the specials to retrieve the police car from outside the Hippodrome. He thought of driving home through the snowstorm last night, his mind wiped clear of everything but the thought that Emma was in danger.

"Yes," he said at last. "I told her about Norris and Edna. She was very shocked. Even though she admitted that Norris had been obsessed with her in the old days, she never thought that he'd transfer the obsession to Lily. Or that he'd murder her because of it."

Edgar didn't tell Emma that Cecily had cried over the telephone. "It's all my fault," she'd said. "I sent her to that evil house. I even asked Edna to look after her. Oh my God, I as good as killed her."

"It wasn't your fault," said Edgar. "You couldn't have known." He'd read somewhere about a case in the thirties when two sisters in France had murdered their employer's wife and daughter. It had been claimed that the two had possessed an almost diabolical bond, that together they could commit crimes they would not even contemplate individually. *Folie à deux*, that was the phrase that had been used. Even though Norris had originally acted alone, Edgar was convinced he wouldn't have continued to kill without Edna. It was Edna's brains and support that had led to the deaths of Vic and Florence. He had thought of Florence Jones as Lady Macbeth but really the Scottish play was being acted out at number twelve Lansdowne Road. *Infirm of purpose! Give me the daggers.* When had Edna taken over? He remembered Edna's shock on seeing Lily's dead body. That had been genuine, he was sure. At what point had horror turned to understanding and then to connivance?

"Tol said that Vic Cutler used to have a historical tableaux act," said Emma. "Do you think Cecily was in that?"

"She was, apparently," said Edgar. "And Lady Jane Grey was one of her most famous poses. I should have shown Cecily the pictures of the crime scene but I

328

wanted to spare her feelings. We might have got to the truth much quicker if I had done."

"You can't blame yourself," said Emma, absolving him as ever. "We all should have suspected Norris. It was always most likely to be someone in the house. Norris had the means and the opportunity. It was just that he seemed so ineffectual."

"But ineffectual people sometimes kill to make themselves important," said Edgar. "And who knows the secrets of a boarding house? The landlord. Look at Christie in Rillington Place."

"I asked Astarte if she could help find Lily's murderer," said Emma. "It sounds mad, I know. But I was getting desperate. I gave her the picture of Cecily and she said, 'There was a man she was scared of. She ran away but he will find her.' That must have been Norris."

"Cecily ran away but he found her through Lily," said Edgar. "Astarte hits the mark again."

"Do you think there's anything in it?" asked Emma. "Or does she just say enigmatic things and we force the truth to fit them?"

Edgar considered. That was what he thought and yet . . . and yet . . . He had heard Emma's voice calling to him through the snowstorm and she, apparently, had heard him say that he was, coming to save her. "It's what kept me going," said Emma, "I knew you were coming for me."

"I don't know," he said at last. "Maybe we knew that truth all along but we just couldn't see it."

"I asked Astarte about us once," said Emma. "She said 'He's not going to leave her.'"

Edgar glanced at Emma who was looking down at her hands. He had told her that Ruby had released him from their engagement but hadn't given any more details. But, even if Ruby hadn't spoken first, he knew he would still have left her for Emma.

"Astarte isn't always right," he said.

"She said that she saw somebody swinging," said Emma. "I thought at the time that it was Cecily but I suppose it was Norris. He'll hang, won't he?"

"Unless he can plead madness," said Edgar. "Yes."

Emma was silent again. Edgar guessed that she shared his reservations about the death penalty. But then Emma looked up and said, in a completely different voice, "How's Bob? Apparently he tried to see me last night but they wouldn't let him in."

"He's all right," said Edgar. "A bit cross with himself for letting Edna drug him like that but he couldn't have guessed what her game was. It was a freezing cold night, you couldn't have expected him and Barnes not to accept a cup of tea. Bob's quite pleased that he recovered so quickly though. Apparently Barnes is still feeling ropy. Bob's his old self again. In fact, he's gone to see the show at the Hippodrome tonight. Betty arranged for him to watch backstage."

"Are they really an item, Betty and Bob?" asked Emma.

"I think they will be," said Edgar. "She's a nice girl, Betty. She and Janette have been absolute bricks, helping out with the other lodgers, carrying on with the show."

"What about Mr Entwhistle?" said Emma. "Where will he go now?"

"I'm going to see if Mrs M can take him in," said Edgar. "At least for a bit. She would look after him, I'm sure."

"I like Mrs M," said Emma. She said, rather diffidently, "Do you know what Max will do now? It was kind of him to come to the hospital with me last night. Apparently all the nurses were in a flutter over him."

"I think Max will go to London and carry on with his life," said Edgar. "I think he was badly shaken by Florence's death though."

"Do you think he was in love with her?"

"I don't know," said Edgar. "I don't know anything. Look how long it took me to realise that I was in love with you."

"But you worked it out in the end," said Emma. "That's the main thing."

To Bob's biased eyes, the tableaux were better than ever this evening. The music was beautiful, the scene changes seamless and the poses, seen at such close quarters, incredibly graceful. Emma might say that it was degrading for women but how could that be when the women were in control now? Only the Lady of Shalott scene disturbed him. Betty looked so pale and deathlike as she lay on the chaise longue with the flowers all round her. The one thing the DI had told him about Emma was that this was the scene Norris had tried to re-create with her. It was hard to imagine and Bob didn't even want to try. Of course Emma was blonde, like Lily. Betty was a brunette really, a much hardier flower. All the same, he was relieved when the scene was over. And, as she changed position, Betty looked stage right and wiggled her feathers at him. Even in the dark, Bob felt himself blushing.

"It's a bit old hat, all this nudity," Harvey Broom complained to Joe. "What are you trying to do to me? America's a very conservative country, you know."

"This is just to please the proletariat," said Joe, who considered himself a bit of a Marxist on the quiet. "Max Mephisto is the real attraction. Wait till you see him. And his daughter! What a beauty."

"I've got enough pretty girls," said Harvey. "What I want is a magician."

"And you'll get one," said Joe. "After the interval."

"I hope so," said Harvey, looking down at the peanut shells in his hand. "These damn nuts are giving me dyspepsia."

Max knew that he was working well. Sometimes, the audience just carried you on waves on approval. You could almost feel them wanting to believe, like that moment in *Peter Pan* when the theatre-goers clap to show that they have faith in the green light that is Tinkerbell. When he moved amongst the audience he found himself putting in extra bits of business, crushing a man's glasses in his hand only to have them appear, unscathed, in the other, conjuring a cigarette box from a purse only large enough to hold lipstick. The gasps and laughter followed him as he moved amongst the expensive seats. He couldn't see Joe and his American friend but he hoped they were watching closely.

When Ruby appeared it was clear that she too was on sparkling form. They worked perfectly together, anticipating each other's smallest gesture, adding extra lines of banter that made the audience rock in their seats. Heartbreak, thought Max, as Ruby twirled her way into the vanishing box, was certainly a powerful motivator. Lucky in cards, unlucky in love. Just before they went on, Ruby had told him that she had broken off her engagement with Edgar. "I don't want to talk about it," she said. "As an impartial observer," Max had told her, "I promise you that you're doing the right thing." Ruby had laughed at that before smoothing her stage face back on. Now she smiled and dimpled up at the Royal Circle. The love from the audience can't compensate for real love but sometimes, thought Max, it comes a very close second.

The final trick, with Max disappearing, worked perfectly. As he stepped into the cabinet Max thought of Florence asking if he could make her disappear. He wished that he could have spirited her away from Vic Cutler and Brighton and the life that had eventually killed her. Who knows what Florence could have achieved on her own, what they could have done together? But it was too late. Just for a second, Max saw the vanishing box as an ominous object, something that devoured innocent women and destroyed them. But that was rubbish. Edgar had told him, during a brief telephone call that afternoon, that the murderer was not a malign piece of stage furniture but an insignificant little theatrical landlord. Anyway, there was no time for these morbid thoughts. Max swivelled the false back of the cabinet, waited the requisite two minutes and then swung himself back in. Then he opened the door to acknowledge the applause.

Max was surprised to find that Harvey Broom was a small rather diffident man with thick glasses and a soft voice. He realised that he had been expecting a Hollywood tsar, a tycoon with a cigar and a paunch. Broom was hesitant and almost shy. His main concern seemed to be his stomach. He refused champagne and asked a bemused Toby if he could fetch him a glass of milk.

But Broom had no hesitancy about Max.

"You're just what I need," he said. "You see, it's this film with a magician, a real Svengali type who seduces all the girls, until he finds true love, but then it's too late and she doesn't love him."

It sounded depressingly familiar. "I can't play the leading man," said Max. "I'm forty-four."

"No, you're not the hero," said Broom, selecting a pill from a Tiffany box. "Tony Malone is the hero. You're the anti-hero. The kind of part Claude Rains plays. But you'll get plenty of screen time. It'll make you a star."

"How do you know I can act?"

Broom rocked to some inward joke. "I've seen you on stage. You can act." He turned to Ruby, who was sitting on the sofa talking quietly to Joe. "And you, young lady. Want to go to Hollywood?"

"It depends," said Ruby, lifting her chin. "Are you making me an offer?"

Broom laughed out loud this time. "Am I making her an offer, she says. This is Harvey Broom. Of course I'm making you an offer, honey. Pretty girls are a dime a dozen but pretty girls who can do magic . . . I can make you a star too."

"Max and Ruby are contracted to do a TV show in February," said Joe. "When do you need them in Hollywood?"

Max looked at Ruby and raised his eyebrows. It seemed impossible that they were having this conversation, backstage at the Hippodrome in Brighton, in a week when so many awful things had happened. But Harvey was taking the matter seriously, getting out a diary for 1954 and flipping through the pages. "Sure. That works. We won't need them until June at the earliest. I'll drop by tomorrow with the contracts."

"I'm leaving for London early tomorrow," said Max.

"Then I'll see you in London," said Broom. "I always stay at the Ritz."

Ruby listened in a land of trance. She had come to the theatre tonight thinking that all she had to do was get through the act then she could go home and cry on her mother's shoulder. But, as soon as she had heard their music, something very strange had happened. She had been lifted out of herself, almost as if she was in one of those old-fashioned mesmerist acts. She knew that she was giving the performance of her life but it was almost as if her body was doing it without her. Everything went right. She knew exactly where to stand, what to do, how long to leave it between each piece of business. And, without looking at him, she knew exactly what Max was doing and how much space to give him. It was perfect, she thought dreamily, as she curtsied for the last time, the perfect final performance.

And now this little man was saying that he was going to take her to Hollywood and there was Joe smiling and talking about contracts. Suddenly she felt that she couldn't stay in that room, listening to men talk, for a moment longer. She needed some air, some space, some time alone.

"Excuse me," she said. "I'm going to change."

Harvey Broom stood up politely. "Don't change, honey," he said. "Stay exactly as you are."

"I'll walk you to your dressing room," said Joe. No one queried this although Ruby's dressing room was only three doors away.

Outside, in the corridor, Joe put his hand on her arm. His dark face looked surprisingly kind. She had never noticed before how long his eyelashes were.

"Are you all right, Ruby? You seem a bit sad."

Ruby tried for a laugh. "I'm not sad. It's been a great night. Mr Broom says I'm going to Hollywood."

"You were wonderful out there tonight," said Joe. "But then, you're always wonderful. Don't worry about

Harvey Broom. Don't worry about anything. I'll look after you."

"I don't need a man to look after me," said Ruby. But, as she sat at her dressing room table and started to take off her make-up, she thought that it never hurt to have people on your side. She remembered the look on Joe's face and smiled slightly to herself. This is the future, she said to her reflection in the mirror. She was ready for it.

Author's Note

The Brighton Hippodrome was built in 1897, designed by Lewis Karslake of the London architectural firm Karslake and Mortimer. The building was originally an ice-skating rink but this pastime did not take off in Brighton, as had been hoped, perhaps because of the competition from the roller-skating rink in nearby West Street. By 1901 the building was empty and Frank Matcham, one of the leading theatre architects of the period, was commissioned to convert it into a circus. This is where the Hippodrome gets its name, from the Greek for "course for horses". Paul Bouissac, in *Semiotics at the Circus*, wrote of another Matcham design at the Blackpool Tower: "No other circus in the world can match the temple atmosphere created by Frank Matcham's decoration, its gilded cast iron pillars and freezes [sic], the deep red of its walls and seat rows, the intimacy conveyed by the proximity of the public to the ring." Despite the ornate design, the circus too was unsuccessful and the building was then acquired by Tom Barrasford who commissioned Matcham to carry out further work to create a variety theatre.

The theatre opened on 24 December 1902. In that same year Barrasford took over the 1,250-seat Empire Theatre of Varieties in New Road, almost next door to the Theatre Royal, and renamed it the Coliseum. In 1909 the Coliseum, run by Barrasford's wife Maud, was fitted out as a cinema and changed its name again, this time to the Court Cinema.

The Hippodrome was sold in 1910 to Walter de Frece, who was married to the music hall star Vesta Tilley, famous for singing songs like "Burlington Bertie" whilst dressed as a man. De Frece was knighted in 1919 for his work in providing entertainment for the troops but eventually sold his chain of theatres to pursue a political career. In 1928 the Hippodrome was acquired by Gaumont-British Picture Corporation and became part of Moss Empires, the UK's largest variety theatre chain. Films were shown at the Hippodrome on Sundays (theatres had to close on Sundays but cinemas could remain open).

Between 1902 and 1964 most of the biggest names in variety theatre appeared at the Hippodrome: Sarah Bernhardt, Lillie Langtry, Harry Houdini, Charlie Chaplin, Laurel and Hardy, Buster Keaton, Gracie Fields, Max Miller, the Crazy Gang, Laurence Olivier, Arthur Askey, Tony Hancock, Dickie Henderson. By the 1960s the Hippodrome had become famous as a pop music venue with both The Beatles and The Rolling Stones appearing on the stage that was once built for a circus.

But, as Max Mephisto prophesied, variety was dying. The pantomime *The Frog Prince*, performed at Christmas 1964, was the Hippodrome's last show. The theatre closed early in 1965. There was a plan to turn the venue into a cabaret club but, after a brief spell as a television studio, the Hippodrome became a Mecca Bingo hall. However, like variety, bingo eventually lost its audience and the Hippodrome finally closed in 2007.

The lease was taken by Academy Music Group (AMG), which planned to revive the Hippodrome as a live music venue. It was believed that plans were still in development when a proposal emerged to convert the Hippodrome and-adjacent buildings into an eight-screen cinema with four restaurants. A planning application was submitted in February 2014. A local campaign group, Our Brighton Hippodrome, was formed to oppose this proposal. Our Brighton Hippodrome intends to revive the Hippodrome as a live entertainment venue and to revitalise the surrounding area. In April 2015, a stakeholder group (including AMG, Brighton and Hove City Council and the Frank Matcham Society) embarked on a viability study to identify a future use for the theatre. The Hippodrome is number one on the Theatres Trust's Theatre Buildings at Risk Register and is high on Historic England's Heritage at Risk Register.

Today, the Hippodrome is closed but inside, incredibly, a great deal of Matcham's opulent design remains. Mecca Bingo preserved much of the interior and you can even still see the signs to the "special fauteuils". To find out more about the campaign to save this unique Grade II listed variety theatre, see the Facebook page "Save the Brighton Hippodrome" or go to the website www.ourhippodrome.org.uk. Thanks to the "Our Hippodrome" website for this information.

The Hippodrome has seen a lot in its time but I need hardly say that the events of this book are entirely imaginary. Nor do any of my theatre employees or artistes resemble anyone ever employed by the theatre.

Acknowledgements

Thanks, as ever, to my editor, Jane Wood, and agent, Rebecca Carter. Thanks to everyone at Quercus and Janklow & Nesbit for working so hard on my behalf. Thanks to Marjorie Scott-Robinson and Lavender Jones for all the information about Brighton in the 1950s. For further details about the Hippodrome and its fight for survival, go to www.ourhippodrome.org.uk. For information and tours of the police cells in Bartholomew Square email: info@oldpolicecellsmuseum.org.uk. I should just add that Bartholomew Square, although definitely the headquarters of the Brighton police in the 1950s, was not actually called a square until the 1980s. This note is especially for Holly.

There are many real places in this book, including Lansdowne Road and Montpelier Crescent, but all the people and events are entirely imaginary.

Love and thanks, as always, to my husband Andy and our children, Alex and Juliet. This book is dedicated to Veronique Walker and Julie Williams with thanks for their constant support and friendship.

Elly Griffiths
2017